THE
PRODIGY
PROJECT

Teresa,

Try to guess which zany, take no prisoners character you inspired?

Enjoy!

— Doug

P.S. — Thanks for all the great help over the years!

THE
PRODIGY
PROJECT

Doug Flanders, MD

Prescott Publishing

This novel is a work of fiction. Any references to real people, events, establishments, organizations, or locales are intended only to give the fiction a sense of reality and authenticity. Other names, characters, places, and incidents portrayed herein are either the product of the author's imagination or are used fictionally.

The Prodigy Project.
Copyright ©2010 by Douglas R. Flanders.

www.flandersfamily.info

Library of Congress Catalog Number: 2010940215

ISBN: 978-0-9826269-2-4

FIRST EDITION

10 9 8 7 6 5 4 3 2 1

*To those who fight
human trafficking worldwide.*

*To my adoptive parents and others
who take in orphans.*

*To my lovely wife, twelve wonderful children,
and beautiful daughter-in-law.
You are the inspiration
for the pages that follow.*

PROLOGUE

Audible bleeding. That's what we call it when the blood is hitting the floor so hard you can hear it. An improvised explosive device, or IED, had opened the spigot on the kid lying on my surgical table. You could hear him bleeding across the room, maybe in the next room. Technically, he was a grown man, but I couldn't get over how young he seemed. I'd spent the last four weeks in Iraq trying to save soldiers like this one—soldiers not much older than my own children.

When did we start sending children to fight our wars? I wondered, not realizing how prophetic that thought would soon prove to be.

I'd given five units of blood in as many minutes, thanks to the high capacity transfusers the Army provides for such occasions, but I knew it wouldn't be enough. In a war zone, giving anesthesia is less about keeping patients asleep and more about keeping them alive.

The surgeon was clamping and cauterizing everything he could see. I was reaching for more blood when I heard someone call my name.

"Lieutenant Colonel Gunderson? Colonel Richter needs to see you in his quarters right away."

"Well, you can tell the Colonel I'm a little busy right now, but he's welcome to come give me a hand if he wants to chat."

We're a little looser about the chain of command in the medical corps than in the rest of the Army. I didn't even bother to look at the specialist passing along the order.

"I'm sorry, sir, but Major Vasquez is to relieve you, immediately, and you're to come with me at once."

Now I looked at the doorway. Even the surgeon paused and turned.

It wasn't a specialist after all. It was someone from the military police. One of the nurse anesthetists from my unit, Major Vasquez, was standing next to him. Vasquez glanced at me furtively and then avoided further eye contact as I gave her a quick report and left with the MP.

What little adrenaline I had left was suddenly in full swing. *Whatever's going on, it can't be good.*

We left the OR and walked down a hallway, our boots thumping as we went. In the civilian world I'd have worn some comfortable tennis shoes, but not here. Here it was combat boots around the clock. Another hallway branched to our right and led to x-ray. Ahead lay the main entrance and triage area, where injuries were sorted according to their seriousness.

The air was fresher in the hallway than in the operating room. It wasn't as stifling, and there was no smell of blood. The temporary medical facility we had established was air-conditioned, keeping it at least twenty or thirty degrees cooler inside than out under the desert sun. It was one of the perks of being in the medical corps, except for those on the very front lines who worked out of the back of modified Humvees.

We waded through a host of soldiers with minor injuries waiting to be seen. Some of them I recognized, but most I didn't. Several looked at me expectantly, thinking that I might be coming to see them. Expectancy gave way to puzzlement when they noticed the MP escort.

Yeah. Well, I'm puzzled, too, I thought.

The MP held the door for me as we exited the facility. The sun's reflection off the white sand was painfully bright. I knew I wouldn't make it thirty seconds without my sunglasses.

Back home in Texas it was late spring and temperatures were on the rise, but nothing like here. Here it was blazing hot. My eyes were already starting to water as I paused to slip on my shades.

"This way, sir," the MP said, trying to hurry me along.

"I know where the Colonel's quarters are," I responded more forcefully than I'd intended.

I disliked being rushed—especially without any kind of explanation—but I despised leaving a patient in the middle of surgery. Although Vasquez was a skilled replacement, it didn't feel right to walk away.

This better be good.

The MP showed no emotion. We trudged along in silence. Soon I was sweating, and not just from the heat.

I attempted to mentally retrace everything I'd said or done in the handful of weeks that I'd been in Iraq. I'd taken care of many wounded soldiers. Most had lived, some had died; but each had received my absolute best. They deserved nothing less.

I always tried to act as though it were my own son or daughter who lay wounded on the OR table. It's the same principle I apply to my private practice in the States. If an elderly man comes in, I treat him the way I'd want my grandfather treated. I try to give a middle-aged woman the same care I'd want my wife to receive. Lots of doctors do this. It's just a little twist on the Golden Rule that helps us keep perspective when we're tired or overworked: *Do unto others as you'd do unto a family member.*

Yes, I felt certain I wasn't in trouble for any medical issue.

Could it be something technical with the Army? The Army had been fairly lenient with the medical corps in the past, but the big push for political correctness was quickly changing all that.

Anyone who's ever worked in an operating room knows the innuendo's so thick you could cut it with a scalpel. Tasteless jokes are served up as the main entrée. I had laughed at my share—and even repeated a few of the funnier ones.

Could that be it? Maybe I'd offended someone and was about to be reprimanded. But why would they pull me out of a critical case to give me a tongue-lashing?

Then a horrible thought struck me: What if there's something wrong with my family? Maybe this interruption has nothing to do with me at all. Maybe it's the Army's way of breaking the news to me about some illness or accident at home.

I'd spoken to my wife earlier that morning, just before she'd tucked the kids into bed for the night on the other side of the planet.

I checked my watch. They'd be starting a new day now—the oldest two doing calculus with their mother on the couch, the middle ones eating breakfast, the babies still asleep.

No, an emergency at home seemed improbable. But then again, with eight people to worry about, anything was possible.

I was still wracking my brain when we arrived at Colonel Richter's quarters.

"Go ahead, sir," the MP told me as he held the door. I entered the room, but he closed the door behind me and remained outside.

Richter was seated at his desk with maps of the city spread out in front of him. Having known him to always be in complete command of both his personal appearance as well as his soldiers, I was surprised to find him looking a little haggard. It was subtle, but enough to convince me something big was amiss.

Leaning over his right shoulder was a medium-sized, muscular man in camouflage fatigues similar to the desert BDU, or battle dress uniform, the Army uses. He wore no insignia of any kind, not even a nametape. He glanced up at me as I entered the room, said a few more words in hushed tones to the Colonel as he pointed to something on the map, and then stood loosely at attention, his hands at his sides. He was deeply tanned with a thick mustache in the Iraqi style, but looked more Mediterranean than Arabic in origin. He'd blend in easily enough at a distance, if that were his intention.

"Gunderson, glad you're here," Richter gave me a half-hearted smile. "Sorry about the short notice and mysterious circumstances, but the Army needs your help, and we need it now. Full explanations will have to wait. We know you've got a Master's in microbiology and your thesis was on biological weapons, but—"

"So my family's okay?"

"Yes, yes, they're fine. And you're not in any kind of trouble, either. I just need to know whether you can identify anthrax under a microscope?"

"*Anthrax?*" I sure hadn't anticipated that question. "Well, yes. Of course, I can. It's one of the simpler organisms to identify due to its unique appearance. Even an undergraduate microbiology student with some basic skills—"

"Gunderson, time is critical. Forgive me for interrupting, but I need you to meet Mr. Smith here."

He nodded to the man on his right.

The name *Smith* didn't sound very Mediterranean to me, and I was immediately suspicious. Nonetheless, Mr. Smith took his cue and began.

"Lieutenant Colonel Gunderson, you are in this theatre at this time for a very specific reason. When you were selected a year and a half ago—"

"Right after the 9/11 bombings?" I said.

Smith held up a finger and then continued. "When you were selected a year and a half ago, right after the 9/11 bombings, but more precisely, right after the anthrax attacks against Senators Daschle and Leahy, we hoped never to involve you. In fact, we hoped you'd never need to know about your true purpose here."

"My true purpose? What do you mean? I'm a doctor. I'm here to save lives."

"Yes, of course. And certainly, helping individual soldiers as an anesthesiologist is important. However, we wanted your expertise as a microbiologist for an even bigger purpose—identifying biological weapons in the field. The anthrax used against Daschle and Leahy was identified as Iraqi in origin because it contained bentonite."

He was right. Bentonite is a kind of finely powdered clay used to separate anthrax spores when they're blown into the air, or aerosolized. I'd covered that in my thesis. It's a method of weaponizing anthrax unique to Iraq.

"But why do you need *my* help? Isn't that the job of the UN weapons inspector?"

Richter and Smith looked at one another knowingly.

"Yes, well, that would be Plan A," Smith cleared his throat. "Unfortunately, for reasons that will soon become apparent, Plan A is unacceptable for this particular assignment. Plan B was my special assistant on this mission—a young PhD from the University of Michigan, who is dying in your OR even as we speak."

"You mean the kid I just left to Major Vasquez a minute ago? He wasn't a soldier?"

"Not in the traditional sense, no. He was on his way to meet me and to examine the anthrax when he was caught by one of those homemade bombs that seem to be everywhere. Clearly, the Iraqis realize the importance of what we've discovered and are trying to protect it. If you can make a positive identification of the anthrax, we can destroy it before things get out of hand."

"So, I'm the back up to the back up?"

"That's right."

"Is there anyone backing me up?"

Smith smiled, "Let's just say I've taken an undergraduate class or two and have had a lot of on the job training recently—but I'd really like a professional second opinion for this one."

"Alright," I said. "Then let's go."

"Congratulations," Smith said, extending his hand. "From this moment forward, you are more than a soldier, you're a certified US government asset."

I wasn't exactly sure what that meant, but I held off asking since everyone was in such a hurry.

"Gunderson, the first thing we need to do is to get you a different weapon," Colonel Richter said. He reached into his desk drawer and pulled out a pistol very much like the 9mm Beretta I had at my side.

"It looks almost identical to the one I've got," I said, laying my weapon alongside the new gun.

"Looks can be deceiving. Pick it up."

I hefted the new pistol and immediately noticed the extra weight. "It definitely weighs more," I admitted. "And the handgrip seems a little bigger."

"To the untrained eye, you'll be carrying a standard issue sidearm," Smith explained. "However, the bullets are made of a depleted uranium and titanium alloy that is twice as dense as lead. Each round has additional powder to propel that extra weight. The clip only holds eight, so use them sparingly."

I'm fairly familiar with depleted uranium—I've seen several soldiers come in with the shrapnel. "So, basically, I'm getting an armor piercing pistol?"

"Oh, it's better than that. You can stop a truck with this gun. The bullets tend to burst into flame upon impact—something inherent in the depleted uranium—so just aim for the fuel tank and watch the fireworks," Smith answered.

"I didn't know we made pistols like this," I commented, duly impressed.

"Technically, we *don't*—which is why you have to give that one back as soon as this mission is complete," Smith grinned. "Richter has some new paperwork for you, which we can discuss in the Humvee. Let's get going."

I grabbed the papers and saluted the Colonel.

"Good luck, Gunderson," he said, rising to his feet and saluting in return.

I followed Smith to the Humvee and hopped in. As he pulled away, I flipped through the papers and read over my new orders. "It says here I'm being discharged home for a family emergency."

"Yeah," Smith answered over the knocking of the diesel engine, "that's what they'll tell your unit. Of course, your family will think you're still in Iraq."

"Won't I be?"

"Not for long. This is the last sensitive site we know about in Iraq. Once you've confirmed the anthrax, you'll be heading for The Farm at Camp Peary in Virginia to get briefed on your new role as an agent."

Smith careened across the desert, leaving huge clouds of dust in our wake.

"From there you'll go to the Army Research Institute of Infectious Diseases in Fort Detrick. They'll bring you up to speed on all the latest biological weapons technology. Iraq is only one of many places on the planet where the US government has some major cleaning up to do. As of five minutes ago, you became the head janitor—and you're going to need a really big mop."

I let all that soak in as I folded the orders and put them in my pocket. I'd heard of The Farm before and knew it was where they trained new recruits for the Central Intelligence Agency.

Apparently, I'd just joined the CIA, which is why Smith had called me an "asset." For some reason, I always thought that the CIA would be a little more formal about it. Maybe this was their version of a field promotion.

Smoke was rising in the distance ahead of us. I pointed, "Is that where we're headed?"

"Yeah. The IED had gasoline and oil mixed together, so it's still smoldering."

"I'm sorry about your friend. I doubt he'll make it."

"I know, and I hate it. He actually came to us—not the other way around. He had a real sense of duty, not just to his country, but to mankind in general. He saw his work with biological weapons as being on par with nuclear disarmament. It may have been unrealistic, but he wanted to see everyone, especially the US, give up biological weapons for good."

"Is that why the UN weapons inspector is being left out of this? I mean—maybe we had something to do with the anthrax?"

"There's no maybe about it. We just need to make sure this is the real stuff and not a decoy. Once it's destroyed, all the anthrax we know about in Iraq will be accounted for. The US of A takes a big, black eye in world opinion either way, but it looks better to say that you never found weapons of mass destruction than to admit that you provided the technology to develop them. Let's face it, we trained Osama bin Laden, we backed the Taliban for years, and for a long time Iraq was our biggest ally in our undeclared war on Iran. It's like raising pitbulls: They're terrific guard dogs right up until the day they turn on you."

"So we're like some sort of top-secret extension of the EPA?" I asked. "We go around cleaning up biological weapons messes before they get out of hand?"

"You got it, Gunderson. We're like the Environmental Protection Agency on steroids."

We wound our way through a barricade and were quickly waved on by the guards, who seemed to know Smith. We had climbed out of the Humvee and were heading into a storage building when we heard an explosion behind us. Smith pushed me to the ground.

Looking back, we could see that both guards had been ripped to shreds.

"We've got to make that identification, and then I'm calling in an airstrike with incendiaries," Smith shouted, pulling me to my feet. "We need to make sure this stuff is completely destroyed."

As we scrambled for the door, an Iraqi woman in full burka emerged from the smoke and destruction. She was walking towards us with outstretched arms, like some strange desert mummy. Smith shouted at her in several languages, but she didn't seem to hear. Her belly appeared nine months pregnant, and we both thought the same thing: suicide bomber. Our guns were instantly in our hands.

"Get inside," Smith barked at me. "I'll handle this."

He shouted a few more things at the woman as I reached for the door and ducked inside. Two loud shots left my ears ringing as I stumbled into the warehouse. He probably had the same kind of gun they had given me, maybe better.

Smith was instantly on my heels. He handed me a mask and some gloves, then led me to a microscope already set up with a sample. I looked at it briefly. It was definitely the real deal. We quickly ran through several more samples, all clearly anthrax.

"That's it. I'm calling it in."

We tossed aside our masks and gloves, and he got on his satellite phone.

"We've got about forty-five seconds to clear out of here," he told me as he hung up and we ran for the door. I started for the Humvee, but he pulled me towards the left hand side of the building instead.

"No time!" he shouted. "Just leave it!"

We ran full speed towards the side perimeter. I caught a glimpse of the woman in the burka lying face down in a pool of blood just yards from the fallen guards.

The bomb she had under her burka never detonated. She lay on top of it awkwardly, tilted to one side with her left leg drawn up and her arms wrapped around it protectively.

I got a sickening feeling in my stomach and began to wretch even as I ran. Maybe it wasn't a bomb after all.

Smith reached the next barricade ahead of me and shouted the warning: "Thirty seconds! Thirty seconds! Pull everyone back now!"

One of the guards got on his radio even as he began to run himself. Everyone seemed to know what to do. We had made it about two blocks when I heard a high-pitched whistling sound, followed by a massive explosion that knocked us all to the ground. A wave of heat passed over us that made the desert seem cool.

And then it was gone.

Behind us a huge fireball reached to the sky. It seemed to just burn and burn, like an oil tanker on fire. I wiped my chin and shielded my eyes.

"Come on," Smith shouted. "You've got a plane to catch."

Within the hour, I was on my way back to the States. I had carried the modified Beretta for less than forty-five minutes, but what a life changing forty-five minutes it had been.

As far as my family knew, I was just finishing out my ninety days of "boots on the ground" as a reservist anesthesiologist in Iraq. Since I had been in the IRR, or Individual Ready Reserve, instead of a regular reserve unit, I barely knew my fellow soldiers. None of them would follow up on my "family emergency." They'd leave that to Colonel Richter, which would leave me in the clear.

The plane sailed though the air with ease. The only turbulence was the turbulence inside my mind. The sun was setting on the horizon, leaving a red glow across the sky. I pulled down the window cover and closed my eyes. But I could still see the red.

CHAPTER

1

Was it a baby or a bomb under her burka?

The uncertainty was eating at me—a spiritual moth nibbling at the fabric of my soul. Now I understood why so many veterans struggled after returning home. It was all the unanswered questions left lying on the ground.

A little over five years had passed since the spring of 2003. I'd worked on numerous assignments all over the world, but it was that first one that still haunted me. A strange sense of guilt would wash over me like the desert heat, unbidden and merciless.

I'd always been ambivalent about my role as a military doctor. The military was all about blowing things up and killing people. Being a doctor meant putting things back together and healing.

Until that day in the desert, I'd been able to compartmentalize. I could separate what the military did corporately from what I did individually. I was safe in a little cocoon called the operating room, far from the fighting front.

And then I wasn't. The walls had been torn down, and I was in the thick of it.

As it turns out, I received training from the CIA and the Army, but worked for neither. In the wake of 9/11, a new anti-terrorism agency had been formed. Its actions were off-the-record and its funding off-the-books.

As far as I knew, the agency that recruited me didn't even have a name. We were just an invisible extension of Homeland Security. The American people had given the green light to do whatever it took to fight the war on terrorism. So now, when the government shifted into high gear and stepped on the gas, I was a big part of the engine that roared to life.

There were different divisions within the new agency, each of which specialized in handling a different type of threat—conventional, chemical, nuclear, or biological.

My area was biological. I'd helped to stop so many exotic dangers that I'd nearly lost count. I knew I'd saved numerous lives, but that was little consolation in moments like these—moments when my mind went back to that crumpled form lying in the sand.

How many lives must be saved to make up for the one that is lost?

Fortunately, I wouldn't have to do this much longer. With Presidential elections just around the corner and the public's memory of past events starting to fade, we all knew our agency was headed for the trash heap. I'd done my bit to make the world a safer place and was ready to move on. Maybe I'd be able to leave my guilty feelings behind, along with the job.

Despite my busy schedule as a doctor and my unpredictable assignments as an agent, my wife, Lauren, and I had somehow managed to have two more kids since Iraq. That brought the total up to nine, but the oldest two were currently taking classes at the local community college and could hardly be counted, since we saw so little of them anymore.

At the moment, I was eating my Saturday morning breakfast while admiring our newest addition, Matthew.

Matthew was the cutest little cherub you could wish for, with blonde hair from Lauren's side and coal black eyes from mine. He had just celebrated his first birthday and was in the quintessential "wonderful ones" stage.

Lauren was spooning oatmeal into his eager little mouth when she caught me gazing at him. Only, I wasn't really looking at Matthew. I was staring past him, off into space, and thinking about a different baby. A baby that wasn't.

That's when she asked me the age old question that wives always seem to ask at such moments: "What are you thinking?"

Before I could stop myself, I mumbled something about the "duality of man." It was vague enough, but not my usual evasive response. Those few words were the tip of the iceberg.

If I weren't careful, I'd end up telling her all about Iraq, my subsequent training as an agent, and my double life over the last five years. How all of our "vacations" had really been missions for the US government. How she and the kids had been my cover and alibi in a world of international intrigue.

Basically, I would end up saying more than I wanted to say, and more than she had clearance to hear. Someday I'd come clean to her. But not yet.

The fact that I had said *that* much kind of startled us both, I think. We just looked at one another, uncertain how to proceed. It was one of those laugh or cry moments.

Lauren fixed me with a penetrating gaze. I could sense her struggling to bite back unasked questions, could feel my heart pounding in my chest as she studied me.

I looked away, afraid to let her look any more deeply into my eyes. What secrets might she be able to read there?

She watched quietly as I reached for another strip of bacon, shoved it into my mouth, and chased it down with a swig of orange juice. I was grateful when Matthew finally broke the silence.

"Ahhh," he chirped, leaning forward in his seat and opening his mouth wide. He rubbed a gooey hand on the front of his shirt to say *please*, and Lauren aimed another spoonful of oatmeal in his direction.

"The duality of man?" she finally said.

"Yeah."

She gave me a weak smile. "You mean how men can be both terrific and terrible at the same time? *Born to kill* written next to a peace sign? That kind of duality?"

"Yeah, that kind."

"Well, that's a new one."

She coaxed Matthew to take another bite of cereal.

"Aren't you supposed to just say, *Nothing*, and change the subject? You know, pretend you're one of those World War II vets who never talk about it?"

"What makes you so sure this is about Iraq?" I asked defensively.

Lauren tilted her head and cocked an eyebrow. "Well, first of all, *I* didn't say it was about Iraq, *you* did. Second, you were clearly referencing that old Vietnam movie, *Full Metal Jacket*. You've made me watch it at least half a dozen times, so I know…"

She offered the baby another loaded spoonful, but he clamped his lips tightly and turned his head.

"All finished?" she asked in a cheerful tone. Matthew nodded vigorously.

"…and third, but most important," she continued, looking back at me, "you didn't have that so-called thousand-yard stare for the first fifteen years of our marriage. It only started five years ago, when you came back from Iraq. It doesn't take a math degree to put two and two together."

I had to be careful. *She knows me too well.* I nibbled at another strip of bacon.

"Well... I was also wishing that I'd studied harder in college...."

Lauren stood up and walked to the sink to retrieve a damp washcloth. "I think I liked your first answer better," she smirked.

"I'm serious."

"You have a Master's degree and you're a medical doctor, Jon. Forgive me if I don't follow your logic."

Matthew squirmed as she wiped off his sticky hands and face. Then lifting him out of his high chair, she set him on the floor and told him to run along and play.

"That's just it," I said, "the Master's degree. Most people see those extra letters on your lab coat and assume you're extra studious, but the exact opposite is often the case. At least, it was for me."

Lauren sat back down at the table and turned her attention to the barely touched plate of food in front of her. Like most mothers, she was usually the last one to start eating and the last one to finish.

Stabbing a large strawberry with her fork, she said, "Now you've really lost me."

"Alright," I explained, "half the kids in college start out pre-med—at least, that's what they tell their parents. Within a semester or two, it's obvious who's going to make it and who isn't. Those who aren't move on to other things, except for characters like me with more tenacity than brains. Somehow, that 2.0 GPA freshman year didn't register as a handicap until it came time to apply to medical school and nobody wanted to talk to me. So I got a Master's degree to prove I was 'worthy,' then reapplied. That was about the time I met you."

"But what does *that* have to do with Iraq?"

"Well, if I hadn't goofed off my freshman year, I could've gone straight to medical school and skipped the Master's in microbiology. Without that extra degree, the Army never would have sent me to Iraq. I mean, normally they wouldn't send an anesthesiologist overseas at all. They usually keep the anesthesia docs stateside and send nurse anesthetists to the field."

I finished off my orange juice before continuing, "But they weren't just taking care of soldiers in Iraq. They were also looking for biological weapons—and they thought I could help do both. It was my graduate school training, not my medical training, that ultimately landed me in Iraq."

"They told you this?" Lauren asked.

"Basically."

I knew I was saying too much. It was a miracle I'd kept my role as an agent secret for so long. I didn't want to blow it now.

Mulling it over, she asked tentatively, "So you don't resent me and the children?"

I could hear the lump in her throat, could see her eyes tear up as she said it.

"Of course not," I assured her. "That's absurd. Why would you even ask such a thing?"

"Well," Lauren shrugged, "if I'd kept working instead of getting pregnant and staying home with the kids, you would never have joined the reserves in the first place, Master's degree or not."

We both knew it was true. We had needed the money. I couldn't have worked any more hours than I was already working at the hospital, and Lauren was determined to stay home with the baby. Patriotism is one thing; practicality is another.

I reached over and grabbed her hand. "Sweetheart, I've never resented you or any of our children, and I never will. I'm the luckiest man alive, and I thank God for all of you every single day. Any sadness I feel has nothing to do with you or the kids—can't you see that? You're not the *cause*. You're the *cure*."

She leaned forward to hug my neck. "Jon?" she whispered.

"Yes?"

"Are you ever going to tell me about it?"

"About what?"

"About whatever happened in Iraq that has you so melancholy and staring off into space several times a week."

"Someday," I said as I stood up and patted her on the shoulder. "Someday."

I turned to go to our library which doubles as my home office. I didn't know it then, but as I walked away, Lauren said a little prayer for me. *Lord, let me have the old Jon back. Do whatever it takes, even if it hurts.*

It's the kind of prayer I'd be afraid to pray, but Lauren's the type who puts faith before fear. It's just one of the many ways in which she is a better person than I am.

I felt my cell phone vibrating and checked it. It was Smith calling. Turns out, his name really *was* Smith—Eric Smith. His dad was English and his mom Italian, so I'd been half right about his origins.

Ever since Iraq, he had been my handler. We'd covered a lot of assignments together. I couldn't believe he had another mission for me this close to elections. Maybe he just wanted to talk. I shut the door and answered the phone. Most of our kids were still asleep, so I could speak freely for a little while.

"Hello?"

"Hey, how's it going, buddy?"

"Alright, I guess…"

Smith paused, picking up on my tone. I'm fairly transparent to those who know me, which is not a good trait for an agent. Then again, I'm not your typical agent. What other agent would drag a wife and nine homeschooled kids along on most of his missions?

"Let me guess. You're thinking about Iraq again, aren't you?" he accused.

"Of course I am," I answered defensively. "Don't act like you don't think about it, too. I know it still bothers you as much as it does me."

"Sure it does. But look, that was five years ago. And besides—you didn't shoot her, I did. And we were both cleared by the internal investigation."

He rattled off the speech as if he'd rehearsed it a million times.

"After the incendiary strike, we'll never know if she was carrying a bomb or not, but everyone agrees we couldn't have taken the chance under the circumstances. Let's face it—we wouldn't even be having this conversation if we'd gotten blown to bits like the guards at the gate. Your kids have a daddy today because of a decision I made then. I can't change what happened, but you've got to let it go."

"Alright," I agreed. I wondered whether he was trying to convince me or himself.

"Good. Now let's stop having this conversation and focus on making the world a safer place for everyone— especially those beautiful children of yours. Neither of us created the biological weapons mess left over from the Cold War. We're just the clean up crew."

"The Environmental Protection Agency on steroids?"

"Exactly. Now you're talking my language."

I didn't mention it, but Smith hadn't been in the field since the incident in Iraq.

Most people have this vision of the battle-hardened warrior who gets tougher and more intense with each subsequent conflict. Pure myth. The human nervous system doesn't work that way. It's exactly the opposite.

The more pain and misery you see, the less you want to see. Young soldiers are an asset, not only because of their physical prowess, but also because of their mental resilience. Their "horror" tanks are still empty.

Although Smith was still fairly young, he'd seen a lot more action than I had. After Iraq, I think he decided his tank was full. After five years in the field, dragging my family along, I couldn't help but think that maybe my tank was getting full, too.

"So tell me what you've got this time," I said with resignation.

"Let's just say that it starts with an all-expense-paid vacation for you and the whole family, along with a few guests. It will be similar to Europe, but with a few twists we'll discuss in greater detail later. But know this: It dwarfs the European assignment by several orders of magnitude."

Europe had been the perfect assignment for an agent with a large family, if such a thing is possible. I'd actually had a great time with the wife and kids touring many of the major cities while gathering critical information.

The result was the complete shut down of a huge bio-weapons program run by old Eastern Bloc scientists selling to the Middle East and Africa. No one ever suspected that the goofy tourist with tie-dyed clothes and eight kids in tow was actually the centerpiece of an intelligence operation.

"How could anything be bigger than Europe?" I asked.

"By several orders of magnitude—trust me. We're talking entire *nations* at risk. This isn't just some bloodthirsty tyrant trying to poison his neighbors."

"So our satellites picked up some suspicious heat signals?"

That was how the European assignment had started—our satellites picking up five star restaurants with bio-weapons kitchens in the back.

To keep large quantities of infectious bacteria alive, you need big incubators to maintain the germs at a constant temperature. When these incubators are hidden in remote areas, like the mountains or the desert, satellites quickly spot their infrared heat signatures—they practically stand out like glowing beacons. It then becomes a fairly simple task to destroy the labs with little collateral damage due to their isolation.

Initially, the Soviets and others tried to move their labs to university campuses as a protective measure. But that was too obvious, and the advent of various watchdog groups quickly made it impractical as well.

Hiding a bio-weapons lab in the heart of a restaurant district was the latest evolution in the game. With lots of ovens going at all hours of the day and night, it was easier to hide from the heat sensing satellites. Fortunately, we'd developed a computer algorithm that could sift out the background heat of the ovens and pinpoint the incubators.

My job was to confirm on the ground what we'd seen from the sky. All I needed was a fancy infrared camera, courtesy of the US government, plus a hearty appetite for world-class food.

"The threat's a little different this time, possibly even revolutionary," Smith replied. "Let me give you the details in person. Meet me at the usual place in fifteen minutes."

Revolutionary? I thought.

CHAPTER

2

I hung up the phone and headed for the bedroom to change clothes. What had Smith meant by *revolutionary*? I told myself not to read too much into it. It might be nothing.

After all, revolution is the most overused word in the English language. A revolution in flavor. A revolution in men's underwear. A revolution this. A revolution that.

The closest most of us have been to a revolution is standing next to an angst-ridden teenager in a Che Guevara T-shirt outside of Starbucks.

A true revolution is big. Really big. It's a seismic shift in the way the world works. It changes our daily lives in a profound manner.

Whenever there is a giant leap forward in our ability to kill one another, it's called a Revolution in Military Affairs, or RMA. It's not the kind of revolution most people want. It's the kind of thing that can put entire nations at risk.

Could that be what Smith was talking about? But how could anybody attack an entire nation with a biological weapon? Sure, one could contaminate a local water supply or aerosolize something over a region, but the sheer size of a nation makes the logistics impossible.

Of course, port cities are vulnerable to biologicals. We'd established that fact with "Operation Sea Spray." Our own government released *Serratia marcescens* over San Francisco Bay back in the 1950's and made a whole lot of American citizens sick with those supposedly benign bacteria.

Perhaps, if someone coordinated the simultaneous release of a highly infectious agent in several major port cities, then they could count on person-to-person transmission to magnify the effects. Still, it was a long shot, given that only a minority of cities in any particular nation are big seaports.

I finished tying my running shoes and then headed for the front door.

"Going for a jog, Dad?" Aaron, my third oldest, asked as he looked up from his laptop.

"Yeah, just a couple of miles."

"Can I come with you?"

Before I could even answer, a chorus of voices rang out from the other room, "Me, too! Me, too!"

There is rarely such a thing as "alone time" in a large family once everyone is awake. I can't even use the restroom without the little ones lining up outside the door, knocking and asking questions. Privacy? Forget it. It was a good thing Smith had called me early. Then again, after five years of working together, he probably knew when to call.

"Little guys, *please*," I said, raising my hands in the air as several of the younger kids rushed into the room. Three-year old Joshua was at the back of the pack, jumping up and down and shouting, "Me, too! Me, too!" with an excited smile on his face, thinking he was getting in on some big kid adventure.

"*Please*," I repeated, "Daddy needs some quiet time."

I heard a few mild protests and some collective grumbling before the children accepted my decision as final and turned to go.

"What about me?" Aaron asked hopefully.

"Sorry, son. Next time, alright?"

"Sure, Dad."

Aaron gave a half-hearted smile and went back to his computer, but he was clearly disappointed. He is the tallest and most athletic of our children, but this really wasn't about running. It was about the fact that he wasn't a little boy any more, and he wanted to be treated like the man he was becoming, not just another one of the kids.

As I headed out the door, I promised myself that this would be my last mission. I couldn't keep disappointing my kids. The oldest two had gone from adoring adolescents to independent adults in the handful of years I'd been playing spy. Somehow, I had missed the entire transition—a fact our strained relationships reflected.

Outside, the grass was still damp with the morning dew as I headed down the street to join Smith. We always met at the jogging trail just a few blocks from my house to discuss assignments. The trail makes a beautiful mile and a half loop of crushed granite around a fifteen-acre spring-fed lake in the heart of my neighborhood. Smith was waiting at the little wooden bridge that spans the spillway. He joined me as I jogged by.

With the arrival of summer, the dogwoods and azaleas had long since lost their springtime blossoms, but everything was gorgeous, nonetheless. A recent rain had knocked the dust out of the air and cooled things down a bit.

I felt as though I could see for miles, and the green of the trees just leapt out at me. The leaves were so full and waxy that they almost seemed artificial. It was the perfect time of day for a run, in the cool of the morning, before the sun climbed too high overhead.

I took a deep breath of the crisp, clean air and glanced at Smith. "Dwarfs Europe, huh?" I asked skeptically as he trotted along beside me.

"By a long shot."

"Really? Did someone finally develop a delivery system that can spread germs far and wide with relative ease?" I asked.

That had been the Holy Grail of biological warfare for years. Everyone had nightmarish pathogens at their disposal; weaponizing them was the challenge. Thankfully, it had been slow-going work. At least, it had been until now, if I were reading Smith correctly.

"Yeah, it dwarfs Europe. But there's not a new delivery system, not in the way you're thinking. This is something totally new—real 'outside the box' stuff. Tell me, what do you know about retroviruses?"

"Retroviruses?" I shot Smith a puzzled look. The hair around his temples was already damp with sweat. "Retroviruses would make terrible biological weapons."

"Is that so?"

"Sure. Just look at HIV. It's a horrible disease, but for a virus it's extremely fragile. Compared to, say, the flu, it's extremely difficult to transmit, too—requires direct inoculation with infected fluids. You could never do it on a mass scale."

I crouched down to jog under some low-hanging branches, then continued once I could run upright again.

"Plus, we're getting better and better treatments all the time. This can't possibly be about HIV, unless someone's developed some weird mutant strain."

"You're right—this isn't about a mutant strain of HIV," Smith admitted. "And it's not about the leukemia retrovirus, HTLV, either. But tell me how retroviruses work. Specifically, how do they go about infecting things?"

"You enjoy stringing me along, don't you?"

"Actually, I do," he said with a smile. "Now answer my question first, then you'll get yours answered that much sooner."

"You really are sadistic."

I glanced at him sidelong. Smith had shaved his mustache and put on a few pounds since he'd quit doing fieldwork. His tan had long since faded, and he was actually starting to look a little pudgy. I thought about picking up the pace to see if he was getting as soft as he looked, but decided against it, partly because I was getting a little soft myself and didn't want to risk an injury.

"Alright, let's see," I said. "It's been nearly twenty years since graduate school, and HIV was still fairly new back then. But if I remember correctly, retroviruses are basically made up of ribonucleic acid, or RNA. Once they get inside a cell, they use reverse transcriptase to convert themselves into DNA."

"So far so good."

"Then that little piece of viral DNA inserts itself into the host cell's DNA and hijacks the host cell's controls. It causes the cell to stop doing whatever it normally does and turns it into a virus factory instead. Eventually, the cell gets so swollen with these new viruses that it bursts open. The viruses spill out, and the process starts all over again."

"Very good, professor," Smith grinned.

I gave a mock bow and kept on jogging. I knew he'd been reading up on this stuff and had me at a disadvantage, but I wasn't ready to concede yet.

"Now tell me about *endogenous* retroviruses."

"Endogenous retroviruses? As in the kind they use to track genetic divergence?"

"That's the only kind I know about."

"This is making even less sense."

"Humor me."

"Alright. Endogenous retroviruses are simply the remnants of ancient retroviral infections in our ancestors. We call them ERV's for short," I said, raising my eyebrows to let him know I wasn't out of my depth yet. He just shook his head.

"Now whenever a retrovirus infects an egg cell in a woman's ovary, it inserts its DNA into that egg, just like it would any other cell," I continued. "However, sometimes the virus never manages to seize control of the egg. Instead, the viral DNA just sits there, hiding inside the egg's DNA, doing nothing. If that egg is later fertilized, then that little extra piece of viral DNA gets passed on to the future generations as though it belonged there. There are literally thousands of such endogenous retroviruses found in the genes of animals all over the planet, and hundreds of them in human DNA alone. Some researchers think that as much as one third of the entire human genome may actually be viral in origin."

"Go on."

"Well, since these ERV's don't seem to do anything, we refer to them as 'junk DNA'. Their only apparent value to modern science is to act as markers for genetic divergence, since everyone downstream from an 'infection' will carry that extra little piece of viral DNA in every single cell of their body. You can actually tell how closely related two people are by how many endogenous retroviruses they share."

"Excellent. You haven't lost your touch," he said with a smile. "And you managed to hit on the two pieces of information that are critical to what we need to discuss. First, there are hundreds of retroviruses sitting in our DNA like little time bombs just waiting to go off. And second, different groups of people will have different sets of these endogenous retroviruses, depending on who their ancestors were."

30

One of my elderly neighbors was coming towards us with her five Pomeranian dogs. We skirted her, one on either side, as the dogs yapped maniacally.

"Those are beautiful dogs, Mrs. Kinderhaus," I called out as we ran by.

"Why, danke, Dr. Gunderson. They're champions, you know," she said in her heavy German accent.

"That's what I heard," I called back over my shoulder. Then in a stage whisper I told Smith, "Did I mention those dogs are also neurotic and annoying?"

"Yeah, sounds like some of the women I've dated. They're beautiful, but they drive you nuts."

"So you date, then?"

"Of course, I date. What did you think, Gunderson? That I'm a monk, or something?"

"No, I suppose I just thought you were married to your work, that's all."

"Well, not everyone gets to marry the love of their life in their early twenties, like you. Some of us have to work a little harder at it. Now can we get back to the endogenous retroviruses?"

"Do we have to? I'm finding this topic much more interesting," I teased.

"Yes, we do. Now, let's suppose someone had figured out a way to reactivate endogenous retroviruses. In other words, after thousands of years of lying dormant and being quietly passed from generation to generation, imagine these viruses being turned back on. What would that look like?"

"That's impossible!"

"Again, humor me. Just suppose for a second and tell me what it would look like."

I mulled it over. It wouldn't look like a normal infection, obviously. The DNA would already be in place. It would just need to be activated. But how?

"Well, for one thing," I began, "If all that DNA were turned on at once, triggered by, say, radiation or something, then every single cell in your body would be affected at the same time. But if all your cells were hijacked concurrently, then all bodily functions would suddenly and simultaneously shut down. I mean *everything*. You'd just drop over dead as all your cells suddenly tried to turn into virus factories in unison. Of course, once you were dead, the cells of your body would no longer receive oxygen or nutrients, so they'd never have a chance to manufacture even a single new virus. There would be a dead body, but no autopsy in the world would be able to explain why. In essence, the perfect crime."

"Exactly!"

"Oh, come on. That's crazy."

"Is it? Or is it the ultimate weapon?"

"But who would want to do such a horrible thing?"

Smith gave me a look that said, "You want the complete list or just the top ten?"

Although I had been around the block a few times, I hadn't completely given over to cynicism and hoped I never did. But I wasn't naive either.

"Alright, scratch that question. But, *why?*"

"Maybe your neighbor has something you want," he shrugged, "farm land, oil fields, diamond mines, whatever. Maybe you hate him because he has a different skin tone or practices a different religion. Is this starting to sound familiar? It doesn't take too much effort for humans to find a reason to kill each other. That's one of the few truths born out by history. What is unique in this case is that there's no blood spilt, no bombs exploded, not even a single shot fired. There is no damage to buildings, no destruction of bridges and roads, and if carefully carried out, there are no casualties on your own side. You could expose a room full of people to the same triggering agent, and only the targeted individuals would succumb. Expose an entire country, and it becomes a simple matter of walking in and burying the bodies. Everything else that you want for yourself is left completely intact."

"That's horrible!"

We finished our second lap around the lake, left the trail, and began jogging along the neighborhood streets.

"Of course," I went on, "it's no different from any other means of genocide, I suppose. But it somehow seems more unnerving. The mechanism of death is coded into the very blueprints of life."

I gave a shudder as we stopped for a water break. We could see Mrs. Kinderhaus from across the lake turning towards her house with her dogs.

"But how does it work? I mean, how could you possibly activate an endogenous retrovirus?"

"We aren't exactly sure. Maybe with radiation, like you said. The fact is that until a few days ago, we'd never even heard of this stuff. Fortunately, there's a researcher on the project who is having misgivings and contacted us. He's agreed to sabotage the program as best he can and will tell us everything he knows in exchange for asylum."

"Do you think this is the next Revolution in Military Affairs we've all been expecting?'

"It sure sounds like it."

"Where?"

"China."

"Everyone always said the next RMA would come out of China. It sounds like they were right. "

"Which is why we need to send you and your family there a couple of weeks from now."

"Hold on a second. I don't want my entire family turned into some sort of primordial soup teeming with viruses."

"I thought you said it was impossible."

"Well, now I'm having second thoughts, alright?"

"Listen, Jon, there's nothing to worry about. This thing is still in an extremely preliminary stage. The researcher built some kind of proprietary computer program that models DNA manipulations. He says they're still years away from an actual weapon. He apparently thought he was doing cancer research, but somehow found out what the real agenda was. He wants to get out and is fairly certain the project will collapse without him and his fancy computer program."

"Assuming I agree to do this, what's my cover? Some sort of medical conference? I suppose that fits, if the researcher is supposed to be doing cancer research. I won't be responsible for his extraction, will I? You know that would be way too risky with my family tagging along."

"Ah, now that's the beauty of this assignment. We have a team of people joining you. They'll be responsible for the extraction. All you have to do is provide a plausible cover."

"Which is?"

"An international geography competition in Hong Kong."

"Geography competition? You consider that plausible?"

"Not only is it plausible, it's perfect. You have a couple kids who already compete in a geography bee each year, don't you?"

"Sure, but they've never gotten past the state level. Don't you have to be a national champion to go the world championships?"

"That's what's so great. The world championships are held every odd year, but the mainland Chinese haven't been attending. Instead, they've put together their own competition to fall on the even years, starting this year. It will coincide with the Beijing Olympics. It's really more of an exhibition than a competition, so technically you don't even have to qualify—you only need to be invited.

And guess who has two invitations sitting in his car right now?"

We came to a hilly portion of the neighborhood and slowed down considerably.

"You're serious about this?" I asked Smith flatly.

"Yes, I'm serious. But it gets even better. The extraction team will pose as a camera crew doing a story on your family's involvement in the geography competition. Kind of like a reality television show. All you have to do is have fun and let them do the work."

"Why not just send them to do the story and leave my family out of it?"

"Well, primarily to make the cover more convincing, but secondarily to give the team better access to the back stage areas and such. The fact is, we don't yet know the identity of this researcher."

"Whose harebrained idea was this, anyway? Yours?"

"Actually, it was the researcher himself who requested the location. We assume it must be close to where he works. Maybe he wants the cover of an international crowd. Or maybe he's one of the judges—who knows? But, yes, I'm the one who suggested you, when I heard the venue. You've got to admit—it makes perfect sense."

"Sure it does—just perfect. Now all I have to do is convince my wife to drop everything and take a vacation on the other side of the planet without spilling the beans as to what I'm really up to."

"I have faith in you. Besides, you've had lots of practice," Smith said clapping me on the back. It caused my shirt, now drenched, to stick to my skin.

"Who all will be joining us for this little excursion?" I asked, wiping the sweat out of my eyes with my shirttail. "Anyone I know?"

"As a matter fact, one of them is an old Army friend of yours, Ranch Richter."

"Colonel Richter? I haven't seen him in years—at least, not since I ran into him at an Army-sponsored medical conference about a year after Iraq. What's he up to these days? How's he doing?"

"Well, he retired from the military and medicine just after that medical conference you mentioned. Now he's living down in French Polynesia with his wife, flying choppers for the tourists and doing an occasional odd assignment for me."

"What's his assignment this time? Hosting the reality show?"

"No, he's coming along to tote equipment and act as chauffeur. He's been to Hong Kong a few times and knows his way around. The host of the show is an agent we already have imbedded there. Her name is Zhou Li. She speaks the language, has some experience as an actress, and knows a lot of contacts on both sides of the law. She'll be a great asset to our cause."

"Then who'll be running the video?"

"Ah, yes, Hank Sanders, the cameraman. He's the best in the business, whether at the top of a mountain or at the bottom of the ocean. You'll like him."

"Oh, really?"

"No, I take that back. Your kids will like him. He's an extreme sports junky. You'll probably worry that he's being a bad influence."

"Please don't tell me my kids are going to be around some foul-mouthed skateboarder covered in tattoos and body piercings all week. I believe in serving my country, but I have to draw the line somewhere."

"I think he's more of a surfer-turned-snowboarder. But not a single tattoo or piercing, I promise."

I eyed Smith skeptically.

"He does shave his head," he admitted, "but you should be used to that from the military. And I've never heard a single curse word cross his lips. He's more of an intellectual extreme sports junky."

"Now there's an oxymoron for you."

"He may even be a little religious. I think he attended Bible College for a while before he started snowboarding professionally."

"Now you're just making stuff up to make me feel better."

"No, I'm serious. He reminds me a lot of you, only younger. When I said bad influence, I didn't mean he's a bad person. I only meant that he likes to do dangerous stunts. He's actually very nice. He just likes to live life on the edge."

"That makes me feel so much better," I said sarcastically.

"Well, good," Smith said between breaths. We topped a long hill, panting hard, and decided by mutual consent to walk the remaining distance back to the head of the trail.

"Now there's one other guy I'm bringing in, but he won't be travelling with you. He was at the Army Research Institute of Infectious Diseases during your training there. Now he's at the Centers for Disease Control. Do you remember Joel Rothstein?"

"Joel Rothstein? How could I forget? The guy wore Armani suits everyday and smoked like a chimney."

"Addiction is no respecter of persons."

"Yeah, I hear cigarettes are harder to quit than crack cocaine. What's Joel going to be doing if he's not going with us?"

"Well, there's a lot of Chinese nationals that work in research labs around the country, including the CDC, right? It seems to me, if you were going to attack with a new biological weapon, you'd target the Centers for

Disease Control first. That'd knock out the guys who have the best chance of countering whatever it is you're doing. That's why I asked Joel to keep an eye out for anything suspicious."

"I thought you said this thing is years away from fruition."

"It is. I'm just being cautious."

"I like that you're cautious. It's one of your best qualities."

"Thank you."

"Speaking of the Research Institute of Infectious Diseases, I noticed they're finally wrapping up that Daschle/Leahy thing. Didn't I tell you it was an inside job? There was a lot of strange behavior up there when I was being trained."

"You've definitely got a good nose for those kind of things, Gunderson. That's one of your best qualities."

"Thank you," I said with another mock bow. "Now, let's go get those invitations out of your car. I need to get back to my family before they start to miss me."

CHAPTER

3

I walked back up the small hill to my house. I could hear a few of the kids playing basketball on the side next to the garage, but no one was out front when I checked the mail. Fortunately, the mail had already come and was waiting in the box. I slipped the invitations in with the stack and headed for the front door.

Aaron was still at the computer when I came in. "Hey, Dad, check this out. Zipp has a new aerodynamic wheel even better than the 808. It's called the 1080. If you used it for a rear wheel on your triathlon bike, instead of your disc wheel, you wouldn't have to worry about crosswinds as much."

He'd obviously gotten over the jogging snub. He also knew the quickest way to get my attention was to talk about new carbon fiber bicycle parts. I was easy prey when it came to the latest biking gadgets. I suspect it's a mutation of the "racecar gene" found in most males of the species. Besides, Aaron always lays claim to the hand-me-down parts whenever I upgrade.

"Nice. Very nice," I said, looking over his shoulder and laying the mail on the desk next to the computer keyboard. "But what would I do with that nearly new disc wheel sitting out in the garage? Hmm..."

"You could probably sell it on eBay," he paused and looked up at me with a grin. "Of course, if you wanted to let someone on Team Molasses give it a try before you did, that would be nice, too."

Team Molasses was what we called ourselves whenever we raced together as a family. With so many little guys on our family team, we were guaranteed to be "slow but sweet." We even had matching T-shirts made along those lines.

"Interesting idea. I'll have to give it some thought." I said, reaching to pick the mail back up.

"Anything for me today?"

"I'm not sure. I haven't really looked through it yet. Go ahead and check, then let me have the rest."

He quickly thumbed through the stack.

"Nothing for me, but here's something for Nathan and Philip. Looks like letters from the GeoBee. I thought that was supposed to be over for a while."

"Why don't you call them inside? I think they're out playing basketball. I'll be in the library. Tell them they can come in there to get their mail."

I sat down at my desk and looked through the remaining envelopes. There were a few bills and an assortment of ads for anesthesia conferences. I could hear Aaron shouting to Nathan and Philip and knew it wouldn't be long.

All three boys soon came racing into the library. Nathan got there first and leaned over my desk sweating and panting. "Hey, Dad—whatcha got?"

Philip, who was two years younger at age eleven, elbowed his brother aside and planted his hands on the desk just in front of me. "Yeah, Dad, what'd we get?"

A tussle for position quickly ensued, and I had to call them down. "You both got one, so stop wrestling long enough to open them up and see what they say."

Philip had his open in a split-second and began reading in the most formal tone he could muster. "Dear Local Geography Bee Runner-Up: The People's Republic of China wishes to congratulate you on your success. We are also pleased to announce our sponsorship of the First International Geography Competition being held this summer in Hong Kong. This announcement will serve as your formal invitation. If you wish to attend, please RSVP to the phone number listed below so that necessary arrangements can be made. The purpose of this event is to foster goodwill between The People's Republic of China and the other great nations of our planet. It is our goal to make this event as inclusive as possible for all those who share a love of geography and a desire for international cooperation."

"What about yours, Nathan?"

"It says the same thing, except it's addressed, 'Dear Local Geography Bee *Champion.'*"

Philip immediately snatched the invitation away to confirm this difference, then promptly handed it back. He hated coming in second at anything and mildly resented this reminder that his brother had edged him out by one question last fall. Even though he was the youngest of the "big kids," Philip tried to outdo the older ones every chance he got, and often succeeded.

"You know what's funny, Dad?" Nathan began. "I don't think The People's Republic of China participates in the regular GeoBee. I followed last year's World Championships, which were won by Mexico, and I think China was listed as China Taipei, which is in Taiwan. Do you think this might be some sort of political statement? Like, 'So what if we weren't invited, we'll just have our own competition?'"

"Son, I think you've hit the nail on the head. Actually, they may have been invited, but refused to participate since Taiwan was going to be there. China has

41

historically boycotted anything that includes Taiwan. I guess the question for us is, do you guys want to go?"

"Do we want to *go?*"

"Are you *kidding?*"

"Yes!" they answered in unison.

"Do you think Mom will let us?"

By now, both were shouting and jumping up and down.

"She'll have to," I assured them, "since she'll be coming, too. Why don't we make a family vacation of it? We've never been to China and have always wanted to go. This is the perfect excuse."

"Okay, what are you boys plotting in here?" Lauren asked, coming into the library with a smile on her face and a dishtowel in her hands. She brought her two little kitchen helpers, Anna, age nine, and Abigail, age six, along with our three-year-old Joshua who began shouting, "Me, too! Me, too!" again.

"Yes, Joshua. You, too," I said, grinning at him as he came over and wormed his way into my lap.

"Me, too, what?" Lauren asked, sitting down in an armchair with one foot tucked underneath her. "You four are obviously up to something. When are you going to let the rest of us in on your secret?"

"It's the coolest thing, Mom," Nathan said in a serious tone of voice.

"It *is* pretty cool, Mom," Aaron added. His six-six frame was draped over one of our sofas looking nonchalant, but I knew he was just as excited as the other two boys.

"What's cool?"

"Just an international geography bee in China that Nathan and I have been invited to attend," Philip said as though it were something that happened everyday.

"*Really?*" Lauren looked over at me suspiciously.

"See for yourself," I said, motioning for Nathan to give her the invitation.

She scanned it twice, nodding unconsciously as she read. "You're right," she agreed, "this is pretty cool."

"Aww, Mom, you're the best!" the boys shouted, crowding around her.

"But, what's this—it's only two weeks away? You've got to be kidding! Don't they know how hard it is to make traveling arrangements for eleven people? Jon, I'm sure it would be fun, but I don't see how—"

"Please, Mom. Please?" the boys pleaded, hands clasped beneath their chins in a symbol of supplication.

"You've always said you wanted to go to China," Anna pointed out.

"Peese? Peese?" Joshua added, squinting his eyes and making a steeple with his hands.

"Why do you do this to me, Jon? If I say *no*, then I'm the spoilsport. I'm the wet blanket."

The protest was just for show. I could tell by Lauren's tone of voice that she was already onboard with the plan. She'd wanted to tour China ever since she and the kids studied non-Western cultures in school.

"So, I obviously have to say *yes*. But I'd better get a lot of help around this house with chores and packing."

"Yesss!"

"Thanks, Mom."

"Hooray!"

The kids were all laughing and cheering and hugging one another. "China, here we come!"

Seth, our oldest, had been lounging on the back porch, talking on his cell phone to his girlfriend. He spent an inordinate amount of time on the phone, and therefore an inordinate amount of time on the porch. True, his phone did get better reception outdoors, but I suspect he chose the spot primarily because it provided a little privacy from the rest of our family.

Seth didn't actually hear the commotion inside, but he could definitely see it through the French doors. After a quick, "Love ya. Gotta go," he pocketed the phone and headed inside to see what was going on.

"What's up?" he asked with an inquisitive nod of his chin.

"It looks like we're taking the family to China. The boys got invited to—"

"Can Danielle come?" Seth blurted out, cutting me off.

"*What?*" I was stunned.

"Danielle... my *girlfriend* for the last two years?" Seth replied in an indignant tone. "We're both nineteen, which makes us adults. So I think she should be able to come with us."

I sat slack-jawed, dumbfounded that Seth could so quickly make everything in our lives revolve around Danielle. As the oldest, Seth had always been independent. If the rest of us wanted to eat Tex-Mex food, he'd lobby for Italian. If we all bought matching T-shirts, he'd balk at wearing his. If we said his hair looked good short, he'd intentionally grow it long.

Ever since Danielle had come on the scene, Seth's attitude had escalated to a whole new level: sulkiness, outbursts of anger, you name it. But what really got under my skin was the feeling that everything the family did eventually had to be cleared through Danielle. A teenage girl we barely knew was directing our every move from a remote location.

Hormones!

I was mentally vacillating between rage over the situation and compassion for Seth's predicament. I had been a teenage boy once myself, and I'd married Lauren over our parents' protests while still in graduate school. They'd wanted us to wait until *after* I finished medical school. *Right.*

I looked to Lauren now with that *help-me-here* expression, but she just gave me the *I'm-letting-you-handle-this-one* smile.

Everyone else had grown suddenly quiet. Nobody wanted to get caught in the middle of this one. Even Joshua was silent, looking from face to face, trying to decipher what had just happened.

"Seth," I began with forced patience. "I recognize that you are an adult. However, you are an adult that happens to still live under my roof. As long as that is the case, you have to abide by my rules. As you know, one of those rules is that we do not invite boyfriends or girlfriends to spend the night or to go on vacation with our family. If and when you get married, it will be a whole different matter."

"Come on, Dad," Seth pleaded, oblivious to all but his own desperate fear of being separated from Danielle for even a week or two. "It's not like we'd be in the same room or anything. She could stay with the girls, and I can room with you and the—"

"Seth, *please*," I snapped. Seth collapsed back into the chair in a huff and immediately started texting Danielle.

"Turn the cell phone off and listen to what I have to say," I insisted, regaining my composure, "*then* you can call Danielle."

Seth punched the off button dramatically, shoved the cell phone into his pocket, and crossed his arms, staring at me with an air of mock interest.

"Alright, then." I took a deep breath and looked around the room, a strained smile on my face.

"Hey, is something wrong?" asked Grace, our second oldest, as she ambled into the room with her headphones around her neck. She'd been working on a writing assignment for an online history class she was taking during summer school when she heard the cheering. Her paper, entitled "Currency of the Conquered," was about women struggling to survive in Nazi-occupied Europe during World War II. Pretty heavy stuff for a newly minted eighteen-year-old, but she'd been taking dual credit classes at the local junior college for a couple of years already. She found the best way to concentrate on her studies was to listen to a little music. It helped drown out the background noise that inevitably occurs with eight siblings. She'd just finished all the *Switchfoot* songs on her iPhone and was taking a short break when she caught wind of the conversation in the library. Curiosity got the best of her.

Before I could respond, the baby started crying in the back bedroom. "Perfect," I muttered under my breath.

"Well, at least now everyone will be together for the family conference," Lauren said brightly as she went to get Matthew up from his morning nap.

This was getting off to a rougher start than I'd hoped. Little did I imagine how rough it would get before it was over. Unbeknownst to any of us, while we waited for Lauren to get the baby, Seth had already begun to formulate a plan to get Danielle to China without the rest of us knowing about it. In retrospect, I suppose I can't blame him. After all, espionage was in his blood.

CHAPTER

4

While I was busy talking my family into going to China, the cancer researcher we were hoping to rescue was facing an existential crisis of his own—what to do about the girl?

Chen Shih had known Jung Ying, the girl in question, for nearly his entire life. As he sat weighing his options, he stared at a picture of her. The only photo on his desk, it showed the two of them beneath a waterfall. They were supposed to be posing together with smiles on their faces, except at the last minute she had given him a shove. Instead of a smile, he had this crazy, startled expression on his face as he toppled sideways into the water with arms flailing. She was pointing and laughing with such vigor that he wanted to hold the frame to his ear like a seashell to see if he could hear her laughter even now.

They had been coworkers for years and friends for even longer. Both had lost their parents at a young age, so in a way they had become each other's surrogate family. Chen could talk with Jung about anything, no matter how esoteric or technical. They would converse with ease, blithely jumping from one subject to another, hardly pausing for breath. She had always been his sounding board and muse. She had a way of helping him to see things from a fresh perspective, pushing past any mental barriers that stood in his way.

Yet, here he was on the cusp of the biggest decision of his life and he couldn't bring himself to discuss it with her.

It wasn't that he didn't want to talk to her. He wanted desperately to tell her everything. To confide what he had uncovered. To discuss what the best—the safest—the most ethical course of action would be.

But he was afraid.

He was partly afraid that she would talk him out of leaving China. But mostly, he was afraid for her safety.

The way he was leaving China and the sensitive information he was taking with him would make him an enemy of the state. She might be in danger just knowing him, but if they suspected she knew of his plans and didn't report him, then her life would surely be forfeit. The safest thing would be to leave her out of it altogether.

Of course, if she came with him, then they would both be safe. What's more, they'd be together. But would she come? The only way to know was to tell her everything, show her the evidence, ask her to run away with him. But what if she refused? What then?

The thought saddened him. Of all the things he would be leaving behind, she was the one that he would miss the most. Almost from the moment he had contacted the Americans last week, his mind had gone back to her again and again.

Was it selfish to involve her, putting his own desires above her best interest? Or was there something more to it than that? Wouldn't she be just as outraged as he was to learn that their research was being used to develop biological weapons? And wouldn't she miss him as much as he would miss her? Maybe it was selfish *not* to tell her.

He was torn and didn't know how to resolve the impasse.

Chen looked away from the picture and back at his computer screen. He had spent the first half of his day like any other, sitting at his desk, tapping away on his laptop. It served as the link between him and the complex tangle of computer servers he used to test his theories about artificial intelligence, or artificial intuition, as he called it.

Artificial intuition had proven better than expected. Far better. He had found that he could use it to make remarkably accurate predictions about how genetic material would behave under almost any given set of circumstances. He could even make reasonable predictions about extra-genetic inheritance— specifically, how and when methyl groups would bind to DNA and activate or deactivate certain genes without changing the underlying code itself.

In essence, artificial intuition could analyze an intricately complex system and do the seemingly impossible: It could predict the future.

But predictions about genetics weren't the only thing artificial intuition was good for. There was also the stock market. Chen had experienced especially good luck in that area, and his boss, Director Lao, had been particularly pleased. He had insisted that Chen provide weekly reports, and Lao's new Porsche Turbo had appeared shortly thereafter, amongst other things. That little side project alone had done more to keep him in the Director's good graces than anything else.

Then there was the issue of hacking into other less sophisticated computer systems. Artificial intuition was well suited for that, too. Exceptionally well suited. Better, even, than he was willing to let his superiors know. Chen didn't want them to suspect how much snooping around he had been doing of late. But he'd been doing a lot.

One of his early projects had been to remotely hack into the Googleplex in Mountain View, California, from his lab in Beijing. Technically, hacking was too strong a term. As one of China's leading computer scientists, Chen was actually an invited guest. But he was the kind of guest who rummaged through drawers and nosed into medicine cabinets. As the only country with censorship power over Google's massive database, China had greater access to the inner workings of Google than anyone else on the planet. That was all the invitation Chen needed.

He had been looking for some very specific things. First, he had wanted a detailed understanding of Google's algorithms and architecture. He felt that those two things would help him to refine his own system, and so they had. Second, Chen had wanted a sneak peek at the massive genetics database Google was building. This, in turn, would give him a head start on the research that he and Jung Ying were conducting.

The thing that Chen had found, without really meaning to, was his own conscience—that internal scale that weighs right from wrong. It had simply shown up one day like a stray dog that wouldn't go away. And, yes, Chen had made the mistake of feeding it.

It had all begun with Google's motto: *Don't Be Evil.* He'd stared at that simple phrase as if it were a road sign in a foreign language, striving to squeeze some small piece of meaning from it. He'd even asked Director Lao about it. Lao had told him there's no such thing as evil.

"There is only power and those who have the courage to use it," he'd explained. "The rest is illusion, an opiate for the weak."

Chen felt certain there must be something more to it than that.

He had asked a few of his coworkers, but most of them just talked about the yin and yang of life. How there is a little evil in every good and a little good in every evil. That good and evil are just two sides of the same coin. That one would not exist without the other.

But Chen was unsure.

Then someone had pointed out that evil couldn't exist alone. "Evil," it was suggested, "is just a corruption or misuse of something good. A hammer can be used to build a home, or to crush a skull. Same tool, different uses. One good, one evil." That was what really got Chen thinking.

The world is full of tools. Some of them are simple, like a hammer. Some of them are more complex, like the computer program he had designed. The more powerful the tool, then the greater its capacity for good or evil. Nuclear energy can be used to provide electricity for an entire city, or to level it.

But what about artificial intuition? Would it be misused? Was it already being misused? Was cancer research really its ultimate goal, as he had been led to believe, or would artificial intuition eventually be twisted and used for evil?

Those were the questions that had prompted Chen to snoop around. Using the techniques he had developed to hack computers on the other side of the planet, he now began to hack those in his own backyard. What he discovered terrified him. It was as though he saw his life's work as a photo negative of everything he had pictured it to be. Everything light was dark, and everything dark was light.

He learned that his work was being used more for the military than for medicine. Indeed, there seemed to be greater interest in *causing* cancer than in *curing* it.

But the biggest thrust of all seemed to center on endogenous retroviruses. Someone in the government wanted to resurrect those ancient diseases and turn them into weapons. And they were using his technology to do it. Chen understood how Alfred Nobel must have felt when he realized people were using dynamite to blow each other apart.

51

But what could he do? He was only one person. There was a big machine at work, and he was just a small part of that machine. Granted, he was a very important part. Without him, without his artificial intuition, would the entire machine grind to a halt? He wasn't sure, but he knew he had to try. He had to get out, and he would need to sabotage his own creation when he fled.

But to whom could he turn? The Russians? They would gladly use his research for the very same purposes and worse if they could. The Japanese? They had hated the Chinese for centuries and would love to help in principle, but they weren't prepared for an international showdown with the thousand pound gorilla that China had become. The same could be said for the rest of Asia. Europe, as well. Africa, South America, Australia? Forget it. The United States had been his only realistic option.

Chen heard a door opening down the hall from his office. Someone was coming. He quickly logged off the government mainframe. He was daydreaming again, and it was making him sloppy. He was good at hiding his electronic tracks, but if someone actually caught him in the act, he'd have a hard time explaining himself. He didn't want to think of the consequences.

The door to his office popped open. There stood Hui Tong, Director Lao's stoic bodyguard. His meaty face and hands were pockmarked with a latticework of tiny scars. It was the accumulation of a lifetime of giving and receiving blows.

"The Director wishes to see you immediately," announced Hui in his usual terse tone. His eyes were fixed on Chen's computer screen.

"Is something wrong?" Chen asked, following Hui's eyes to the computer. The screen showed Google's simple homepage. Hui didn't respond.

"Well, let me log out, and I will come right away," Chen said, his pulse quickening. He knew something was up. Director Lao didn't call people to his office on Sunday afternoon just to chat. In fact, he seldom called people to his office to chat at all. Had they uncovered something? Had they found him out?

The short walk to the elevators seemed much longer than normal with Hui Tong silently padding behind him. It was the elevator ride, however, that seemed to last forever. Hui Tong was not a large man, but compared to Chen Shih, he might as well have been a giant.

Chen found himself fixating on Hui's knotted forearms and calloused hands. Swallowing hard, he imagined those rough paws around his own neck. He could only guess how many fingers had desperately clawed in vain at those muscular arms. He looked up into Hui's emotionless eyes, pondering the fact that Hui could strangle him before they ever reached the penthouse floor and realizing there was nothing Chen could do to stop him.

Chen nearly jumped out of his skin when the elevator "dinged" and the doors slid open. Hui remained motionless, quietly watching and waiting for him to exit. He stepped out and headed down the hallway, Hui falling in behind him. As they reached the huge mahogany doors, Chen paused and turned. He looked to Hui, wondering whether he should knock or go on in. As if in answer, Hui pushed past him and opened the door.

As they stepped inside, Chen immediately noticed a large and beautiful Persian rug at his feet. It had replaced the industrial looking Berber carpet that had been there just weeks before. Overall, the office had kept its glass and stainless steel modern look, but there were a variety of luxurious upgrades displayed here and there. Clearly, the stock tips were panning out.

Chen looked across the room to where Director Lao normally stood when he awaited guests. A perfectly tailored suit of the finest silk stretched across his thin but rigid frame, making him look like some impossible human kite, taut against the wind, waiting to lift into the sky. Lao's skin was flawless, and he never had a hair out of place. How many times had Chen found Lao looking out that same floor-to-ceiling window admiring the gardens below, his hands clasped behind his back in contemplation? Typically, the Director would ask some rhetorical question, then wait for an answer before turning to address his guest. It was his way of establishing dominance in a meeting.

But today Lao was not alone. His arm was draped over the shoulders of someone smaller, someone female. Chen's heart leapt into his throat when he realized it was Jung Ying. If Lao suspected Chen, perhaps he was questioning Jung.

Relieved that he had not yet confided his plans to her, Chen's initial fear quickly gave way to something else. Why did the Director have his arm around her that way? Lao was not her relative or husband. Chen felt this weird urge to shove Lao away, to challenge him in some way.

"The gardens are beautiful this time of year, aren't they?" he blurted out overly loudly.

Hui Tong looked at him sidelong, eyes narrowing. Chen had broken protocol. He had spoken first. It was the verbal equivalent of a shove.

Lao's arm dropped to his side. Chen gave a quiet sigh of relief. It had worked. Lao and Jung both turned to face Chen. Chen looked first to Jung. She seemed pleased to see him, just as he was to see her. They both smiled. When Lao laughed lightly, Chen turned his attention to him.

"Ah, the man of the hour. Please come in. Have a seat. Both of you sit while we talk."

He gestured for Jung and Chen to take the leather chairs in front of his thick glass desk. He sat opposite them in a large swivel chair. Hui Tong stood off to one side, quietly observing, as usual.

"You two make quite a team," Lao said looking back and forth between them. "No one can be an expert in everything, which is why collaboration is so important. But the two of you have taken collaboration to a higher level. Chen, your skills as a programmer seem to synch perfectly with Jung's skills in the laboratory. The research you are doing together is truly amazing."

"Thank you," Chen replied self-consciously. "That is mostly because Jung is such a good programmer herself."

"You are too kind." Jung bowed shyly to Chen, but didn't return the compliment. They both knew Chen hated working in the lab, although he was terrific with the theoretical side of things.

"Regardless," Lao continued, "I would hate to see anything happen to that synergy. It would be a true loss for our research center and for science as a whole." He fixed his eyes on Chen. Did Lao know something? Was this a threat? Lao's gaze slowly drifted over to Jung. His face was expressionless.

"But we should not dwell on such unhappy thoughts," he continued with a sudden smile. "Let us talk instead about your bright futures here at China's Center for Advanced Research. Chen, I believe you and I spoke briefly the other day about the concept of power. Am I correct?"

"Yes, of course."

"But what is power? Where does it come from? How is it obtained?" He paused for effect, looking them over carefully. Both remained silent.

"How do you think the Americans would answer such questions?" the Director asked, fixing his gaze on Chen again. Did Lao know Chen had contacted the Americans? Was this a taunt? Before Chen could respond in any way, Lao went on. "I can tell you what they would say. They would say that money is power."

Chen looked over his shoulder. Hui Tong was as still as a statue, but doubtlessly coiled like a spring, ready to pounce should Chen try to run. But where could he run, anyway? Chen would simply have to play this thing out and hope that Lao hadn't discovered too much. Lao was naturally suspicious. He probably hoped to bait Chen into giving something away. The key was not to panic. Maybe he was reading too much into Lao's statements. Perhaps his sense of guilt was causing him to imagine things.

"Is that true, Chen?" Director Lao asked.

"Is what true?" Chen said turning back around.

"That money is power. Do you agree with the American philosophy?"

"I know that money can buy a lot of nice things," Chen stated, glancing around the room in an exaggerated fashion.

"Ah, so you have noticed my new decorations. I guess a thank you is in order." Lao nodded to Chen. "But having nice things is not the same as having power, is it?"

"No, I suppose not. But certainly money can lead to power, just as power can lead to money."

"Well spoken. But let me ask you, Jung, what did Chairman Mao have to say about power? I am certain you know."

"Naturally," she replied. "He said that political power comes from the barrel of a gun."

"Do you believe it?"

As he spoke, Lao slipped his right hand into his coat pocket, pulled out a pistol, and aimed it at Jung's chest.

Chen leapt to his feet and stood in front of Jung. His instinct was to protect her. Hui Tong took a step forward, most likely to intercept Chen.

"Please, relax. It's not loaded. I only did this to make a point. Chen, sit down. You can take the gun if it will make you feel better."

Lao laid the weapon on the table and pushed it towards him. Chen sat back down, but left the gun. Jung smiled and gently patted his leg. He was shaking all over, his heart thumping in his chest.

"Chairman Mao and the Americans are both correct," Lao was saying. "Greed and fear are merely different pathways to the same destination—power. Some refer to the carrot and the stick. Others speak of rewards and punishments. But it all boils down to the same thing: greed and fear. If you want to control people, if you want to bend them to your will—which is all power really is—then you must tap into one of those two emotions. Capitalists choose greed. Communists choose fear. And religions grasp for both with their alternating tales of bliss and damnation."

"Surely, it is not that simple," Jung protested.

"Chen, you studied game theory as you developed your computer program, did you not?" Lao asked, "Is what I am saying untrue?"

"Unfortunately, it is more true than not," Chen admitted. He hoped Lao would not detect the nervousness in his voice. "Nearly ninety-seven percent of people make decisions in a self-serving way, often driven by fear and greed, as you have said. In other words, people are fairly predictable, which is why game theory has proven to be so accurate when applied to the social sciences. The vast majority of people will simply do what benefits them the most, even at the expense of others. In the original version of my computer program, I merely took game theory as it applied to self-centered people and applied it to the so-called 'selfish genes' that biologists talk about."

"But what about the remaining three percent of people?" Jung asked.

"Errors and ignorance," Lao answered with a dismissive wave of his hand.

"Or the few remaining saints," Chen said quietly, looking out the window.

"Ah, I forget. You are still young. You have not had time to become old and cynical like me. But the reason I bring all this up is so you will not be alarmed by some of the things that are going to happen at next week's computer conference."

"What do you mean?" Chen asked.

"Let me show you something."

Lao reached into his left coat pocket. He pulled out a small test tube with his left hand and then picked up the gun again with his right. Holding the two items side by side, he rotated them around so that Chen and Jung could see that the barrel of the pistol was nearly identical in size and shape to the test tube.

"What are you trying to say, Director?" Jung asked.

"What I am trying to say is that if Chairman Mao were alive today, he would have to modify his original statement. I think he would tell you that modern political power comes from the barrel of a test tube, not a gun. Science is the new currency of power. It has been said that 'guns made men equal, tanks and planes made armies equal, and nuclear weapons made nations equal.' Now the only thing left to set a country apart in its eternal struggle for power is superior technology."

"But how does that relate to the conference next week?" Chen struggled to keep any hint of accusation out of his voice. "What does the struggle for political power have to do with a handful of computer scientists discussing a lot of theoretical ideas?"

"Well, much like religion, science—especially cutting-edge science like the two of you are doing—can stir up feelings of both fear and greed. Is the technology dangerous? Is there money to be made? New technology is an irresistible magnet to the powerful and power-hungry alike. In other words, there will be some very important people present at your lecture next week, Chen, and they may have some questions to ask you."

"What important people would you be talking about?"

"Military people mostly, including some high-ranking generals from the army."

"What does the military have to do with our cancer research?" Jung asked, seemingly puzzled. Although Chen already knew the answer, he felt it best to play along, even if Lao was on to him.

"In a certain sense, nothing at all, other than the fact that soldiers can get cancer just like everyone else. But there has always been a certain symbiosis between the worlds of military science and medical science, not unlike the symbiosis you two share. I mentioned the importance of collaboration earlier. But collaboration is important for institutions as well as individuals. Sometimes the military helps us. Sometimes we help them."

"Which is it this time?" Chen asked.

"A little of both, I think. They help to fund our research. We share our findings with them in exchange. It actually works out quite nicely. Governments have always spent more on the military than on medical research. You can look at the budgets of any nation on the planet—the numbers aren't even close. But by being creative and willing to collaborate, I've managed to funnel some of those resources in our direction. I just need for you two to help me out by following my lead and playing along. Consider next week's conference an elaborate performance with you, Chen, as the lead actor. Fortunately, you have only one line to learn."

"Which is?"

"*Yes.* Whatever they ask, the answer is *yes.* If you can do that, then you will be back to work in no time, doing what you do best. Beyond that, you can leave the money and the military matters to me."

CHAPTER

5

Chen had spent a restless night after yesterday's meeting with the director. He still wasn't sure how much Lao knew, but it was clear he knew something. The meeting had been too sudden, too strange, and there had been all those weird hints that Lao knew more than he was saying.

There were only two things of which Chen was now certain: First, he needed to sabotage Jung's lab. And second, he needed to take Jung with him to America.

It was Monday morning. Jung would be working in her lab. Chen would definitely see her today, but needed to pick up something from one of their colleagues first. After logging off his computer and finishing the last of the hot tea he'd made at breakfast, he got back on the elevator that had seemed so ominous yesterday, only this time he went down to the ground floor instead of up to the penthouse.

He greeted a few co-workers as he made his way outside. The massive gardens that connected the multi-building research complex still seemed asleep in the early morning sun. Chen strolled along one of the many stone paths until he came to the waterfall. He smiled again at the memory of Jung shoving him into the adjacent pool.

He sat down on one of the benches to gather his thoughts. How many times had he come here to rest and contemplate? The steady sound of falling water soothed his mind.

His eyes traced the outline of the artificial rocks that composed the waterfall and the pool. He had watched the construction crew build the entire structure from chicken wire and concrete just a few years ago. They had stained the concrete a more natural color and then etched in little fissures to make the rocks appear weathered. It was amazing how real it looked.

Chen glanced back toward the tall glass building from which he had just come. Was Lao looking down at him even now? It was probably for the best that he intended to see his friend over in animal housing before going to see Jung. It would be less obvious where he was ultimately heading should Director Lao happen to be watching.

Chen rose to his feet, brushed himself off, and continued along the path past the koi pond with its giant lily pads. The number and variety of flowers along the way was remarkable. Fluorescent orange tiger lilies nodded on their tall stems. The bearded irises stood proudly in their ruffled trim. And thick borders of glossy green liriope outlined beds of alternating light and dark violets in a patchwork of purple.

Chen could hear the dogs barking as he came around a hedge, and he could smell them long before he reached the building. He had to acclimate himself at the threshold before entering the kennels, because the odor was so overpowering. Once he had adjusted, he made his way through the maze of cages to the back of the building.

"Big Bin, what are you doing?" Chen called out when he spotted the friend he had come to see.

Big Bin was seated on a stool with a chicken leg in one hand and a washcloth in the other. His shoes off and his pants legs rolled up, he would take a bite of the roasted chicken and then lean way over to rub his shins with the washcloth.

"Lucky you got here when you did, Chen. My legs are so sad from not seeing you, they're beginning to cry. Look."

Bin gestured towards his shins. Sure enough, giant glistening drops of moisture were forming on them. No sooner would he mop them away than new droplets would appear.

"You've stopped taking your medicine again, haven't you, Bin? Maybe it is a good thing I came when I did."

Chen walked over to Bin's desk and retrieved the pills he knew were hidden in the drawer but seldom touched.

"You know I hate taking those things. I have to run to the restroom every fifteen minutes when I take them. That is hard on my worn-out knees."

No one knew exactly how much Bin weighed, not even Bin. Most commercial scales top out at three hundred pounds. As a teenager, Bin had once gone to the zoo to weigh. He was about four hundred and fifty pounds at the time, but felt so humiliated by the process that he refused to ever go back.

He absolutely loved animals, however, and they seemed to love him. They didn't judge him for his size. The job in animal housing at the research center had been a natural fit.

Chen handed Big Bin his pills along with a fresh bottle of water he found sitting on the desk. Bin reluctantly swallowed a couple of the pills and washed them down with the water.

The weeping of his lower legs was a sign of heart failure. His body was telling him it couldn't take much more. The diuretics helped, but couldn't change his underlying problem.

"If I wet myself, it's your fault."

"You're already wetting yourself," Chen replied, pointing at Bin's shins.

"Good point," Bin laughed.

"Listen, Bin, I hate to bother you, but I was wondering if you have any more of that concentrated cigarette extract you helped brew for the guys in building seven."

"The stuff with a hundred different carcinogens in it?"

"Yeah."

"I think there's still a bottle or two over in the supply cabinet if you need it, but why would you want such a nasty concoction?"

"Well, I *am* doing cancer research."

"I know that, but so is everyone else around here."

Chen opened the door to the cabinet and found the bottles. Slipping one into his pocket, he turned back to Bin. "Let's just say that for my next experiment, I need to guarantee some tumors."

"Well, you picked the right stuff then. Good luck," Bin said as Chen waved goodbye and headed back to the gardens.

Chen put his hand in his pocket and rolled the bottle around with his fingers as he walked along the path to Jung's building. He knew that the key to any good act of sabotage was subtlety. If done right, the victim could go years without ever realizing he'd been undermined.

If a computer system was crashed or a lab smashed up, the damage would be immediately apparent. Help would be called in, the mess would be fixed, and everyone would go on their way. Such methods were certainly inconvenient to the victim, but not nearly so effective as a well-considered act of long-term sabotage. The kind of sabotage Chen was planning.

There were two prongs to Chen's attack.

The first was to introduce multiple viruses into his artificial intuition computer program. Just micro-viruses, really—little bits of code that would create minor errors here and there which would gradually add up without ever being too obvious.

The second prong was to add carcinogens to some of Jung's lab experiments. Again, he would do just enough to create some false trails, possibly leading to years of worthless research. With some luck, by the time Lao unraveled everything, he would be out of funding or would have lost interest in endogenous retroviruses altogether. At least, that is what Chen hoped.

Chen decided to take the stairs to Jung's second story lab. He reached the top and went to her door, but hesitated, his hand upon the knob. He had already crossed the Rubicon when he contacted the Americans last week. By talking to Jung, he would be burning all his bridges behind him. The Chinese had a phrase for what Chen was doing; they called it "sinking the boats and smashing the pots". It meant there would be no turning back. Twisting the knob with new resolve, Chen stepped inside.

Working his way past long rows of massive tables to the back of the lab, he quietly pushed open the stainless steel swinging door that led to the side room where Jung could normally be found.

Jung was alone, seated at a workstation with her back to Chen. Engrossed in her project, she didn't seem to hear him approach. He breathlessly looked over her shoulder and saw a small basket filled with a dozen or so squirming pink rodents no bigger than her little finger. On the left was an equal number of glass beakers filled with an amber-colored fluid. On her right sat a stainless steel pan filled with liquid nitrogen, a quiet fog hovering over its surface.

Chen watched as Jung carefully lifted one of the baby rats. Her small deft fingers worked quickly. In one

64

swift stroke, she snipped the tiny rat's head cleanly from its shoulders with a pair of stainless steel surgical scissors. The head fell into the vat of liquid nitrogen, per accepted international protocol, freezing the brain instantly. To a lab scientist, this was the routine and humane thing to do when harvesting neonatal rat cardiac myocytes, or the living heart cells of a baby rat. The folks from PETA would undoubtedly have a stroke.

Next, Jung grasped the headless little body and used the scissors to split the sternum down the middle, exposing the heart. Carefully, since it was a moving target, she snipped the heart from the chest and dropped it into one of the beakers of amber enzymes and nutrients. The enzymes would separate the heart muscle cells from each other and from the connective tissue that surrounded them. The nutrients would keep those heart cells alive.

A quick spin in the centrifuge would allow her to separate out the healthy heart muscle cells for experimentation. What made baby cardiac myocytes so special was the fact that, left in a Petri dish overnight, they would reform connections to one another. Before long, the bottom of the dish would be lined with a fine layer of heart muscle cells, all attached to each other and beating in synchrony. They would form a pink, pulsating sheet as thin and translucent as tissue paper.

With multiple identical Petri dishes all harvested from the same rat, Jung Ying could conduct a variety of experiments with matching control samples. Cardiac myocytes also had the advantage of allowing her to visualize in real time the changes that were occurring on a biochemical level. If she added one thing, the heart cells might beat faster or stronger. If she added something else, they might slow down or stop altogether. Although not as specific as the chemical analysis she would eventually perform, this immediate, visual feedback was invaluable.

Chen let out a little gasp as he watched the first head fall. He was always shocked and a little sickened to watch how the cells used in their experiments are actually harvested. He would help out in the lab as needed from time to time, but much preferred to stay at his computer and leave the blood and guts stuff to others—others like Jung.

Chen's gasp startled Jung, and she turned to see who was behind her. When she saw Chen, she smiled. "Sneaking up on me?" she teased.

"Sorry, I did not mean to disturb you. I forgot how brutal lab work can be."

"You're not afraid of a little old mouse are you," she said waving the headless, heartless body at him.

Chen pulled back, and Jung laughed. "Give me ten or fifteen minutes to finish this up, then we can talk."

"Okay... Maybe I'll just wait in the other room. There is something I need to tell you, but it can wait until you're done."

Chen slipped back through the swinging door, feeling a little queasy. Before him, at least a hundred small boxes rested in rows on large heavy worktables. Each box had a lid of leaded glass with several cables going to and from it. Inside every box was a single Petri dish full of neonatal rat myocytes, beating in rhythm. Chen thought it resembled a nursery for aliens out of a science fiction movie.

Each box was equipped with several high-tech features that served to regulate the conditions inside: A small heating element and a self-adjusting gauge kept the temperature constant. A timer systematically dripped nutrients onto the samples at precise intervals. A tiny camera carefully tracked changes to the baby heart cells and sent the information via continual live feed to Chen's experimental computer program, thus creating an ongoing feedback loop.

The variable, and thus the crux of the experiment, was the small radiation emitter in the corner of each box. By exposing the cells to different frequencies, the hope was to find a frequency that would induce changes, however subtle. They could then focus on that frequency. If there proved to be a correlation between a given frequency and harmful changes, they had found something.

What Jung and Chen were doing—or at least, what they *thought* they were doing—was trying to find a link between low-grade radiation and cancer. Sure, everyone knows that gamma rays and x-rays cause damage to DNA. And, if DNA is damaged in just the right spot, then cancer will not be far behind.

But what about the alleged, controversial connection between brain tumors and cell phones, or leukemia and power lines? Is there really a correlation or is it just a fluke?

Jung's experiment itself was fairly straightforward, similar to the child's test to see if beans grow better in sunlight or artificial light. Only this was a little more sophisticated, and the true objective lay more with how the data was processed than with the data itself. That is where Chen's new computer program came in.

Chen's program was designed to make predictions about complex systems. Those predications were modified as new information became available. By having a continuous flow of new information, the predictions could be constantly refined and updated. It was a dynamic form of game theory that attempted to emulate the workings of the human brain. In essence, it was an effort to combine the speed and storage capacity of computers with the efficiency and elegance of human thought.

Chen looked around. He was here to sabotage the experiment, and it wouldn't take long. He originally planned to get Jung to help him, but since he had some time to kill anyway and he wasn't totally sure she would cooperate, he decided to go ahead and get started.

He found a stash of "Pipette Man" precision droppers hanging on a stand in the corner. Pulling the bottle of concentrated cigarette extract from his pocket, he used one of the droppers to draw up a little of the dark liquid. He then walked around the room randomly lifting the lids of the lead containers and dripping microscopic amounts of the elixir onto the Petri dishes inside.

The heart cells in the first dish stopped beating almost instantly. Chen adjusted the amount of fluid delivered by dialing a knob on the Pipette Man, then continued on.

The next sample slowed its beating noticeably, so Chen decreased the amount delivered again. After about seven or eight samples without any noticeable changes, he was done.

He cleaned up the dropper, hung it back on the rack, and returned the bottle of elixir to his coat pocket.

Chen then walked over and cracked the swinging door open to check on Jung. She was finishing up by tossing the diminutive and lifeless bodies into a biohazard container. She set the beakers of enzymes and miniature hearts into a warmer and then wiped down her desk. After carefully washing her hands, she took a deep breath and turned toward Chen. He held the door for her.

"So what did you want to tell me?" she asked sweetly.

"I'm quitting the research project."

"You're what?"

"I'm finished. Done. Leaving."

"*Leaving?*" she seemed shocked, maybe even a little scared. "To go where?"

"To America."

"But how will you get there? And what will you—"

"I've already made arrangements—and I'll figure the rest out once I get there. I just know that I can't stay here."

"Why not, Chen? I don't understand."

"You know that little discussion we had with Director Lao yesterday?"

"Yes."

"All that stuff he was saying about military people being at the computer conference?"

"Yes, but he explained that, remember? It's all about funding. They help us. We help them. No big deal."

"There's more to it than that, Jung. We aren't doing cancer research. We never have been. We're developing a brand new class of biological weapon."

"You must be mistak—"

"No, I'm not mistaken. I hacked into the research center's mainframe using my artificial intuition program. This whole place is nothing more than a high-tech military installation charged with designing and testing a new type of warfare based on endogenous retroviruses. They're calling it genetic warfare, Jung. They lied to us. Everything we're doing here is founded on a lie."

"That can't be true," she said, shaking her head slowly.

"It is true, Jung. I'm sorry, but I'm telling you this because I want you to come with me. I can't bear to leave you behind. Please—come with me to America?"

Jung's eyes welled with tears. She was quiet for a moment before responding. "Can I have some time to process all this?" she asked softly.

"Of course, you can," Chen answered tentatively. "How much time do you need?"

"A few days. A week at the most. Can I let you know at the computer conference this weekend?"

"I'll wait until then," Chen agreed. "That's fair."

It was not quite the answer he had been hoping for. He gave her a grim smile and turned to go, completely forgetting to tell her about the sabotage.

CHAPTER

6

In the week since I had announced our trip to China, our home had become a beehive of activity. Most of our regular routines were abandoned in the mad rush to get ready for our upcoming adventure. Although Lauren normally schools the kids year-round to avoid losing ground on subjects like math and phonics, their already truncated summer schedule was pared down even further to allow time for packing our bags and making the necessary travel arrangements.

As promised, the kids all pitched in to help their mother with the preparations. They washed laundry, sorted clothes, toted suitcases down from the attic, and compiled lists of things not to forget. When they weren't busy doing Lauren's bidding, most of them had their nose in a book, trying to earn extra money to spend on souvenirs abroad. We had promised to pay them each a dollar an hour for the time they spent reading—or, in the case of pre-readers, the time they spent listening to siblings read aloud—and Lauren had given them book logs to track their progress.

This summer reading program has been a long-standing Gunderson family tradition. The children are allowed to choose whatever books interest them. It's not uncommon to find a teenager reading Dr. Seuss aloud to a passel of youngsters in the library. For a couple hundred dollars each summer, we have a family full of avid readers—a bargain by any measure.

In addition to their extra-curricular reading, Nathan and Philip were working feverishly to brush up on their geography. Despite having scant time to prepare, neither was eager to be embarrassed on an international stage, and of course, each hoped to outdo the other if he possibly could.

As for Lauren, she barely slowed down long enough to catch her breath. There's an old adage that says, "Man works from sun to sun, but woman's work is never done." I don't know how that plays out in other people's homes, but it's a fairly accurate account of how things usually go at our house.

The fact is, I couldn't keep up with Lauren if I tried. She gets up earlier than I do, and she goes to bed later. It's not that she's an insomniac—she just doesn't require a lot of sleep, which is handy when you have nine kids to homeschool. I think she actually enjoys sewing, scrapbooking, and working on lesson plans while the rest of us are sleeping and the house is quiet.

When it comes to travel, let's just say that I do the spying, and she does everything else. For most people, the idea of planning a trip and packing for a group the size of our family would be overwhelming. For Lauren, it's a personal challenge—a challenge she has faced and conquered many times.

What was unique about this trip was that we would be on television and possibly even involved in an awards ceremony, depending on how well the boys did in the geography competition. That meant we'd need to wear nicer clothes than we generally wore when traveling, and we'd have to pack some dress clothes, just in case. I'd probably have to shave, too. I hate shaving when I'm on vacation.

"Jon," Lauren called out. "I'm stuck."

I wandered into the kitchen to find our dining table laden with clothes for every member of our family, all lined up in color-coordinated stacks. Lauren stood at the head of the table, hands on hips, surveying the scene.

"What's the problem?" I asked.

"I can't decide whether to put all our dress clothes in a single suitcase and check it, or to pack them in the backpacks with the rest of the clothes," she explained, blowing a wisp of hair out of her eyes as she leaned over to place a clean pair of blue jeans on my stack. "Keeping them separate will make sure they stay neat, but if the suitcase gets lost, nobody will have anything nice to wear. What do you think?"

I knew my wife's desire to travel light was again doing battle with her desire to be prepared. Traveling light would normally win—especially when we're backpacking—but the extenuating circumstances surrounding this trip had Lauren second-guessing herself.

"I'd say go with the one suitcase idea," I told her. "Otherwise, we'll have a big wrinkled mess on our hands when the time comes."

She sighed, still unconvinced.

"You might pack a nice white polo in the individual backpacks, as well," I added hopefully. "They could double as backup dress shirts in a pinch, and if we don't end up wearing them for the awards ceremony, we can use them as casual shirts later in the trip."

"Hmm, that might work," Lauren nodded, considering my suggestion. She gave me a peck on the cheek and said, "Thanks, honey. That's just what I'll do."

I watched as she folded a small red shirt around a diaper, some socks, and a pair of pants, and then carefully placed the bundle on top of the baby's stack.

"So, how's it coming?"

"I'm getting close," she answered. "I'll have to do another load of laundry to get all the white polos washed, but as soon as those are dry, I'll be ready to start stuffing backpacks."

"Don't forget to pack my travel belt."

"It's already in your stack. If you want to hide the money in it before I pack it, you'd better use big bills. You won't be able to fit very many in that little zip—"

"It'll have to wait," I said, rummaging through my pile of clothes to make sure she got the right belt. Then, noticing the look of annoyance on Lauren's face, I attempted to put things back the way I found them and hurriedly explained, "The bank told me it's almost impossible to get Chinese currency in the States. Just don't let me forget to get some before we leave the airport in Hong Kong, alright?"

"Sure thing," she smiled and went back to sorting socks onto the respective piles of their owners.

"How're we doing on passports and vaccinations?"

"The passports are ready to go—although yours will need to be renewed as soon as we get back. And everyone was current on shots except the middle boys. Grace took them to the pediatrician's this morning to get their tetanus boosters. They were going to stop at the grocery store on their way home, but I expect them back anytime now."

"That would explain why it's so quiet. Where are the rest of the kids?"

"I put baby down for a nap so I could concentrate on packing, and the girls are in the utility room folding laundry. I'm not sure what Joshua's up to."

"I think he's in the backyard playing with the dog. What about Seth?"

"His car's gone, so I assume he went to see Danielle."

"Again?"

"Again."

"I wish he'd let us know where he's going when he leaves. He treats this place more like a hotel than a home."

"He's just testing his wings."

"Did we act that way when we were his age?" I asked in an exasperated tone.

"Worse." She raised her eyebrows at me for emphasis. "And you'd better get used to it, because we have at least eight more to go."

"At least?" I teased.

"You heard me."

Lauren has always claimed that she got her college degree in math so she could stay home and multiply. I've always said that, for a couple of Protestants, we'd make mighty fine Catholics, as far as birth control is concerned. We were both getting a little old to be having more kids, but that obviously hadn't stopped us yet. I suspected Lauren was hoping for double digits, and we were just one baby away. I chuckled at the thought.

"What are you laughing at?"

"Nothing. Nothing at all," I told her as I headed back to the library to make a couple of phone calls.

"Honey?" she called after me, "could you check on Joshua and make sure he's okay? Please?"

I agreed somewhat begrudgingly. I had several things I needed to take care of myself before we left, but I figured I could at least talk on my cell phone while I chased down our three-year old in the backyard, so I pulled it out of my pocket as I stepped outside.

The backyard is our little oasis. We did most of the landscaping ourselves, which makes it all the more special. They say you never truly appreciate flowers until you've planted a few yourself. I can testify to the truth of that. I couldn't tell the difference between a daisy and a daffodil until I got a spade in my hand. Now I can name just about anything in the garden.

I dialed my boss from the patio, then meandered into the backyard to hunt for Joshua. Toys were scattered everywhere, and I started picking them up instinctively. I threw a Frisbee onto the porch just as my boss picked up.

"Hey, Mike. Gunderson here. How's everything going?"

"Going great, Jon. I've got the usual administrative hassles, of course, but nothing too bad. It's a lot like herding cats, as you used to say when you were in my position."

Every doctor in our group has to serve a term as president, which allows each of us to experience the administrative side of running our large practice. It's basically a mild form of torture, and no one can stand to do it for more than a couple of years. Mike was a natural, though. He made the job look easier than most.

"Don't remind me. I'm still trying to repress those memories," I laughed. "Any word on baby Einstein yet?"

Mike and his wife Janet were two of the brightest people I knew. They'd been trying to get pregnant for a couple of years, but without success. I always felt a little guilty bringing it up, since Lauren and I have so many, but I'd feel even worse ignoring this important struggle in my good friend's life.

"Our third attempt at in vitro was another failure. I don't mind telling you, it's starting to take its toll—and I don't mean the ten-grand-a-pop either. We can afford the financial end of things—it's the emotional rollercoaster all those hormones send Janet on. I don't know how much more either of us can take. Adoption's sounding better and better all the time."

"That wouldn't be a bad choice," I told him. I'd spotted Joshua in the corner of the yard, wrestling with our dog, Molly.

"No, but it's such a big decision. So many of the kids these days have special needs. I don't know if we are up for that kind of challenge."

"Well, if anyone were, it would be you and Janet."

"Thanks, Jon. I suppose even if we have children naturally, there's no guarantee they'll be perfectly healthy. Having kids is a gamble, no matter how you slice it."

"That's true—but it's definitely a gamble worth taking."

"You would know, wouldn't you?"

There was an awkward pause. I watched as Joshua played tug-of-war with the dog, not knowing what to say.

"Well," Mike broke the silence. "I'm guessing you weren't calling to chat about kids. You are probably trying to follow up on that last-minute vacation request, right?"

"Sorry about the short notice, Mike."

"That's okay," he laughed. "I've grown used to it after all these years. But I expect you to eventually slow down and start paying me back!"

"One day—I promise."

"Let's see—Thursday looks light, so that should be fine. Friday has a lot of requests ahead of you, but I'm one of those requests. I could let you have my spot, but you'll owe me."

Joshua seemed to have won the wrestling match. His back was to me, but I could see Molly dancing around his heels, begging for a rematch.

"If you don't mind adding it to my tab," I answered, "it would sure help me out."

"No problem. Now, the following week you were already scheduled off, so I think you're good to go."

"Excellent. I really appreciate it, Mike."

"Don't worry about it. Just bring me back a nice souvenir or two from China as a down payment on your ever-growing tab!"

"That's a deal. See you when we get back, buddy."

I hung up and called to Joshua, who spun around, smiled broadly, and trotted toward me, munching on a half-eaten biscuit as he ran.

Problem was, we hadn't had biscuits for breakfast—we'd eaten cereal.

"Hey, sweetie, where'd you get that—that biscuit?"

Joshua's little eyebrows shot up with enthusiasm. He swallowed the bite in his mouth and answered proudly, "Molly brought it home. It's good."

"*Molly?*" I repeated. I looked down at the dog, who continued to stare fixedly at the biscuit, licking her chops and wagging her tail. "But where—"

That's when I noticed our gate standing open. Just beyond it, our neighbor's garbage can was toppled, its contents strewn far and wide.

Suppressing my gag reflex, I abruptly knocked the biscuit out of Joshua's hand, frightening him in the process. Molly pounced on it immediately and darted off with her prize clenched between her teeth, drool dripping from her chops. Joshua watched her go and began to cry.

"Oh, baby, I'm sorry," I said, soothing him. "We just can't eat stuff the doggy brings home. It's nasty." I made a face.

"*Nassy,*" he echoed, imitating my look of disgust.

I brushed the crumbs off his shirt and made him spit a couple of times. No telling how much he had eaten, or what else had been mixed in with it at the bottom of the trash bag. *Yuck.*

I carried him inside and asked Lauren to clean him up further while I gathered the neighbor's garbage.

"Oh—and don't forget to put my Crossing Guard prototypes in the kid's backpacks," I reminded her as I retrieved a fresh trash bag from under the kitchen sink.

"Those Kevlar things?" she answered doubtfully. "I don't know, Jon. The kids packs are already tight, as it is."

"Come on, honey. They're lightweight and hardly take up any room at all—that's the whole point. But they could save our lives if something crazy happens. How am I supposed to sell these things to the general public if I can't even convince my own wife of their importance?"

"I'm sorry, Jon. I'll make room if you want. But it's not like we're going into a war zone, you know."

That was debatable, but I let it slide and headed back out to deal with the trash.

The fact is, kids can't wear flak jackets to school every day. They shouldn't have to. Nevertheless, year after year, as sure as the changing of the seasons, another group of school children is gunned down. What can be done to end this national epidemic?

That was the question that had given birth to the "Crossing Guard", an invention I was currently trying to patent. The motto for the Crossing Guard is this: "Simple ideas—Saving lives". And it really is a simple idea.

It's just a medium-sized oval sheet of Kevlar that can be inserted into any briefcase or backpack. It's lightweight and unobtrusive, but when the shooting starts, a kid can hide behind it as he runs for the exit. Not the perfect solution, maybe, but it's a start. At least it gives our kids a fighting chance.

Like any new invention, there's a huge lag between creation and production. Crossing Guard wasn't commercially available yet, but I had a lot of prototypes lying around the house and insisted our kids use them, especially whenever we traveled abroad. Guns might be outlawed in China, but it always pays to be prepared.

I'd just finished gathering the last of our neighbors' strewn garbage when Grace pulled into the driveway with the boys. Before she'd even come to a complete stop, Nathan and Philip jumped out of the Tahoe, laughing their heads off.

"Dad! Dad, you're never going to believe what happened."

"Let me tell, let me tell," Philip insisted.

Grace and Aaron grabbed the few bags of groceries and came over to join us, Aaron looking a bit sheepish.

"What's up?" I asked, lifting the lid to our own garbage can and depositing my trash bag inside.

"Aaron totally passed out when he got his shot!" Nathan blurted.

"Yeah, we thought he was kidding around, but he wasn't."

Aaron shrugged. "I'm not sure how it happened. Maybe I shouldn't have been trying to watch."

I smiled sympathetically. "Don't feel bad, son. I get a little queasy around needles myself."

"But you're a doctor," Aaron protested.

"It just depends on which direction the needle is pointed. It always feels different when it's pointed at you. Like the difference between major and minor surgery."

"What's that?" Grace asked.

"It's minor surgery if it's on someone else, but it's major surgery if it's on you!"

Everybody laughed as we headed into the house. I mussed the back of Aaron's head. "You going to be okay?"

"Yeah, just a little embarrassed is all." Strong and muscular, Aaron was loath to display any sign of weakness.

As the kids recounted their story to Lauren, I headed to our bedroom. There was one last thing I needed to do before I'd be ready to travel. I wanted to make sure I packed a little ketamine for the trip.

Ketamine is a powerful anesthetic. It's seldom used in America, except in very small doses, because it tends to leave patients hung over after surgery and will make them drool quite a bit unless it's mixed with a little atropine. Similar in action to PCP, ketamine sometimes causes nightmares, as well. Its street name is Special K, but a person who takes it recreationally can end up in a terrifying world of sensory deprivation.

That's the bad part.

The good part is that ketamine relieves pain, renders unconsciousness, and supports respiration and circulation in otherwise healthy people. It works quickly and doesn't require a bunch of fancy equipment—just a needle and syringe. Since it's cheap and doesn't need refrigeration, it's the agent of choice for medical missionary work and remote military operations.

I've also found it to be handy in a tight spot— especially when I can't carry a gun, like in China.

The military supplies every combat soldier with an automatic injection device called the Mark I to be used in case of nerve gas exposure. These are similar to the EpiPens people use for allergic reactions, except instead of delivering a single shot of epinephrine, the Mark I contains two injectors, one for atropine and the other for pralidoxime chloride.

With a little ingenuity and a blatant disregard for the warning labels, the Mark I can be made to inject Ketamine and labeled to look like a big EpiPen. Then it can be carried anywhere in the world, and nobody asks questions.

It can be used in a pinch to render an enemy unconscious and then quietly escape. There's no mess, and it's relatively humane—other than the bad dreams and the drool. Like tagging game with a handheld tranquilizer gun. That's why I never leave home without it.

CHAPTER

7

Chen and Jung wandered among the Terra Cotta Warriors admiring their exquisite craftsmanship. They had flown to Xian from Beijing the previous night and were getting a rare and up-close tour of this marvel from China's ancient past. The military men and computer programmers who would be attending the computer conference that evening were milling about, as well, murmuring and pointing out various items of interest to one another.

"Do you think each of these ceramic soldiers was modeled after a particular person?" Chen asked. "The fact that they're all so unique in size and detail certainly makes me wonder."

"Maybe," replied Jung. "But I think the goal was to capture a type of person rather than a specific person."

"How do you mean?"

"Well, for instance, officers are distinguished from ordinary soldiers by the style of hat that they wear."

"Okay."

"And generals are indentified by their ornate jackets."

"Yes, I can see that. But what I mean is the facial expressions and hair, the things that identify them as individuals," Chen said, turning to look at Jung as he spoke.

It had been a week of misery for Chen. Jung had not yet given him an answer, and it was eating at him. In addition, he still didn't know how much Lao had uncovered. It was becoming difficult to keep up appearances.

How many people had stopped Chen in the hallways to ask if he were okay? It was virtually impossible for him to fake enthusiasm, and he had always been so enthusiastic about his work in the past, back when he thought he was actually helping people.

Now he was forced to tell his co-workers that he was nervous about his presentation; that he didn't like to give public speeches. It was true enough and seemed to satisfy everyone's curiosity, but he obviously couldn't disclose the primary reasons for his discomfort.

Luckily, he had stayed busy. He had the speech to prepare, of course, along with his normal work to perform. He had also planted a few more micro-viruses into his artificial intuition program. He kept a record of all the micro-viruses on the thumb drive he now carried in his pocket, just in case. He figured the thumb drive could be used as a bargaining chip if Lao ever confronted him.

In addition, he had spent some time monitoring Jung's lab to see if the alterations he had made were being incorporated into the database. They were, but he decided not to document that fact anywhere. It would serve as a safety net, if he were forced to turn over the thumb drive.

"I'm getting to that," Jung answered. Her words pulled Chen out of his reverie. "What I think is that each facial expression is representative. In other words, one is happy, one is sad, one brave, one fearful. The goal, I believe, was to capture all the wonders and weaknesses of man. It's just that it took a whole army to do it."

"Interesting," said Chen. He walked up close to one of the horses and laid his hand on its head, feeling the upright hollow ears, and looking to see how deep they were.

"Don't touch the display, please," one of the docents called out to Chen.

"Sorry," he responded, surreptitiously dropping his thumb drive inside the hollow ear as he stepped away. If Lao were to spring a trap now, at least he wouldn't find condemning evidence on Chen's body. Lao would have to let him go in exchange for the drive's location.

"Which of those emotions are you feeling right now?" Jung asked, unable to read her friend's expression.

"All of them," Chen said. "All of them."

That had been in the afternoon. Now the evening had arrived. Chen stood in front of the mirror in his hotel room straightening his tie and smoothing his jacket. He heard a knock at the door. Showtime.

Chen grabbed his papers before answering the door. Jung and Hui Tong stood waiting outside the door together. It was strange seeing Lao's bodyguard in a suit and tie. With his knotted arms covered up, he almost looked civilized. Almost, but not quite. There was a brutality in his eyes that could not be disguised.

Jung, on the other hand, was the picture of elegance. Chen had only seen her dressed up a few times, and it had been awhile. Her black dress was form fitting and sleeveless. Its color served to accentuate the porcelain skin of her slender arms and neck, while perfectly matching her ebony hair. Chen was speechless. It was only when Jung's ivory skin took on a blotchy pink color that Chen realized he was staring, mouth slightly agape.

"We must hurry," Hui said gruffly.

They gave each other awkward smiles and followed Hui down the hallway. When they got to Director Lao's room, Hui knocked. Chen gave Jung another nervous glance and saw her looking at him with an amused grin. It was his time to turn red.

The door opened. Director Lao stood before them in full military uniform.

"Director Lao? I—I don't understand," Chen stammered, trying to shift his focus from Jung to this new revelation.

"Director Lao. General Lao. I wear many hats. All men of significance do. I simply choose the one most appropriate to the need. Today, that means wearing my General's hat. Come, we do not want to be late."

The four made their way across the compound to the meeting hall. They passed several soldiers along the way, each of whom saluted Lao with great pomp. It was odd realizing Lao had this other, separate life. It felt strange, like a child who discovered his father had a second family he never knew about.

After signing everyone in at a table manned by some junior officers, Lao introduced Chen and Jung to a variety of people congregating in the conference center. Once they entered the meeting hall itself, they waited in the back momentarily. A man dressed in an ordinary suit and tie stood at the podium finishing up his presentation. His small round glasses gave him the air of a college professor.

"In conclusion," he was saying, "America meets all the historical criteria for a Chinese colony. Raw materials are extracted, processed into goods, and then sold back to the colony at a premium. The colony thus becomes indebted and financially dependent on the sponsor country, which in turn loans more money to the colony at whatever interest rate it deems appropriate. This creates a self-perpetuating cycle that is not easily broken. Furthermore, to relieve overcrowding in the sponsor country, excess population from the sponsor country can be sent over as colonists. These new colonists tend to be more highly educated than the indigenous peoples and should therefore obtain positions of power within the colony. This will help to further insure favorable policies and practices towards the sponsor country. Thank you."

The speaker gathered his papers and stepped down from the podium. The master of ceremonies, a colonel, stepped forward and thanked him. Then on the large screen behind him, there appeared the words: "*AI: Artificial Intuition* by Chen Shih."

"The time has come," Lao whispered. "Follow me."

Lao led Chen along the side aisle toward the front, while the MC gave some introductory remarks Chen didn't quite catch. Jung followed after, and Hui Tong brought up the rear. When they reached the front, Lao motioned for Chen to go to the podium. Lao and the other two took the seats on the front row that had been reserved for them.

The colonel handed Chen a remote control to advance his slides. After nodding his acceptance, Chen turned to face his audience. He had anticipated giving his presentation to a room full of programmers like himself. When Lao told him a few military men might be present, he failed to mention that the conference was being held on a military installation just north of Xian. The location for the conference hadn't been chosen just to be close to the Terra Cotta Warriors. This was a military meeting, plain and simple. There were a whole bunch of soldiers present and only a handful of programmers, not the other way around.

Chen was determined to play along, to tell them what they wanted to hear. Maybe that would appease Lao and get him to lower his guard a little. Of course, it might just make him all the more suspicious.

Chen thanked everyone for the opportunity to share his research, especially General Lao, his mentor. He said a few words about the greatness of China and her bright future. His voice cracked slightly. He looked over at Jung, who smiled encouragingly. She mouthed something that looked like "good job," but he wasn't completely sure.

Chen had heard that beginning a speech with a joke helps set an audience at ease. These people didn't look like the joking kind. He surveyed the sea of crisp uniforms and stern faces before him, glad that he had chosen more of a visual gag than an actual joke for his introduction. He pushed the advance button, and a picture of a giant mousetrap appeared on the screen overhead.

"Most advancements in computer science in general, and in artificial intelligence in particular, have revolved around the idea of building a better mousetrap. The emphasis has primarily been focused on two areas: faster speeds and bigger memories. We have made commendable progress. As it now stands, computers can transmit data over a million times faster than human neurons. Furthermore, with the Internet connecting every computer on the planet, memory is essentially infinite. In essence, we have built the best mousetrap ever made. This is great—unless you're trapping elephants."

Chen advanced to the next slide, which showed an elephant stepping on a mousetrap and crushing it. He smiled, but got little response from the audience. *Tough crowd.* He wasn't sure if it was a dumb joke, if it was too late in the day for everyone, or if military men were just naturally stoic. He forged ahead.

"In essence, all of our energy has been poured into what psychologists typically refer to as Type II thinking—logical, data driven, mechanistic, left-brain, so to speak. What has been completely ignored is that type of thinking that practically defines us as humans, Type I—creative, intuitive, organic, right-brain, if you will. What I hope to show you today is how I have been able to teach computers to think like humans. By combining the elegance of human thought with the speed and memory of computers, I have broken through to a new frontier in artificial intelligence, and the results have been dramatic."

Chen advanced to the next slide. It showed the phrase "More Memory" with a big X drawn through it and the words "Learning to Forget" written alongside. Below this, the words "More Speed" were also crossed out and replaced with "Simple Shortcuts."

"These two concepts are the essence of my work," Chen explained. "First, we must teach our computers which data to forget, or at least to ignore. Second, we must find simple shortcuts that increase our efficiency, independent of speed. This is essentially what the human brain does when it thinks intuitively. It ignores all the unimportant information and focuses on one or two details that really matter."

A heavy man in the third row yawned, but the rest of the audience seemed surprisingly attentive. Most were staring at the screen above Chen's head rather than looking directly at him. He advanced to the next slide and continued.

"Let's start with memory. Chimpanzees have nearly photographic memory, much better than their human counterparts. Yet despite their amazing memories, they lack the basic reasoning skills found in even very young humans. Likewise, so-called idiot savants often have photographic memories, but seem unable to use them in practical ways. Both are functioning in a primitive way, if you will, heavy on memory, but low on processing.

"I would submit that computer science is at an idiot-savant stage. It remembers every detail, but doesn't know where to go from there.

"We have already established that the Internet makes memory nearly infinite. Thus, the challenge is not one of storing information, but of processing it. This is the basis for Internet search engines that sift through that immense sea of data to find just the right piece of information to match a keyword or phrase.

"Google has had great success with their page-rank system, which can quickly sort through the minutiae to help users find just what they are looking for. It is this ranked or prioritized approach to information that I have applied to other forms of problem-solving as well. I like to think in terms of a sculptor chipping away at the excess marble to reveal the object hidden beneath."

Chen looked around the room. Jung was smiling and nodding. He noticed the smooth white skin of her arms again and looked away before he started to blush.

That is when he spotted the young man standing in the back of the room. He was a few years older than Chen and hadn't bothered to dress up, just blue jeans and a T-shirt.

Chen had heard rumors of a computer programmer at the research center, working on a similar project, who had fallen out of favor with Director Lao about the time Chen had arrived. Could this be him? Was he being brought back in to keep an eye on Chen and his work?

Maintaining his composure, Chen advanced to the next slide and continued.

"This brings us to the issue of speed. If I want to cross the street, I can simply walk across, or I can go in the other direction, around the world, and get there from the other side. Both arrive at the same point, but one is obviously more efficient.

"The way we are currently using our computers is like taking the long way around. We just keep trying to go faster and faster, hoping to make up the difference, instead of simply walking the few steps over. What I have done is to teach computers to walk directly across the street, just like a human would.

"You see, in most seemingly complex systems, there are some very simple underlying rules. This is true in virtually every sphere of life. Our brains, in fact, are hardwired to uncover these simple rules, but we do so subconsciously. Intuition is merely the name we give to this innate ability that we all possess. This is why humans are so quick to stereotype. We see a pattern and apply it across the board, often unaware that we are even doing it.

"Over the next thirty minutes or so, I hope to show you how I have trained computers to forget the unimportant and to find the simple rules. I will give you the nuts and bolts of what I like to call Artificial Intuition."

CHAPTER

8

Chen concluded his lecture and thanked everyone. He had tried to give enough detail to be convincing, but not so much that his work could be easily continued once he was gone. The young man in the back had remained nonchalant throughout the lecture, but Chen sensed he was paying careful attention, despite his demeanor.

Chen took the front row seat between Director Lao and Jung that had been reserved for him. Jung took his hand and held it in her lap with both of hers, smiling at him proudly. It was the first time they had held hands since they were very young, yet it felt natural under the circumstances, and he did not pull away.

After some concluding remarks from the colonel, everyone stood to leave. Jung continued to hold Chen's hand. Hui Tong looked uncomfortable. Chen wondered whether it was the suit Hui was wearing, or if being a bodyguard simply pushed him into high alert whenever there was a crowd.

Director Lao turned to face Chen. "Several of the Generals want to speak with you privately," he told him. "Hui will take Jung back to her quarters, while you and I meet with them." Glancing down at Chen and Jung's intertwined hands, Lao added, "I won't keep him long."

Jung immediately let go.

As Chen followed Lao around the edge of the stage, he looked back. Hui was leading Jung to the exit of the auditorium. She, too, turned to look, and their eyes met briefly. She gave a quick smile and was gone. Chen thought of all those concentration camp victims in Germany during World War II. How the Nazis would separate them, men and boys to one side, women and girls to the other. A simple fork in the path, and one might never see his mother or father or sister or brother again.

Lao led him to a small conference room. Several generals were standing just inside the door, talking informally when they arrived. After Lao made introductions, everyone took a seat around an oval wooden table in the middle of the room. Chen spotted the young man who had attended his lecture at the far end of the table. He was leaning back in his chair with hands clasped behind his head, the encircled "A" of an anarchy tattoo clearly visible on the inside of his left forearm.

"Who is that?" Chen asked Lao in an undertone when the young man was neither introduced nor even acknowledged.

"No one of consequence," the young man answered, having overheard the question despite Chen's attempt at discretion.

"This," Lao answered, ignoring the comment, "is my son, Yen-Chou."

"*Steven*, if you please," the young man interrupted.

"Yen-Chou insists on using a Western name. He seems to think it improves his status in the international hacker community," Lao noted, shooting Steven an irritated glance.

"Until he left us to pursue other interests, he worked many years doing computer counter-intelligence at the Center for Advanced Research. Even now, he helps us with an occasional assignment. Since part of this brainstorming session is to explore the capabilities of your new program as it relates to counter-intelligence, I wanted him here. Nothing that will be said in this meeting is beyond his clearance level, so speak freely."

Chen could only guess at the nature of the obviously complicated relationship between Lao and his son. He couldn't give it much thought, though, because the General with three stars was already speaking.

"Gentlemen, let us begin." His voice was gravelly and authoritative. "Mr. Shih, General Lao has told me quite a bit about your approach to analyzing data. I like what I've heard. I have some very specific applications in mind, which I have been assured are all possible, but I would like to hear your opinion."

"Yes, sir," Chen nodded.

"Let's start with the basics. Battlefield integration. This is where most nations have focused their information technology resources. The current thinking is that by using computers to coordinate all the fighting forces, whether by land, air, or sea, the overall effectiveness of any military campaign can be increased by thirty percent or more. I admit that this is a big jump, but not big enough to ensure total dominance. Naturally, our own teams are working on this, but I want something more.

"I'm thinking that if our enemy's entire campaign is being directed by computers, why not seize control of those computers? Take over their system remotely, possibly without their even realizing it until it's too late? We could even make them fight against themselves. Instead of battlefield *integration*, we could create battlefield *disintegration*. And if we gain remote access over their nuclear weapons, they would truly be at our mercy. Computers have become indispensable to modern warfare, and that makes them an Achilles heel which can be exploited."

There was that concept of power again. Maybe these military types were all the same. They all jockeyed for control—but who was in control of them? Chen wondered if he would get the same "there's no such thing as evil" speech from this guy that he got from Lao.

"Steven here seems to think your program might be able to 'intuit' the way other computers generate random numbers and use that as a backdoor to breaking their encryption," the three-star General said.

He gestured towards Steven, who just smirked in a casually annoying way.

"Yes, sir," Chen replied, "That's entirely possible. Detecting patterns and making extrapolations from them can be employed in an infinite number of ways. Breaking encryption is an obvious choice, because it's normally a long and expensive task. But it could be made quicker and cheaper using the shortcuts inherent in artificial intuition."

"Excellent. Then let's discuss selective elimin... I mean, selective isolation."

The General cleared his throat and glanced at Lao.

"You see Mr. Shih, in every nation there are individuals, not unlike yourself, who are, well, unique. These individuals are often instrumental in the smooth functioning of that nation's defenses, particularly in the arena of technology. Now, if these unique people could be identified and hindered in their work—or better yet, if they could be recruited away—it would be a great blow to that nation, especially during time of war.

"The Israelis have developed an algorithm to analyze communication patterns within terrorist organizations and thus identify the ring leaders. They have used it with great success. By neutralizing a few key terrorists, they have been able to dramatically reduce terrorism. And they've done it in a way that minimizes bloodshed and bad press. Obviously, Israel is not going to share that technology with us, but I think your artificial intuition will be able to do the same thing. Am I right?"

"Yes, I think so, sir," Chen answered quietly. He disliked this line of discussion. He glanced at Steven who was poker-faced, as was Lao.

Chen wanted to object, but said nothing. His protest would be registered when he fled the country next weekend. For today, his answer to every question would be "yes," just as Lao had instructed.

"Very well then, that brings us to our final topic."

Chen knew it had to be endogenous retroviruses. His snooping around had told him that was what the military was most interested in. Apparently, they were saving the worst for last. He looked at the General and waited.

"General Lao tells me that your cancer research has focused on activating and deactivating bits of genetic code without actually altering the underlying DNA itself. Can you explain?"

"Well, sir, in the past, cancer research has mainly focused on damage to or alterations in DNA proper. But current research has uncovered two other mechanisms that can influence or manipulate DNA, only without all the classic mutations most people think of.

"First, there are transposons—sometimes called 'jumping genes.' These are simply bits of DNA that can reposition themselves within the genome. Then, once they are in a new genetic neighborhood, transposons alter which traits get expressed and which get suppressed in that area. There is no net gain or loss of DNA—just a reshuffling of the deck, so to speak. We see this behavior primarily in plants, like corn."

"And the second mechanism?"

"The second is methylation. When stressed, an organism can add or remove methyl groups to a string of DNA. This essentially turns that region on or off. Of the two mechanisms, this is the most promising. If we can create the right type of stress, then we should essentially be able to activate good qualities and deactivate bad ones. We have tried experimenting with different types of stressors, including chemical and nutritional. We are currently focusing on the effects of all forms of radiation. My job is running the results of our trials through my artificial intuition program, looking for patterns."

"And have you discovered any?"

"Yes, sir."

"And they are?"

"Well, it has become apparent that what researchers once considered 'junk DNA' isn't junk at all, but merely quiescent genes waiting for the proper stimulation so they can be expressed."

"And you can provide this stimulation?"

"In a rudimentary way, yes. But our findings require more refinement before they will have practical applications to cancer."

"But you discovered something else, didn't you? Another pattern?"

Chen didn't want to admit it, but it was clear that the General already knew everything he was going to say— like a good lawyer who never questions a witness without knowing in advance what his answers will be.

Now, Chen was in the witness box. He was on trial, not just for his own life, but for the lives of millions.

"Yes, sir," Chen conceded, meeting the General's eyes.

"Go on."

"Well, sir, it seems that most of the genes that are preferentially activated are viral in origin. You see, many of the quiescent genes found in junk DNA were actually brought in and deposited by viruses long, long ago."

"Endogenous retroviruses?"

"That's right, sir. I assume General Lao has already gone over—"

"Yes, but I want to hear it from you."

Chen willed himself to continue, "Well, sir, when I provide certain types of stressors, as I mentioned, what I find is…"

"Yes?"

"What I find is that these endogenous retroviruses tend to get switched on a lot. It happens far more frequently than pure chance would predict. Almost as if they were primed and waiting for just the right trigger.

"In other words," Chen admitted in defeat, "I've not yet found a cure for cancer. Instead, I've discovered a way to resurrect a host of deadly viruses from the ancient past."

The General smiled at Director Lao. It was a big toothy grin. The interview was over.

CHAPTER

9

Hank Sanders was in heaven, or at least what he imagined heaven to be like. Clear skies and blue water as far as the eye could see. His bank account indicated he could stay in paradise for sixteen months, seventeen tops. That gave him plenty of time to heal, and then he would head back to southern California and the purgatory known as "the real world." Perhaps he would settle down and find a regular job, maybe even sign up for some night classes and finish his degree.

He leaned forward in his cushioned lounge chair and rubbed his left thigh. It was still atrophied from the cast he had worn up until two weeks ago, just before he'd arrived on the island. At least his tan was starting to look normal again, but the muscle would take more time to rebuild. He was in his early twenties and had the aura of a natural athlete—not overly tall like a basketball player, or overly big like a football player, but somewhere in that middle ground occupied by professional soccer and tennis players.

He heard the creak of wood behind him. Someone was walking along the dock that led to the little thatch bungalow he would be calling home for the foreseeable future.

He took a long slurp from his drink to get the last few drops then turned to see one of the seashell-clad girls who worked as attendants at the resort. He lowered his Maui Jim shades to get a better look as she sauntered towards him. She had a new beverage, something cold and colorful, in her right hand. With her left, she balanced a silver covered platter above her dark shoulder.

A little early for lunch, he thought, squinting at the sun and running his hand across his smooth pate. He hadn't worn a watch since he had arrived. He hoped this might be a mid-morning snack, but something in his gut told him it wasn't.

"Another drink, sir?" the girl asked, quietly stepping up beside him and extending the new glass in his direction.

"Sure." He eyed the mysterious tray suspiciously while taking the glass from the Polynesian beauty. "What's that?" he asked, nodding towards the silver dome and looking into her coal black eyes.

"It's for you," she replied smiling. Her teeth were so white they nearly sparkled. He couldn't help but think she would be perfect for a toothpaste commercial. *Or maybe a shampoo ad,* he mused, glancing at the silky black hair that fell around her shoulders.

The girl shifted the weight of the platter to her other hand.

Suddenly, Hank couldn't believe he was on a tropical island face-to-face with a gorgeous woman and thinking about television commercials. *Occupational hazard*, he told himself, giving his head a quick shake to clear his mind.

That and a string of bad relationships. Technically just one bad relationship, but it had left such a strong aftertaste that it had soured all the others that followed.

"Sir?" The girl raised her eyebrows expectantly, still awaiting a response.

"Sorry," Hank said, smiling back. "What did you say?"

"It's for you," she repeated, lifting the lid and offering the contents to him.

It wasn't a bomb, thankfully, but it wasn't hors d'oeuvres, either. It was a satellite phone. Hank picked it up with some hesitation and placed it to his ear.

"Hello?" he said tentatively, wondering who might have tracked him down at such a remote locale. He had not intended to be found.

"Hey, how's my favorite extreme sports cameraman doing?" sang out the overly enthusiastic voice on the other end.

Hank was simultaneously relieved and annoyed. "How did you find me?" he asked.

"You know you can't hide from me, Hank. Besides, I've got a great opportunity I think you'll want to hear about. Why don't you meet me in Los Angeles so we can discuss the details." The sales pitch had begun.

Hank waved the girl away with a quick thank you. "Listen, Smith," he said into the phone. "I'm still recuperating from that last 'great opportunity' you brought my way. It will be months before I'm up to speed. Isn't there someone else you can call?"

"Hank, you know I only want the best. That's why I always give you first shot at these things. Besides, there are no stunts involved this time, so you don't need to be *completely* recovered anyway. And best of all, I'm willing to give you a fifty percent increase on your usual fee, since it's such short notice."

"Don't con me. It's always short notice," Hank said accusingly. "But let me do the math here—no stunts and you'll increase my fee? This must be a really dangerous assignment. Call it double my usual, since I'll be working injured, and I'll listen to your pitch. But if I say *no*, you'll fly me back here and leave me alone for at least a year. Agreed?"

"You've got my word on it. Now, if you'll look to the horizon on your left."

Hank did as he was instructed. Just coming into view was what appeared to be a small bird floating over the ocean, but Hank knew it was one of the helicopters that served for transportation around the smaller French Polynesian islands. In moments he would begin to hear the hum of the blades and be able to make out the details of this high-dollar taxi. "I see you were counting on my saying *yes*," he observed dryly.

"I *knew* you'd agree. I just wasn't sure how much it would cost me."

"I guess I should have asked for more."

"Hey, wait until you hear the assignment before you start regretting the price. Besides, I told the pilot to buy your lunch as soon as you're packed. That shouldn't take long—you'll be relaxing in the restaurant in no time."

"You're too generous."

"Oh, and listen, Hank. The pilot is an old Army buddy of mine. He'll be working on this assignment, as well. You'll have some time on your hands once he gets you to Papeete—direct flights to Los Angeles don't leave until late—so I'll arrange for your dinner there, as well. Try to get some sleep on the plane, if you can. I want you fresh when we meet tomorrow morning."

"I guess the lay-over flight through Hawaii is out of the question?" Hank hinted.

"Sorry, my friend. Time is of the essence. I'll see you in the morning."

The line went dead. Hank closed the phone and set it on the little table beside his chair, next to his barely touched drink. The helicopter was clearly audible now and would be touching down any minute. As Hank limped back to the hut to get his stuff, he had a feeling he was going to regret this.

He stuffed his few possessions into a leather backpack and headed for the helipad. The chopper came down nice and gentle. It was an older model, but obviously well cared for, probably even refurbished at some point. Pontoons had been added somewhere along the way, as well. Hank had been around plenty of helicopters while shooting videos over the years, and he knew a good one when he saw it.

The pilot remained in his seat, carefully filling out the helicopter's logbook as the blades slowly came to a stop. *Typical high-strung, meticulous personality*, Hank thought as he watched, hanging back a bit to give the pilot a chance to climb out.

He looked early to mid-fifties with sun-leathered skin and hair quickly going to white, but still fairly full, despite being cropped short. He had a trim build, about five foot ten or eleven, and carried himself confidently.

Hank extended his hand as the pilot walked up. "Hank Sanders. I appreciate the lift. That's a nice bird you've got there. It looks like somebody's been taking good care of her." *The quickest way to a pilot's heart is through his wings*, Hank reflected.

"Oh, thanks," replied the pilot, looking back over his shoulder briefly. "I'm Ranch Richter. I've been flying *Suzy* here for nearly four years now. Bought her about three years back when the outfit I was working for down here went under. You know much about choppers?"

"I've learned a little while heli-skiing."

"Ever fly one yourself?"

"No, never had the privilege."

"Well, throw your stuff in the back, Sanders. We'll eat while they refuel *Suzy*. Then if you're interested, I'll let you take the stick once we're over the water."

"Really?"

"Sure. I don't think you can do much damage out here. It's not like flying through snow covered mountains. Besides, the controls are linked, so I can help you out as need be."

Hank tossed his backpack into the helicopter. *Leather seats, not bad,* he thought, then followed Ranch to the one and only restaurant on the island.

They dined at a small outdoor table, enjoying the sunshine and light breeze. A waiter filled their water glasses and took down their food order before leaving them alone to make small talk.

"So, Smith tells me you're pretty good with a camera, Sanders," Ranch commented cordially.

"Oh, the cameras are no problem—just point and click these days. It's being in the right spot at the right time to get a good picture. That's the real work."

"Is that how you hurt your leg? Being in the right spot?"

"Yeah, I had a snowboarding accident on my last assignment. To get really great footage, you've got to snowboard backwards in order to film the 'star' doing his stunts. Needless to say, the person behind the camera has to be just as good as the one in front of it, maybe even better, and certainly more careful."

Hank shrugged his shoulders sheepishly, "Anyway, being careful isn't exactly my strong suit, or I wouldn't be in this business in the first place. So I ended up with a broken leg, a couple of cracked ribs, and a minor concussion."

Hank didn't mention that he was helping to bust up a large drug ring working out of Aspen at the time, or how many Hollywood stars were copping plea bargains as a result. It might come across as agent-to-agent bragging.

The waiter returned with their dinners, and both men tucked in hungrily.

"You ever been to China before?" Ranch asked after savoring a few bites of the house specialty, coconut-encrusted fish smothered in mango sauce.

"Is that where we're headed?"

"That's what Smith said, but I didn't get many details."

"Well, it's more than I got. He only told me he needed a good cameraman and that there wouldn't be any dangerous stunts. Still, that doesn't say much. He did mention that you and he were old Army buddies."

"Technically, Smith never served in the Army. But, yeah, we worked together in Iraq about five years ago."

"I assume you flew Apaches. Those are nice machines."

"I wish. No, the last thing I flew for the military was a Huey over in Vietnam, thirty plus years ago. Had several of them shot out from under me and lived to tell about it. I shoved the last one I ever flew into the ocean myself, to make room for the next guy trying to land on the ship's deck. Those were some crazy times. People try to compare Iraq and Vietnam, but the two aren't even close."

"What did you do in Iraq, if you weren't flying choppers?"

"Same thing I'd been doing in the States for the couple of years preceding it: pushing papers around. Officially, I'm a surgeon, but with every promotion in the military, I found myself doing less and less operating and more and more administrating. I'd occasionally assist other surgeons, but didn't trust myself to be the primary surgeon on anything bigger than a hemorrhoid."

Ranch pushed the rice around on his plate with his fork as he talked, searching for any remaining flakes of fish.

"Once I got out, I had my retirement and my pilot's license, so I returned to my first love—flying. I tote tourists around down here, and Smith throws me a bone every now and again, so I make out all right. The kids are grown, doing their own thing, and my wife loves living here. So, honestly, I can't complain."

"Do you ever miss it?" Hank asked, wiping his mouth on his napkin and pushing back from the table.

"Miss what?"

"Operating."

"Not as much as I thought I would. Maybe it's because the Army weaned me off of it slowly, rather than making me drop it cold turkey, like most retiring surgeons have to do. But, yeah, sometimes I miss it."

Ranch looked off in the distance with a wistful expression. Hank wondered if he'd hit a sore subject and realized Ranch was probably older than he looked.

Snapping out of his daze, Ranch clapped Hank on the shoulder. "Well, Sanders, we'd better get to Papeete. They should be finished fueling *Suzy* by now, and it's about time for your flying lesson."

After Ranch paid for their meal, they headed back to the chopper and climbed inside. Ranch checked his instruments carefully and radioed in his position and destination. Hank tentatively put on his headset and brought the mouthpiece around. He could hear Ranch speaking to him through the headset over the now muffled sound of the blades gaining momentum.

"Can you hear me alright?"

Hank nodded yes and gave a thumbs up.

"Just push that little red button on the control stick when you want to say something," Ranch continued, pointing to the small button.

"Okay," Hank said, depressing the button as he spoke.

Ranch smiled.

As the helicopter lifted into the sky, Hank watched the huts shrink below him. The water took on multiple shades of blue. *Leaving paradise, all too soon.*

"You don't have much stuff," Ranch's voice came over the headset as he motioned with his head towards the back seat.

"I like to travel light," Hank responded, pushing the button.

"The only people I ever met who traveled that light were a couple of snipers I knew back in Vietnam."

"Whoa, now—you've got the wrong idea," Hank said. "The only thing I shoot is a video camera."

"That so?" Ranch eyed him with mock suspicion, "Then where's all your equipment?"

"First of all," Hank defended, "I'm on vacation, and I don't like to take my work home with me. Second, I could never afford all the high-dollar stuff my employers want me to use. I might do an underwater gig one month, and then jump out of a plane the next. I supply the talent. It's up to them to supply the tools."

"I'll take your word for it," Ranch said, smiling. "Now, here, hold the controls like this," he demonstrated. "The two sticks are linked, so I'll hold mine loosely with my left hand while you drive. The foot pedals rotate us side to side—I'll work those. And I'll control our lift, with my right hand, like this."

Hank heard the engine surge and felt the helicopter lift suddenly. Taking firm hold of the stick, he looked to Ranch for further instruction.

"Now, to tilt left, pull the stick to the left. To tilt right, pull it right, just like you'd guess. Pulling back tilts us up; pushing forward tilts us down. Just try to keep the front edge of the blades parallel with the horizon. I'll control the lift and the side-to-side rotation, like I said, so you just concentrate on keeping us level."

Hank tried to keep the blades level, but it was harder than it looked. He would start to drift to the right, then over-compensate to the left, while unintentionally bringing the nose too far down at the same time.

"It's a little like balancing a BB on an ice cube, isn't it?" Ranch prompted.

"Definitely."

Hank had started to get the hang of it by the time they reached Papeete, but did not find it nearly as easy as Ranch made it look. The years of practice showed. Plus, some people just have a knack for such things. Hank suspected Ranch was one of them.

CHAPTER

10

It's amazing how quickly time passes when you're busy raising a houseful of kids. They actually seem to grow before your eyes. I find myself calling them by the wrong names, not because I've forgotten, but because I just can't believe they have grown up so fast.

All of our kids favor, so it's easy to mistake one for the other. This is especially true when they're dressed alike. The matching clothes they wear when we travel may make it easier to count heads, but they also make it easier to confuse names.

People marvel when they hear we have nine kids. I think they must subconsciously envision a room full of toddlers. They usually say something like, "I don't know how you do it," as they imagine all those runny noses and dirty diapers.

Fortunately, our kids have all arrived one at a time, and usually a couple of years apart. So after about the fourth or fifth child, the older children have been both eager and able to help with the younger ones. That makes all the difference. In a way it's gotten easier, not harder, the more children we've had.

We've assigned each of the older kids a younger "partner" whom they are responsible to help dress, feed, and generally keep an eye on. With nine children this would imply four pairs of kids, assuming Lauren's in charge of baby Matthew. We actually have only three pairs. Aaron is with Joshua, Nathan with Anna, and Philip with Abigail. Seth and Grace are off the hook, since both stay so busy with their college classes. We typically rotate partners once a year, so everyone gets a chance to bond with everyone else.

So where does all that leave me? Well, if our house were a construction site, I'd be the guy leaning on the shovel, telling everyone else to dig a little deeper. I make such useful comments as, "Partners help partners get shoes and jackets—it's time to go!" or, "Aaron, will you change Joshua's shirt? He spilled milk on himself at breakfast."

On the whole, I think our system works pretty well. Whenever we travel, I keep an overall head count, double check hotel rooms for items left behind, and lend a hand to anyone who might be having trouble with a younger partner. In other words, I'm not totally useless. But I'm not critically important, either, which leaves me open to casually pursue my extracurricular governmental activities as needed.

The day soon arrived for us to leave for China. Our bags were packed, our tickets purchased, and our passports ready, so we piled into our fifteen-passenger van—the only vehicle that can accommodate our crew—and headed to Dallas/Fort Worth International Airport. It's a two-hour drive from our small town, but it's easier and faster than trying to catch a connecting flight with so many little ones in tow. Besides, our family can practically fill up a commuter plane, which makes it difficult to book adequate seating on short notice.

Upon arriving at DFW, we took the trolley to our terminal. The kids loved this. The planes looked like toys as we observed them from the elevated tram. We checked our one bag of dress clothes, but toted everything else onto the plane.

It was a little inconvenient trying to stuff so many backpacks into the overhead bin, but we couldn't afford to lose anything. Imagine being stranded in a strange city and having to track down clothing for eleven people in multiple sizes, including extra-tall, using public transportation and a Chinese phrasebook. The hassle factor alone would be astronomical.

Fortunately, since we were "travelling with small children," we were allowed to board early. I felt a little guilty about going to the front of the line with such a big group, but it was probably for the best.

"If you need anything, I'm Katie," came a gentle voice.

Lauren and I looked up to see a young blonde flight attendant. "Okay," we answered together.

"Are they all yours?"

I gave Lauren a knowing grin and let her field the inevitable list of questions we'd both answered a million times before.

"Yes, they're all ours."

"Any adopted?"

"No."

"Any twins?"

"No."

"So you've given birth—what, seven times?" the flight attendant asked, trying to count all the faces.

"Actually, nine," Lauren answered. "The older ones are ours, too."

"Oh my, that hardly seems possible. I'm nearly thirty and neither of you look much older than I am. How long have you been married?"

"Twenty years—nearly half our lives."

"The better half," I said, nudging Lauren with my elbow.

"For *one* of us, maybe," Lauren laughed, nudging me back.

"You guys are too cute," the flight attendant smiled. "I have to get back to work, but I'd love to visit more once we're in the air."

The other passengers began to file slowly onto the plane, checking seat numbers against their boarding passes. Eventually, the last one was strapped safely into his seat, and the plane began to taxi down the runway.

I don't know why, but I always enjoy the take-off. There's something about feeling my back pushed against the seat and seeing the earth peel away beneath me that I find exhilarating. Although millions of others share that same experience everyday, it reminds me of what a unique time we occupy in history. No Roman centurion, no Viking explorer, no Spanish conquistador ever experienced the thrill of lift-off that so many of us take completely for granted.

Once the plane had leveled itself, I looked back to check on our kids. The older ones were reading, the smaller ones were drawing on notepads Lauren had given them for the trip, and the baby had already nodded off.

That was one thing I could say about our family— we traveled well. Maybe practice really does make perfect.

The flight attendant returned.

"Your kids are so well-behaved," she whispered. "We always draw straws to see who gets the section with the most kids. But now the flight attendant in first class is begging me to trade. She only has one kid up there, but I think he's auditioning for a remake of *The Exorcist*."

As if on cue, we heard high-pitched wailing from the front of the plane. "But I don't want soda. I want a lemon slushy. Give me a lemon slushy now!"

There was a crash and splash. A bedraggled, middle-aged attendant appeared from behind the first-class curtain. Her jet-black, dyed hair was plastered to her forehead, and her shirt was soaked. She marched straight to the restroom in the back of the plane with the obvious self-control of a seasoned professional.

"It's only Sprite. It's only Sprite," she muttered as she squeezed past.

The younger flight attendant suddenly had a look of inspiration. "I'll bet you guys homeschool, don't you?"

"Why, yes, we do," Lauren answered.

"That's a reasonably safe assumption for a family our size," I added.

"Well, I just got engaged. My fiancé and I've been discussing the possibility of homeschooling our kids someday," she said, flashing her oversized engagement ring.

"Oh, how pretty," Lauren enthused.

"I'm going to make an improvised lemon slushy while Julianne cleans up, but then I would love for you to tell me more about homeschooling. One of my good friends just had her second child, and she's been talking all about it."

I elbowed Lauren as the flight attendant disappeared into first class. "Another Gunderson apprentice. You'll have half of China homeschooling by the time we leave."

"I hope so," she grinned and pulled out her crocheting.

I watched her work for a while. I'm so proud of my wife. Outside of work, I'm simply known as "Lauren's husband." Many of our acquaintances don't even know what I do for a living, but they know all about Lauren. She's a local legend—the woman with nine kids, who teaches them calculus at home!

The remainder of our flight was quiet. Lauren visited intermittently with Katie, the flight attendant, while I looked out the window, daydreaming about what lay ahead. We were to meet with Hank, the cameraman, at LAX. Filming would begin as soon as we arrived.

As we debarked the plane, I saw someone with dark sunglasses and a ridiculous paisley sport coat holding up a cardboard sign with "Gunderson" written across it in big, bold letters. It took me a second to realize it was Smith.

Next to him stood a trim young man about six feet tall with a dark tan and a clean-shaven head. He hefted a fairly large video camera onto his shoulder when he spotted our family. He limped just a bit as he moved towards us, possibly from the weight of the camera. Clearly, this was Hank.

"Act natural," I hissed at everyone, but proceeded to assume a big, fake smile myself. Joshua tripped and started crying. I had to help out by holding him, while his partner, Aaron, took his backpack and Lauren carried the baby.

"Get a close up of the tears," Smith instructed, hamming up the Hollywood producer role he was obviously playing. Once the toddler had settled down and we were all standing around feeling awkward, he practically shouted, "And, *cut!*"

"I'm sorry about that Mrs. Gunderson," he apologized. "It's all about ratings these days—and that means drama. And what could be more dramatic than the tears of a dear, sweet child like this one?"

He patted Joshua on the head, who eyed him suspiciously. I think Smith was enjoying himself.

"That's okay," Lauren replied. "Part of the price tag for our free trip, I suppose. I assume you must be the producer, and this is the cameraman who will be travelling with our family?"

"Yes, of course. I'm Eric Smith, and this is Hank Sanders. Once you leave this airport, I'll hand you over to our Hong Kong affiliate, Zhou Li. Hank, as you mentioned, will be with you for the duration."

We shook hands all around, then Smith asked to talk with me privately about the trip. He had Hank shoot more footage to distract the others while we stepped away.

"Pretty convincing, *Eric*," I whispered once we had moved to a quiet corner. "But aren't you breaking regulations to be here?"

"What part of this operation looks like we're following regulations?"

"Good point, but you'd better hurry up and tell me what you need to say before one of the kids wanders over."

"Don't worry—Hank will keep them busy. I need to give you the code phrases we're using in the extraction."

"But I'm not supposed to be involved in the ex—"

"I know, but I still want you to be up to speed with what's happening. Our mystery researcher sent us half the specifications for a new scrambler the Chinese have developed. It's designed to keep us from spotting their surface-to-air missile radar and taking it out. In other words, they can see us, but we can't see them for a counterstrike."

"Alright, so—"

"So, he sent top secret information to demonstrate his legitimacy, but also included instructions for us to follow. Once we've done as he's asked, he'll give us the other half of the plans as identity confirmation, along with further instructions."

"And you're going along with this?"

"What choice do I have?"

"I guess you're right. So what are our instructions?"

"When we hear echoes of Chinese friendship going around the world, we are to tell the messenger, 'Nixon would be proud' and await further instructions."

"That's it?"

"Do you see why I wanted you to know? It's cryptic enough that we need everyone to keep their eyes and ears open."

"Echoes of Chinese friendship. Tell the messenger 'Nixon would be proud.' Interesting."

"Maybe it'll make better sense once you get there."

"I sure hope so."

We headed back to the others and found Hank chatting with Grace while the rest looked on patiently with their partners. Seth nodded towards Hank and rolled his eyes at me. I think he was vaguely repulsed by the idea that someone was showing interest in his little sister.

Hank had rolled up his cargo shorts on one side and was showing Grace a long scar down the side of his thigh. The video camera was off and just sitting on the ground. Hank had clearly found something more interesting to do than shoot footage of a bunch of kids.

"Nasty scar you have there, Hank," I interrupted. "From the size of it, it looks like you got a plate put on the outside of your femur instead of a rod through the middle. You must have broken the bone in multiple places."

Hank's head snapped up, and I think he was mildly embarrassed. I could see he had clear blue eyes.

"That's exactly right, Dr. Gunderson," he stammered.

"Most surgeries leave a characteristic scar, so it's pretty easy to tell what's been done. For instance, if you had gotten a rod in your femur, the scar would have been smaller and higher up. Probably higher than you'd want to show off in public."

Hank blushed slightly and quickly rolled his shorts back down. Seth grinned.

"What do you say we grab some lunch, everyone?" Smith called out, motioning for us to follow him.

The food wasn't bad for airport fare. It helped pass the time while we waited for our flight. Smith prattled on about how documentary filmmakers don't get the respect they're due and what a public service they provide. He expressed his ambivalence about reality TV. Sure it paid

115

well, but it was hard to find good original material. He said he was grateful to our family for letting him film our adventure, especially since it tied in with so many things that were of current public interest—world travel, big families, and of course, academic competitions featuring brainiac homeschooled kids.

If I hadn't known him for five years, I would have bought his shtick, hook, line, and sinker. I had to suppress a laugh a time or two, covering it with a fake cough.

At the other table, Hank regaled the kids with stories of daring stunts and extreme sports adventure. The younger ones were enraptured, as were the middle ones, but Grace acted aloof and only vaguely interested. That usually meant she was utterly fascinated, but I would never have told Hank that.

Seth seemed to think that Hank was the coolest person he'd ever met, despite Hank's poorly camouflaged interest in Grace. As far as he knew, Hank was the complete antithesis of his boring old dad. Hank was single, carefree, and travelled all over the world to face extreme challenges of every kind. Seth would never have even put us in the same room together, much less on the same team. Life is sometimes funny that way.

Feigning boredom, Grace pulled out a book to read. I knew the conversation must have really piqued her curiosity, because she was going to such great lengths to hide it.

"Extreme sports junkies are not as bad as you think," Hank said, looking directly at Grace. "A lot of us are actually good guys."

Grace kept reading her book and, without looking up, said, "I don't classify people as good or bad." Then she turned a page.

"You don't?"

"No, I don't. I simply think of them as somewhere along a continuum of maturity."

"*A continuum of maturity?* What's that supposed to mean?"

"It basically means that people mature at different rates. Some people mature quickly, some more slowly," Grace closed her book and looked Hank straight in the eyes, "and some never grow up at all."

"Nice," is all he said, as we heard the boarding call for our plane announced over the loudspeaker.

CHAPTER
11

The plane ride to China was uneventful, albeit long and tiresome. The trick was to break it up into small bites that we could handle. We would watch a movie for a while, then eat a meal, then work puzzles, then eat again, then read a book.

Somewhere in there, most of us got a nap—except Lauren, who used the quiet times to crochet. She has always claimed that keeping her hands busy helps her to think. The more she has on her mind, the faster the thread flies through her fingers. By the time we reached Hong Kong, she'd completed a good three yards of handmade lace.

At the airport, our local producer and chauffeur were waiting to meet us. The chauffeur was my old Army buddy, Ranch Richter, but we acted like complete strangers. He didn't look like he'd aged a bit.

The producer, Zhou Li, was strikingly beautiful. She was athletically thin and, at five feet six, fairly tall for a Chinese woman. I had to wonder why she was a struggling actress and not a big star already, but I don't know much about the politics of Chinese movie making.

I remembered reading somewhere that the industry has a bias against people born outside the big cities; they're viewed as country bumpkins. Maybe she was just a small town girl struggling to make it in the big city?

Whatever the case, the real issue was why was she working for us? Money to pay the bills until she got her big break? A grudge against an oppressive government? A forced abortion at some point?

It was only later that I learned her full story. Her father had been a high-ranking government official, and she had grown up with all the corresponding privileges. He had financed her acting career—until he fell out of favor with his superiors and was demoted in disgrace.

Although she hadn't made it big as an actress, her beauty had attracted the attention of a young but powerful drug-smuggler who dabbled in the movie industry. They dated for a long time. Her father's old connections kept her boyfriend out of trouble, and her boyfriend's connections allowed her and her father to exact a small amount of revenge against a system that had turned on them. Her father eventually died. Then her boyfriend was killed, and she was captured in a British led sting operation in Hong Kong. Alone in the world, she had cut a deal and been an agent ever since.

Today, Zhou and Ranch hadn't been able to find a vehicle large enough for all of us, so they'd leased two minivans instead. We split our group, with Lauren taking the three girls and two littlest boys. I got the four oldest boys and Hank. Zhou drove the lead car with the girls. Ranch followed close behind with the rest of us.

The hotel was absolutely breathtaking. Clearly no expense had been spared. There was exotic marble everywhere, and all the furnishings seemed to be gilded. It was enough to make a Saudi Prince proud. I was told the hotel had been recently updated, but this was beyond a simple renovation. Apparently, the Chinese sponsors of the competition were trying to make a good impression. I was just glad I didn't have to foot the bill.

Lauren forgot to remind me about getting cash at the airport, but remembered at the hotel. Fortunately, the hotel was big enough to provide a currency exchange for their guests. I got the equivalent of about seven hundred dollars in bills and hid them in my travel belt before dinner.

We decided to eat at the hotel, which had an excellent restaurant, then turn in early to shake off the jet lag and get ready for the next day's competition. The boys convinced me to let everyone swim after dinner, since there was a miniature water park built into the hotel. This provided an easy way for everyone to freshen up and allowed us to skip bathing the littlest ones after such a long trip. Call it laziness, but it seemed the most practical thing to do at the time.

We ended up having a blast, and I think Hank got some great footage for the fake documentary. He seemed to spend a disproportionate amount of time focused on Grace, but she was wearing a modest, one-piece swimsuit that was Lauren-approved, so I tried not to worry.

Looking back, I think it was Grace's overall wholesomeness that so captivated Hank from the beginning. He had seen his share of wild girls over the years and knew they were a dead-end trail. I suspect he valued Grace primarily because she valued herself.

In fact, it would probably not be exaggerating to say that Hank was crazy about Grace from the moment he met her. Studies have shown that the blood flow patterns inside the brains of people in love look suspiciously similar to those of schizophrenics. I think that explains a lot.

We all slept like logs, then enjoyed a ridiculously opulent breakfast buffet the next morning. The boys still blame the buffet for why they didn't do better in the competition. They claim all their blood was being shunted to their stomachs and away from their brains. To hear them tell it, they could barely stay awake, much less compete. *Excuses*.

They actually did better than I had expected, which may reflect how tough the competition is in our home state of Texas. It may also mean that the Chinese stacked the deck with weak opponents when they sent out the invitations. I can't say for sure, but of the fifty who made it to the finals, twenty-seven—just over half—were Chinese.

The morning competition consisted of a written exam to thin the field from five hundred competitors to fifty. In the afternoon, those fifty would answer questions on stage until a winner was declared.

While the boys took their written tests, the rest of us played ping-pong on some tables that had been set up to keep the families busy. We had just finished our second game when Nathan joined us with a Chinese boy about his own age. They had been given a couple of hours for the exam, but both had finished early. Nathan is a quick test taker; evidently, the other boy was, too.

"Who's your new friend?" I asked smiling at the teen.

"This is Chen. We finished at about the same time, so he asked if I wanted to play some table tennis. He says he can't believe I have eight brothers and sisters, so I wanted him to meet all of you, as well."

After everyone was introduced, the boys played a match. Lauren needed my help with the little ones, so I spent the morning chasing after Joshua and waiting patiently for everyone to finish their tests.

After the last exam had been handed in, all the contestants and their families reassembled in the auditorium for some entertainment by a local acrobatic troupe while the tests were graded and the rankings tabulated.

Nathan missed making the top fifty by just two positions. Philip was number forty-nine, however, and I think he felt vindicated when he got to be up on the stage and his older brother didn't. There's nothing like a little sibling rivalry.

Our new friend ended up getting the only perfect score on the written exam, but had rejoined his own group before the announcement was made, so we didn't get to congratulate him.

Lunch was delicious. I'm not a big fan of Chinese food, but then again, most of my experience has been at various "Super Buffets" in America. I'd always been told that the authentic stuff was worse—chicken feet and eels— but what they served that day was terrific, like the difference between eating fresh seafood in a coastal city and eating frozen seafood somewhere inland.

The competition began promptly after lunch. Philip was eliminated in the first round. He actually had what should have been a fairly easy question: What is the most visited landmark in China? Unfortunately, we hadn't begun our sightseeing yet, and he didn't know.

He could have given a top-five list fairly easily, but wasn't certain which was number one. We watched him deliberate for a moment before answering with a grin, "McDonalds?"

This drew quite a few laughs from the Americans and Europeans, but the judges gave Philip a stern look. I don't think they shared his sense of humor. Sometimes the truth hurts.

Most of the competitors were actually quite good, so it took a while to get down to the final three. I learned a lot of obscure geographic trivia in the process.

The last three contestants were a girl from Germany, a boy from India, and our new friend, Chen. It was funny how we all felt a certain sense of pride at seeing someone we knew, however briefly, in the final three.

Chen ended up winning, although it took six more rounds to find something the other two didn't know. The German girl finished third and the Indian boy second. Each was given a large trophy and an opportunity to say a few words. The Master of Ceremonies held the microphone in front of the girl first.

"Yes, I would just like to say *thank you* to the people of China for hosting this wonderful event. I've had a great time and will cherish the memories always." She gave a big smile and a small bow to the host. He bowed back and moved to the boy from India.

"Well, I thought the questions were a lot easier than I would have expected at first."

The host went visibly cold at the insult.

"However, they got progressively harder, which is how it should be, so that was good."

The host relaxed a little.

"I have never lost an event in my life, so clearly the competition was decent."

He looked at Chen when he said this, ignoring the girl. Everyone present was starting to feel awkward by this point.

"So— congratulations."

He extended his hand to Chen with a forced smile and, mercifully, quit talking.

Chen shook his hand graciously; then spoke into the microphone himself. He looked over the audience and then straight into the central television camera and said something in Chinese. You could see many of the Chinese people throughout the room nodding in agreement.

Chen then turned to the Indian boy and said something in what I assume was Hindi. The boy smiled and nodded.

Next, he turned to the girl and said something in German, but I could only make out a few words, something about friendship. She smiled shyly, and Chen looked back at the big television camera.

"Let today be the beginning of a new age of friendship between China and all the people of the world!"

he said in crisp clear English with a touch of a British accent.

He then proceeded to repeat the phrase again in Spanish, then French, and then Italian.

Suddenly it hit me. I was hearing echoes of Chinese friendship going around the world, and everyone was hearing those echoes in their own language. This kid wasn't just the winner—he must be some kind of messenger for our defector!

I shot a glance at Hank who had picked up on it, too. We both started making our way down to the stage. Chen continued to give the salutation in at least ten or twelve more languages, but I lost count.

"Where are you going?" Lauren asked.

"I want to get some close-up footage," Hank volunteered.

"I thought I'd go congratulate our new friend," I said.

We got down to the stage just as things were wrapping up. "Hey, Chen," I waved to him, practically shouting over all the commotion.

"Hi, Mr. Gunderson," he said waving back at me.

"Congratulations. That was quite a performance you gave."

"Thank you."

"Nixon would have been proud."

"Kissinger, too," he replied with a knowing smile.

I didn't know what else to do. The ball was in his court now. I waved goodbye as Hank and I headed back to join our crew.

Apparently, our scientist had a family. I assumed Chen was his kid and was in on the arrangement. The scientist would undoubtedly want an extraction for his entire family, including Chen, but that really wasn't my job. I had done my part. A little sightseeing and we would be on our way home. Chen seemed like a nice young man, though. I hoped it all worked out for him and his family, whoever they were.

I gave Hank a "What now?" look. He just shrugged his shoulders and started putting away his equipment. Now we waited.

"Hey, Dad?"

I turned around and found Nathan holding out a small USB thumb drive.

"Chen asked me to give this to our cameraman if he won. He didn't say what it was, but said Hank would understand. Maybe it's some pictures or video for the documentary? Who knows?"

Hank and I looked towards the stage, but Chen was gone.

"Okay, great."

I took the small storage device and handed it to Hank.

"Now listen, kids. I need everyone to take their partners to the restroom and help them get freshened up while I give Hank a hand loading the equipment. We may get stuck in traffic, so it's important that we all use the facilities before we leave."

Everyone knew the drill.

Hank and I headed to the minivans. Ranch was there waiting. Zhou followed us out. She was the only one with a computer. It was one of those miniature laptops that only weigh two or three pounds. She dug it out of her stuff, and Hank plugged in the USB.

"Dr. Gunderson, it's asking for a password," Hank said.

I thought for a moment. A *password?* "Try 'Nixon' or 'Kissinger' for starters."

Hank carefully spelled out each attempt, his fingers hovering deftly over the keys.

"Bingo! Kissinger was it."

"Excellent. What's on the drive?"

"One second. It's taking a little bit to open. These lightweight computers are great, but the processors are so slow. Okay, here we go. It looks like—it's the other half of the scrambler schematics, as promised. Here's our next set of instructions, as well. It's just a street corner and a time—midnight tonight. That's pretty self-explanatory, isn't it? Good job everyone."

"Here come your kids," Zhou said.

"Alright, everyone. Let's load up with the same seating arrangement as before," I said as Lauren and the kids gathered around.

"Zhou has picked out a really nice restaurant where we can celebrate, and Hank can get some final footage for the documentary. Then we're free to relax and enjoy ourselves for a few days before heading back home. No more filming. No more competition. No more responsibilities. Just stress-free fun!"

CHAPTER

12

Chen had less than two hours to orchestrate his and Jung's escape. There was a lot to do, not the least of which was explaining all the details to Jung. She would catch on quickly, but he wished she hadn't waited until just a few days ago to agree to come along. He was pleased she was coming, but she hadn't left him much time to finalize his plans, much less to fill her in on everything.

He dropped his pocketknife into his backpack on top of his change of clothes, then tossed in a pair of scissors for cutting hair. He had briefly considered dying his hair blonde or something, but in China that would hardly be a disguise—it would make him stand out like a sore thumb.

Next, he held up a Ziploc bag of white powder. It was just baking soda, but it looked more illicit in the hotel room than it had in his kitchen. He would use it to stop the bleeding from the small incisions he would need to make on Jung and himself.

Everything was ready. Hopefully, Jung had brought some rubbing alcohol, some silver nitrate, and the hair clippers from the lab, as he had requested. Those items would make things easier, but they weren't absolutely essential. The scalpel and surgical scissors he had asked for would also help, but his pocketknife would work almost as well in a pinch. Chen believed in having a backup plan for everything.

He gave one last look around. This was it. Shouldering his backpack, he stepped out into the hallway of the hotel. He checked his watch again. Ten fifteen. The stairwell was just a couple of doors down. Chen made his way towards it. As he reached for the door handle, the door popped open and a middle-aged couple stepped out. It was no one he knew, and they were so engaged in conversation that they hardly noticed him. Nonetheless, it startled him. He had to pause for a few deep breaths at the top of the stairs.

Jung was just one flight down and a few doors over. Chen made his way to her room and knocked. She was expecting him and opened the door immediately. After checking the hallway, he slipped inside.

"We don't have much time," he told her.

"Very well. What do I need to do?"

"Let's start with the clippers. Do you have them?"

"Yes. I guess you want me to buzz your hair off as a disguise or something?"

"Precisely. Did you bring the other items, as well?"

"Most of them. I couldn't find any scalpels. We mainly use scissors in the lab, so I brought a pair of those. I also brought a razor blade, but it isn't sterile. I'm assuming that's why you wanted the alcohol—to sterilize things? I get the impression you're going to be doing some minor surgery, but I can't imagine what exactly it will be."

"Grab the clippers and come to the bathroom. We can talk while you cut my hair. Then I'll cut yours."

A look of horror passed over Jung's face. "You're not going to buzz mine, are you?"

"No, of course not. I've got some regular scissors in my backpack. We'll just need to shorten it a little. But come on, we need to hurry."

Wrapping a towel around his shoulders to protect his clothes from the loose hair, Chen sat down on the toilet. Jung stood beside him and plugged in the clippers. She sorted through several different attachments.

"How long do you want it?"

"Use the longest one your have. I don't want it too extreme. That would be as bad as no disguise at all."

Jung grabbed the size eight, which would leave Chen's hair about an inch long, and turned on the clippers. He held his chin up. Jung lifted his bangs with her left hand and brought the clippers in with her right. The dog and rat hair she was used to cutting was a lot shorter and coarser.

"Are you sure about this?" she asked doubtfully. "Once I do it, there's no turning back."

"There's already no turning back."

Jung began to cut. Thick locks fell to the floor around the commode. Chen didn't flinch.

"So are you going to tell me the rest of what's going on?"

"Yes, I just don't know where to begin."

"Try the beginning."

"Well, for starters, I don't think our parents' deaths were accidental."

"You mean they were killed?"

"Yes, but not only our parents. Lots of parents. All over China. Parents of kids just like us."

"You mean kids with high IQ's?"

"Yes."

"But why?"

"To give the government complete control over us, so they can use us for whatever purpose they want. No meddling parents asking questions or getting in the way. I found a huge file, Jung. There are hundreds of kids, nearly a thousand so far, who have been gathered over the years. All of them have the same basic story. They get indentified as exceptional, and then both parents die in a tragic accident shortly thereafter. They become wards of the state and ultimately end up working for Director Lao. It's called *The Prodigy Project*."

Jung pondered that for a moment. "Do you remember your parents, Chen?"

"Only barely. It seems like I can remember everything I've ever known so clearly, except for them. They are like phantoms on the edge of my consciousness. Whenever I try to reach for them, they vanish."

"I'm the same way. When I try to think of my father, all I can see is an image of Director Lao, only younger. My mother I can't see at all, but I can remember a snippet of song—something about geese and rain. It makes me think of those rice paddies in Southern China. Maybe it was a folk song—like a lullaby she sang to me each night. I don't really know."

Jung turned the trimmers off. They both stared into the mirror, lost in thought. "Your turn," Chen finally said.

They traded places and Chen got the scissors from his backpack. As he reached for her hair and held it up trying to decide on the optimal length, there came a sharp knock on the door. Jung and Chen froze.

"Answer it," Chen directed. "I'll clean up in here."

Jung shut the bathroom door, and Chen began to quietly clean up the loose hair. The rap came again, only louder.

"Who is it?" Jung called.

"It's Hui Tong. Is everything okay?"

Chen could hear Jung pull open the door. "Yes, I'm fine. Is something wrong?"

"No, nothing is wrong, I just wanted to make sure you and Chen got back to your rooms safely. I checked Chen's room, but no one answered. I thought he might be with you."

130

"Yes, he's here, but he's in the restroom. I think all the rich food has upset his stomach. He's been in there a while."

"Chen, are you okay?" Hui called out.

"Yes, yes. It's just nerves. I'll be fine."

Hui seemed satisfied. "You'll let me know if he doesn't get better?"

"Yes, of course."

Chen listened as Jung shut the door to the hallway, then opened the bathroom door and came back inside. He had finished cleaning up the hair and was sterilizing his pocketknife with the rubbing alcohol he'd found in Jung's bag.

Chen looked up. "Listen, let's leave your hair long for now, just in case he comes back. We are getting short on time, and I don't know how long it will take to do the most important part."

"Which is?"

"Removing the tracking devices."

"That doesn't sound very comfortable."

"It won't be, especially since we don't have any kind of anesthetic. Fortunately, they are fairly superficial."

"No brain surgery then?"

Chen smiled at her joke. She had a gift for helping him relax just when he started to get wound up.

"No brain surgery. Here, look." Chen held up his left arm and showed her a small scar near his armpit.

Jung pulled back her sleeve and saw that she had a matching scar. It was tiny and insignificant, but definitely there.

"Roll your fingers across the scar," Chen said. "Can you feel a bump underneath?"

"Yes, I can. I suppose I noticed it before, but never gave it much thought. They must have been implanted when we were little. I don't remember."

"I don't either, but that's how they keep track of us. It was another one of my discoveries while exploring the mainframe computer. Hui knew I was here before he ever knocked on your door. He was just curious what we were up to. Had you pretended I wasn't here, it would not have fooled him, but it would have definitely made him suspicious. You did well."

"Thank you." She eyed the pocketknife. "So, we're going to cut these tracking devices out without any anesthetic?"

"I'm afraid so. You do mine, then I'll do yours. You can take mine out first since you have more experience with this kind of thing."

"Cutting up lab rats hardly qualifies as experience."

"It's more than I have."

"That doesn't exactly instill me with confidence."

"I'm sorry, but it's the best I can do. Unless we get rid of these things, we won't have a chance. If we remove them now and leave them under our pillows, they won't know we're gone until sometime tomorrow. Hopefully, we'll be out of the country before they ever discover we're missing."

"I understand why we need to do it, but that doesn't make it any easier."

"Watch. I'm going to slap my arm like this." Chen slapped the inside of his left arm until it was red and irritated, then he pressed his right thumb down hard just above the scar.

"What's that all about?"

"The slapping creates a diffuse, mild pain that will distract my brain from the sharper, more intense pain of the incision. Holding pressure will compress some of the nerves and blood vessels in the area to further lessen the pain and bleeding respectively. Now all you have to do is make a small cut on top of the scar. The fat and tissue will bulge out, and you can grab it with the tweezers. The tracking unit should be somewhere in the fat that you snip off with the surgical scissors. We'll double check to make sure, then apply the silver nitrate to control the bleeding."

"What if we can't stop the bleeding?"

"We will, don't worry. I brought some baking soda as a back up. I read somewhere that criminals in America use it to plug up gunshot wounds until they can get to the hospital. Worst-case scenario, we'll have to hold pressure for a while. That would be inconvenient, but it wouldn't be life threatening. Hopefully, we can just cauterize it with the silver nitrate, put a butterfly bandage across it, and be done."

Jung looked unconvinced.

"Come on," Chen urged, eyeing his watch. "We have less than an hour."

Jung grabbed the knife. Hesitantly, she took Chen's arm and held counter traction with her thumb, making the scar between their thumbs taut. Then she made a quick puncture wound with the knife, not too deep, not to shallow. She really was more skilled than she was letting on. The fat bulged out and she grasped it with the tweezers. She could feel the hard nodule and lifted it up.

Chen let out a gasp. He had been trying to watch, to study Jung's technique, but now he had to look away. His pain relief tricks weren't helping as much as he'd hoped. The incision had been tolerable, but the tugging from the tweezers sent a wave of nausea over him that he could barely control. He heard a snip and felt a sharp pain. The tugging sensation was replaced by a dull throb. He looked back. Blood was running onto the floor.

Jung grabbed a washcloth and held pressure. "Here, you hold pressure," she told him. "I'll get the silver nitrate ready."

Chen saw her head turn away from him, then everything started to fade out. When he came to, he was staring up at the bathroom ceiling. It took him a second to get oriented. Then he was embarrassed. "How long have I been out?"

"No more than a minute or two. I saw you slumping through the mirror and caught you before you hit your head on anything. Since your breathing was normal, I went ahead and dried up your wound and applied the bandage. Look, it all worked perfectly."

Chen looked at his arm. Sure enough, there was a tiny bandage and no blood. Very professionally done.

"Your turn," Jung announced brightly as she handed Chen the knife.

"Now wait a second," Chen protested.

"I don't think we have a second to spare."

Jung slapped her arm a few times and held it towards Chen, dutifully applying pressure with her thumb. He placed his thumb opposite hers like he'd seen her do. The tiny scar loomed large. Chen swallowed hard and lowered the knife towards it.

He paused and looked into Jung's eyes. She nodded for him to continue, then turned her head towards the shower. He was glad she wasn't going to watch. He felt self-conscious, afraid of hurting her more than necessary through lack of skill.

He pushed the blade into her skin. It was tougher than he had expected, but suddenly gave way so that he cut a bigger gash than he intended. She tensed, but held still, her eyes tightly closed.

Chen picked up the tweezers, found the electronic pellet after a bit of digging around, then carefully snipped it away. The tissue was strong and sinewy, and he had to snip hard to cut through it. Jung groaned quietly and looked down at her arm. The blood had begun to flow, so she quickly applied pressure.

"Did you get it?" she asked.

"I think so," Chen replied and began to pick at the tissue he had laid on the bathroom counter. There it was, a little metal ball the size and shape of a BB or a small ball bearing. He showed it to Jung. "They're not very big, but they're enormous by today's nanotechnology standards."

The bleeding had slowed down on its own to some degree, but Chen touched it up with the silver nitrate. Jung winced a time or two, but reassured him with a smile whenever he looked up. Once it was fairly dry, he put a butterfly bandage across it to hold the edges together. He looked at it proudly once he was finished.

"You're a regular surgeon," Jung teased.

"Sorry about fainting."

"Don't worry about that. The first time I had to cut into a rat, I actually threw up. In fact, I couldn't stop throwing up until they gave me a shot of something and put me to bed. So on the whole, I think you did really well."

"You mean it?"

"Sure."

"Well, we only have a few minutes left before the lights go out and we make our getaway. We'd better change. We'll wear the khaki and red outfits so we'll look like school kids, but we'll need to cover up with the gray sweat jackets and hoods until we are free from the hotel. I don't think the security cameras will catch us when the power is down, but I want to play it safe. We'll dump the jackets later."

Jung stared at him for a second or two.

"What's the matter?" he asked.

"Well, are you going to take the bathroom or the bedroom to change?"

"Oh, sorry. You stay here. I'll take the bedroom."

Chen stepped into the hallway as Jung closed the door behind him. He could hear her shuffling around behind the door. Carrying his backpack to the bedroom, he quickly changed into his khaki pants and red shirt, then slipped on his gray jacket and pulled up the hood. He would remind Jung not to look directly into any cameras, just in case.

The bathroom door opened.

"How do I look?" Jung asked, turning in a circle.

"Like a gray Ninja in a skirt."

She pretended to fluff her hair even though the hood was up. "Think it will catch on as a fashion statement?"

"Absolutely. It'll be all the rage by the end of the season."

They smiled at each other and fell silent. "How much time do we have?" she asked.

Chen looked at his watch. "Seven minutes. That's enough time to cut your hair if we hurry."

"Do it, then." She folded down her hood and flipped out her hair. It struck him as a singularly feminine thing to do. She walked into the bathroom and came back with a towel. "Here, tuck this around my neck."

He did so, then began to quickly trim her hair. When he was done, she admired it in the bedroom mirror. "I really do look like a school girl, but it's been a long time since I felt like one. Maybe never."

"We've been older than our age since the day we were born," he said.

"Yes, we have," she nodded knowingly.

"Let's get by the door. It's almost time."

As they waited by the door, she whispered, "So, how did you arrange for a power outage at the hotel? Did you hack into their computers?"

"No. Their security system was on a closed circuit, so I couldn't get in. At least, not very easily. I had to shut down power for a big chunk of the city instead. It was easier to hack the electric company than the hotel. I'm just hoping Hui doesn't decide to check on us again when the lights go out. Hopefully, he'll trust those precious little beads sitting on the bathroom counter in there."

"Shouldn't we put them under our pillows, like you said before?"

"Good point, but I don't have time to take mine upstairs. I'll have to leave it on the extra bed in this room." Chen ran to the bathroom, grabbed the two pellets, deposited one on each bed, and then raced back to the door just as the lights went out.

As they carefully slipped out into the hallway, Chen took Jung's hand. A sliver of moonlight, peering through the windows at the end of the hall, kept things from being completely dark, but just barely.

No such luck with the stairwells. They carefully felt for the railings and descended slowly, feeling for each step. After a couple of flights, the lights suddenly came back on. It was only the faint battery-powered emergency lights, but it was blinding for a moment. Startled, Jung froze.

"It's okay. It's just the battery-powered lights. The back-up generator won't kick on for a little while yet. Once it does, it will take a minute or two for the security system to reboot. The outside lighting won't come back on at all until my program lets it, which gives us another four minutes. We can actually go faster now that we can see, which is good."

Jung seemed reassured, and they both hurried on. As they came to the bottom flight, they noticed a young man dressed in black jeans and a black T-shirt leaning against the wall next to the emergency exit. He was looking at the ground and smoking a cigarette.

Chen glanced at Jung. "Come on," he whispered and proceeded forward with his head down to avoid eye contact with the stranger.

As they reached the last step, the young man said quietly, "Someone turned off the smoke alarm for me."

The voice was vaguely familiar. Chen glanced up furtively. The young man was blowing out a cloud of smoke that obscured his face, but as it cleared, Chen recognized him. It was Steven, Director Lao's son.

"Good evening, Chen, Jung," he said nodding at each in turn. "Going out for a stroll?"

He dropped his cigarette and stomped it out with a broad grin. He was in control of the situation now and was enjoying it.

Chen felt a surge of panic. Something in him wanted to punch Steven on the nose and run like mad. Another part wanted to try to bluff his way out, but the gray hooded jackets in the middle of the night made that highly unlikely. Steven was no fool. Instead, Chen just stood there, as if frozen.

"Cat's got your tongue, I see," Steven laughed, "so I'll make this easy. I know you probably don't have much time."

He reached into his back pocket and pulled out a Tazer. Chen backed up a step and put his arms out behind him, instinctively protecting Jung.

"It's not what you think," Steven said. "You have GPS tracking devices imbedded under your skin. The Tazer will disable them, so they can't track you. It fries the electronics. That's how I got away the first time. I won't lie—it hurts like mad, and they'll come looking for you as soon as the signal goes dead, but you won't stand a chance otherwise."

"Why would you help us?" Chen asked.

"I have my reasons. It's more than I can explain in the time we have. Suffice it to say, Lao ordered me to follow your electronic tracks, to see what you have been up to. You did a good job hiding them, but I've been on both sides of this game much longer than you have. I've discovered a lot. Maybe not all, but enough. I wanted to wait until you were gone before turning anything over to my father. He'll be furious, of course, so I'll need to make a good show of trying to catch you. Just don't do anything stupid, or I'll have no choice but to help him. He knows my skill level. I can only play dumb for so long. Now let me see your arm."

Chen unzipped his jacket and pulled out his left arm. He pushed up the sleeve of his shirt, revealing the bandage.

Steven looked surprised. "You knew about them?"

Chen nodded. "We removed them. They're upstairs on our beds, resting quietly."

Steven seemed impressed. "That's even better. You'll have a head start. I can wait until they discover you're missing. But after that, I become the hunter."

He reached for the door and held it open for them.

"Thank you," Chen and Jung said sincerely as they stepped through it.

"Good luck," he answered, "and don't let me catch you."

Steven closed the door behind them as they hurried away from the hotel, around the corner, and into the darkness of the night.

CHAPTER

13

It was about twenty minutes after midnight. Lauren was sound asleep with the baby snuggled up against her, their breathing deep and rhythmic. At the risk of waking Matthew, I pulled back the covers ever so slightly to get a glimpse of his angelic sleeping face. He stirred a little, pursed his lips, and made a few sucking sounds before settling back down. *So sweet.*

I looked over at the girls. All three were tangled up in a heap of limbs. They had started the evening in the standard Gunderson manner with two older children on the outside of the bed and a smaller child tucked in between, to keep the younger one from rolling off the bed in the night. Within short order, however, the girls had wadded up all the blankets and gotten so crooked on the bed that I didn't know how they could rest at all.

Just two rooms and four queen beds took care of everyone. The oldest two boys lucked out and didn't have a little one sandwiched between them.

We always tried to get adjoining rooms when we could. When we couldn't, we figured the boys could fend for themselves. After all, Aaron is already bigger than I am.

I couldn't rest, even though my part of the mission was over. All I had left was some sightseeing with the family and a plane ride home. Ranch and the others should have picked up the researcher by now and would be smuggling him out of the country. I just needed to put my head on my pillow and drift off to sleep.

I lay down, but sleep still didn't come. I was shifting around, trying to get comfortable, when I thought I heard a faint knock at the door. Easing out of the bed so as not to disturb Lauren and Matthew, I stuck my head in the entryway and listened.

The knocking came a little louder, so I walked to the door and looked through the peephole. There stood Ranch. He was looking around uncomfortably and preparing to knock a third time.

I opened the door a crack, and he pushed his way in.

"We have a problem," he whispered.

"Give me a second to grab some pants and my room key. We can talk outside. I don't want to wake everyone up."

I slipped on my jeans and some flip-flops and grabbed my wallet with the room key, then followed Ranch down the hall a few doors to his room. He put a hand on the doorknob and looked back at me with a "brace yourself" look.

"What's going on?"

"You'll see," he said, opening the door.

Hank was standing just inside the entryway, leaning against a television cabinet. He acknowledged us with a nod as we entered, then looked back into the room without saying anything. Beyond him, Zhou sat in the corner of the room with her arms crossed. She glanced at us briefly, then turned her attention back toward the opposite corner, just out of my field of vision.

As Ranch ushered me further into the room, I followed Zhou's gaze, my eyes gravitating to the corner where I assumed the action was. There, sitting side-by-side on a small sofa, were two Chinese adolescents in what looked like school uniforms. The boy had on khaki pants and a red polo shirt. The girl wore a khaki skirt and a red polo that matched the boy's.

They both looked at me expectantly, each clutching a small backpack. The boy, I suddenly realized, was our friend Chen, although he had evidently gotten a haircut since the last time I had seen him. The girl looked vaguely familiar, but I wasn't sure.

"What are they doing here? Where's the researcher? Are these his kids?"

"Meet the researcher—*and* his partner," Ranch said with a forced grin, gesturing toward the two.

"But they're just—"

"That's what we said."

At this point, Chen stood to his feet and made formal introductions. "I am Chen Shih, as you know, and this is Jung Ying, my associate."

I had to suppress a laugh when he used the word *associate*, because it sounded so official coming from a couple of school kids in uniform.

The girl joined him in standing and both bowed slightly.

"Nice to meet you, Jung. And nice to see you again, Chen." I nodded my head to each in turn. "Forgive me, but as a father of children about your own ages, I have to ask, *Where are your parents?* Especially at this time of night."

"Neither of us *have* parents," Chen answered matter-of-factly. "They died when we were young."

"But if you're orphans, doesn't that make you wards of the state or something? Surely, someone is responsible for you?"

They looked at each other sheepishly.

"I guess you could say that Director Lao is responsible for us," Jung said. "He runs the research institute where we live and work."

"Unfortunately, he is also trying to use our research to build the new biological weapon I contacted you about," Chen added. "He thinks it will put him in the history books."

"If he succeeds in what he's planning, he'll definitely make the history books, the same way Hitler and Stalin did. Even so, you're both still minors. We can't just whisk you away."

I looked around the room at the others. Everyone shrugged. No one wanted to get involved in international kidnapping. Then again, none of us wanted to see hundreds of millions killed by some new bio-weapon, either.

"We just went through all this before you got here," Zhou said. "They say they're emancipated minors."

"That's right. We're emancipated. That makes a difference, doesn't it?" Jung asked in a high sweet voice.

She had the hint of a British accent, much like Chen. It was cute and endearing, despite the hour of the night and crazy situation.

"Explain to me how that works?" I asked, somewhat doubtfully.

"Well," began Zhou, "It's a way to get around international child labor laws. In general, China doesn't worry too much about such things. However, these kids were destined to be in the international spotlight, so the government wanted to make sure everything looked squeaky-clean. By emancipating them, the government could claim that the children were working of their own freewill."

"So why can't they just *quit* working of their own freewill?"

"Well, what is true on paper and what is true in reality are two different things. There are lots of ways to manipulate them, even though they are supposedly emancipated. For instance, Chen felt certain they would threaten to harm Jung to keep him working."

143

"We're also confident our parents' deaths were not accidental," Chen added, reaching out to grasp Jung's hand. She nodded soberly. "And we aren't the only ones, either. I've seen the files for hundreds of kids just like us, whose parents have mysteriously died."

"I'm sorry about your parents. How old were you?"

"I was three and Jung was two. It was about ten years ago."

"And you've been at this 'research institute' ever since?"

"Yes."

"And when you say kids just like you, I assume you mean really smart kids."

"Yes."

"How smart, exactly?"

"What do you mean?"

"I mean, surely they've tested you at some point?"

"Oh, of course, they test us all the time. It's just, well…"

He seemed stumped for words.

"It's just that beyond a certain point, the tests cease to be meaningful," Zhou filled in. "These two are off the charts."

Chen's hesitancy had been humility.

I thought this all over for a few moments. "Well, I think our duty is clear, both to these children and to everyone else on this planet." I looked around the room. Everyone was nodding slowly and thoughtfully. "So how do we use this emancipation angle to get them out of the country?"

Zhou gestured towards the children.

"Adoption," Chen stated and began pulling some paperwork out of his backpack. Jung smiled brightly and nodded her head. Apparently they had worked it all out.

A grin spread across my face. Now, I realized why I was here. Smith had set me up. The agency wanted me to adopt these kids, so they could get them out of the country legally. I looked over at Ranch and Hank.

"So *that's* why Smith brought me in on this mission, isn't it?" I asked.

"I don't think Smith knew," Ranch said.

"But Lauren and I will still have to adopt these two kids somehow as part of the extraction, won't we?"

"Not you and Lauren."

"Then who?"

Ranch pointed to Hank with his thumb. "Him."

"*Him?* But Hank's single. Don't you have to be married to adopt in China?"

"Hank and Grace, I guess I should say."

"Hank and Grace!" I turned on Hank accusingly. "This was your idea, wasn't it? You've had your eye on Grace this whole trip!"

Hank held up his hands. "I swear, Dr. Gunderson, this wasn't my idea. Those two kids thought up the whole thing." He pointed towards the couch. Still doubtful, I turned back around to see what they had to say.

"I'm sorry, Mr. Gunderson. I had to make some quick decisions. I analyzed the situation for optimal success, and Hank and Grace made the most sense. They are closer to the right age to adopt, plus they don't already have a bunch of children like you and Mrs. Gunderson."

"They also don't have a marriage license!" I protested, glaring at Hank again.

"Hear him out, Gunderson," Ranch said.

I turned my attention back to Chen.

"You see, Mr. Gunderson, I was in the preliminary testing room with your son Nathan at the geography bee. I got the names of Hank and your daughter from him, and then later snapped a few pictures of them with my camera. I have taken the liberty of preparing a variety of documents to make it all work out, including a marriage certificate, which I have here."

He handed me a pile of paperwork. Adoption forms galore and there, right on top, a marriage license with Hank and Grace's names on it.

"We can make it official at the American consulate in Guangzhou just before we get the adoption papers approved. Obviously, it will be a marriage on paper only and can be undone once we get to America and other legal arrangements can be made."

"This just seems so complicated."

"Yes, but doing it legally and officially will be the greatest possible insult to Lao, and will silence any protest he might make to the international community afterwards."

"How am I supposed to explain all this to Grace? And *Lauren!* She has no idea what I've been doing these last few years. None of them do."

I looked at Ranch pleadingly. He was the only one in the room who knew my whole story.

"Lauren's a smart woman, Jon. She probably suspects more than she lets on. I imagine she may even be relieved to have some of your strange behavior explained."

"You may be right. She caught me staring off into space, thinking about Iraq again, just before Smith called with this assignment. You think I should tell Lauren and Grace separately—or together?"

At that point, Zhou interjected. "Not to rush things, but we have only five and a half hours before Chen and Jung are supposed to report for breakfast. Their absence will certainly be noticed at that time, if not before. We've got to get to Guangzhou, complete all the paperwork, and then get them out of the country before then. What we are doing may be legal, but that doesn't mean it will be honored so long as we remain on Chinese soil."

"Together it is, then—but I'm not looking forward to this."

I pushed past Hank and headed for the door. He quietly mouthed the word, "Sorry," as I went by.

Yeah, me too! I thought as I stepped into the hallway.

CHAPTER

14

The hallway was empty. Granted, it was half past midnight, but in big cities that doesn't mean much. In fact, it sometimes means things are just getting started. Certainly for me, on that night, that's what it meant.

The hotel had assigned us adjacent rooms, but not adjoining ones like we preferred. I had a key to each room in my wallet. Lauren and Seth had the duplicates. Since I'd be getting both Lauren and Grace out of our room, I would need one of the older boys to babysit while we talked across the hall.

I slipped quietly into the boys' room, hoping to get Seth up without disturbing the others. Aaron was alone in their bed.

"Where's Seth?" I whispered, giving Aaron a gentle shake.

"Went downstairs for a snack. Said he was hungry," Aaron answered groggily.

"When?"

"About midnight, maybe a little after. I'm not sure."

"*Great.* Your brother has a real gift for…" I trailed off, unable to express my frustration with my oldest son at that point.

Aaron was fully awake now. "Is something wrong, Dad?"

"Sort of, but I can't really explain it all right now. I need you to come next door to watch the baby and your little sisters while I take Grace and your mother across the hall to talk with Ranch and Hank."

Aaron looked at the clock and back at me suspiciously, but didn't say anything. As he began slipping on his clothes, I attempted to rouse Nathan in the next bed.

"Nathan, sorry to wake you, but Seth's downstairs getting a snack, and Aaron's going to be in my room babysitting. I'm leaving you in charge of this room for a little while. Aaron will be right next door, and I'll be across the hall in Hank's room, if you need us. Okay?"

"Okay," he answered, rubbing his eyes and looking around. "Is something wrong?"

There was that question again.

"No time to explain. Aaron and I will be right back, okay?"

"Okay." He rolled over and pulled the covers up around him. He didn't seem too alarmed. Probably wasn't awake enough to fully appreciate the tension.

Once Aaron was dressed, we slipped into the hallway. A hotel employee was coming toward us. Housekeeping, perhaps? We returned her polite smile and watched as she disappeared around a corner. Then we crept into the room where Grace and Lauren slept.

"You can rest on the sofa while I wake your mother and Grace. I'll put some pillows around the baby so he won't roll off, but listen for him. If he starts to stir, you may have to hold him."

Aaron stretched out on the sofa while I went to wake Grace. I figured she wouldn't question me as much and could be getting ready while Lauren extricated herself from baby Matthew. I gave her a gentle shake, but she's such a sound sleeper that I nearly woke the other two girls trying to get her up. She finally cracked open an eye and groaned, "What is it?"

"I need your help with something important. Aaron will watch the girls while you and your mother come next door so I can explain. Just throw on some clothes while I get Mom up."

"Sure thing, Dad." She carefully lifted Anna's leg off her stomach and sat up on the edge of the bed. Then she stood up, grabbed some clothes off the nightstand, and shuffled into the bathroom to change.

I took a deep breath and went to Lauren's side of our bed. I stretched my hand toward her, then hesitated and pulled it back.

After twenty-plus years of marriage, I knew my wife fairly well. I knew we didn't keep secrets from each other. My role as an agent over the last five years had been the only exception to that rule, albeit a major one.

I also knew that she would eventually understand and forgive me, but that there would be a window of time prior to that understanding and forgiving during which she would feel very angry and betrayed. That window of time would begin the moment I woke her and would end at some unknown point in the future. Very likely, it would be an extremely uncomfortable time, especially once she found out what we were planning for our oldest daughter, Grace.

Finally, I forced my hand forward, shook her gently, and whispered her name.

"*Lauren?*"

She startled slightly, snapped her eyes open, and looked down at Matthew to make sure he was okay. He had apparently begun nursing again while I was gone and was still quasi-attached, though sound asleep. Once she realized he was safe, she turned her attention to me and asked, "What is it sweetheart?"

"I know it's late, but we need to talk."

"Sure, go ahead," she whispered back, "but keep your voice down. I don't want to wake the children."

"Well, it's a little more complicated than that. Aaron's going to watch the little ones so I can take you and Grace across the hall."

"What does Grace have to do with this? Is she sick or something?"

"No, Grace is fine. I just need her help, as well as yours. Get dressed, then I'll explain everything."

"Okay, just give me a minute."

Turning her attention back to the baby, she managed to break suction and pull herself free without waking him up. Matthew smacked his lips together a few times, then settled back down as she tucked some pillows around him. She headed for the bathroom with her clothes just as Grace was coming out.

"What's going on, Mom?"

"Ask your dad. He hasn't told me anything yet."

Lauren went into the bathroom and shut the door. I held my finger to my lips, motioning for Grace to hold her questions.

We waited in silence for Lauren to change, Grace leaning against the wall, I standing mute at her side. I don't know how she felt, but my heart was in my throat. This was definitely the moment of truth.

Lauren opened the door to the bathroom, then she and Grace followed me into the hall. I quietly shut the door, and they both looked at me expectantly. Grace acted a bit annoyed at being woken up, but Lauren didn't seem bothered at all. Our babies had been waking her up at all hours of the night for the last twenty years, so in a certain sense, this wasn't a big deal to her. She was used to it.

"Remember the kid who won the geography bee today?" I asked, uncertain how to start.

"Of course," they answered in unison.

"Jinx," Grace said, shooting a smile at Lauren. I was glad to see her lighten up a bit now that she was more awake.

"Well, he's here at the hotel. Right now. With a friend."

"You dragged us out of bed to tell us *that?*" Grace asked incredulously.

"Jon, *what* is going on?" Lauren wanted to know. "What can his being here possibly have to do with us— especially at this time of the night?"

"Well, it appears that he and his friend need our help."

"Our help? At—" Lauren pulled her head back to squint at her watch, "at nearly one in the morning? Where are their parents? They should be in bed at this hour. And we should, too, for that matter."

"That's just it. They don't have parents. He and his friend are orphans. And, not only that, but they're seeking political asylum in the United States, as well."

"Political asylum?" Grace snorted. "What do they expect *us* to do? Smuggle them out of the country?"

"Actually, yes."

"Jon, seriously. That's absurd. We don't even know them. Besides, I'm sure it's illegal."

"Not if they're formally adopted."

"Adopted? Jon, is this some kind of joke? Is Hank hiding around the corner with a camera, waiting to get some juicy footage?"

"Lauren, I'm not—"

"Can't they see we have plenty of children already? I'm sure they're great kids, that someone would be happy to help them. But not us. Not when we already have nine of our own."

"Well, actually," I grimaced and scratched my neck, "it's Grace they want to adopt them."

"*Grace?*"

"*Me?*"

"And she'll need to do it before six o'clock this morning."

"Oh, this just keeps getting better."

Lauren eyed me skeptically, then raised her voice long enough to call out, "Okay, Hank. You can come out now. The prank's over."

Turning back to me, she whispered, "Even if this weren't a joke, it should be obvious that Grace is still a child herself."

"Technically, Mom, I'm an adult now. I just turned eighteen."

"Do not encourage your father with this elaborate ruse."

"Lauren, I know I'm asking a lot of you, but please at least meet the kids and hear the rest of their story before you make up your mind. There's a lot more at stake than you realize, but I can't discuss it in the hallway. Just come into Ranch's room and meet them first."

"How is Ranch involved in this? Was this *his* idea? He seems much too level-headed to be mixed up in a stunt like this."

"I'll explain everything as soon as we get out of the hall."

I walked over and tapped lightly on Ranch's door. He opened it immediately and invited us inside.

Over all, Lauren and Grace were handling things a little better than I expected. They were probably too tired to fight, and they thought I was joking, anyway. I slid around the corner to let the girls into the room.

As Grace came in, she looked at Hank with a smirk and said one word: "Nice."

Hank held up his hands defensively again. Grace's smirk vanished once she saw the kids and realized this wasn't a prank. Behind her, Lauren let out a little gasp and held her hands to her mouth.

"Oh, Jon, you're not joking," she whispered, looking at me in shock.

I shook my head. "No. I'm not."

Lauren looked back at the children in their red and khaki school uniforms. Nobody said anything as she slowly surveyed the room, taking everything in. Zhou nodded with a stiff smile. Ranch waved at her apologetically. Hank just stared at the floor and avoided eye contact. Grace had begun to grin like a Cheshire cat. When Lauren glanced back at me, she had a real look of confusion on her face. I gestured toward the children as if to say, "Let them explain".

As Lauren turned her attention back to the children, Chen formally introduced himself and Jung.

"Mrs. Gunderson, I am Chen Shih, and this is my associate, Jung Ying." There was that word "associate" again. They both gave a bow.

"It's a pleasure to meet you both," Lauren began tentatively. "Oh, and congratulations on winning the geography competition today. You must have studied very hard. I know my boys sure did."

"Thank you," Chen answered with another bow.

"Um… Jon tells me that you're orphans and hope to be adopted. I'm so sorry about your parents. It must have been terribly hard on both of you."

"We were both very young at the time," Jung interjected. "It is only as we have gotten older that we have come to understand the magnitude of the situation."

"You see, Mrs. Gunderson, we believe that our parents were murdered, and that we are being used by the Chinese government to develop a biological weapon that could be used to murder millions more," Chen said.

"I—I don't understand. You're both children. How could you be making a biological weapon?"

"They are very special children, Mrs. Gunderson," Zhou explained. "When Chen approached our agency a few weeks ago about extraction, we assumed he was an adult, since he's a senior research scientist. He kept his age secret until he could explain, in person, the details of his plan for adoption and escape. Further proof of his prodigy status." Zhou gave a smile and nod to the children, who glanced at each other sheepishly.

"You say he contacted your agency? What does a travel agency have to do with all this? I'm getting confused here."

"Zhou's not a travel agent, Mom. She's a spy. And I'm guessing Dad is, too," Grace leaned slightly forward and peered at me. "Isn't that right, Dad?"

Now it was my turn to put my hands in the air defensively. "Whoa, now. *Spy* is way too strong a term for my level of involvement."

Grace gave me a look. She wasn't buying it.

"Your level of involvement?" Lauren seemed incredulous. "Jon, are you saying you're a part of this—this—whatever it is?"

"Well, sort of."

"Sort of? As in, sort of *pregnant*?"

Ranch let out a snort, but became very serious again when Lauren glared at him. She turned back to gaze at me, her eyes narrowing. She pointed her index finger at me and said, "You've got some explaining to do, and quick!"

"Well…you know how I'm in the Army Reserves, right?"

"Yes."

"And, you know how I sometimes go to medical conferences as a substitute for the ordinary weekend drill?"

"You're stalling, Jon."

"I'm getting there. Anyway, from time to time—in the past—I've agreed to complete a few non-military governmental assignments while attending those conferences."

"Like repeatedly sneaking off with that silly camera of yours the whole time we were in Europe?" Lauren accused.

"Precisely."

"I knew there was something fishy about you and that camera, but I never could put my finger on it."

"That camera was a highly sensitive infrared scanner that we use to detect biological weapons manufacturing," Ranch explained. "Your husband helped shut down one of the biggest operations in the world and saved untold lives in the process. You should be proud."

"So you're in on this, too?"

"I'm afraid so. In fact, I'm the one who identified Jon as a potential agent nearly seven years ago, then helped recruit him when we were together in Iraq. Your husband has a unique combination of skills that are very valuable in this line of work."

"Told you Dad was a spy."

Lauren shot Grace a look of irritation, "You stay out of it."

"Sorry," she apologized.

"So that explains all the angst you have had of late about graduate school and serving in Iraq. I knew something wasn't adding up. It's beginning to make better sense now, though. What about all those mission trips to South and Central America? Did you have some non-military governmental assignments then, too?"

I nodded, "I'm afraid so."

"And Africa?"

"Same."

"What about all those conferences in the States?"

"Usually pre-assignment training."

"So pretty much everywhere we've gone in the last five years has been somehow related to these government assignments?"

"Pretty much," I grimaced.

"Jon, you never cease to amaze me."

I wasn't sure Lauren meant that as a compliment, but I didn't have time to ponder it, because at that instant we heard shouting in the hallway.

Someone was banging on a door with all his might. Above the din, we could hear Seth's panic-stricken voice calling, "Mom! Dad! *Help!* They've kidnapped Danielle!"

CHAPTER

15

I stepped into the hall. Seth was frantic. Aaron had just opened the door to our room, and Seth was trying to push past him in his search for me. "Seth," I hissed, "over here." He turned and looked at me, tears in his eyes.

Now Nathan opened his door, as did several other guests up and down the hallway, looking for the source of all the late night commotion. We were going to have an audience for whatever was about to unfold, unless I could quickly get Seth inside one of the rooms.

"Dad—*Dad!* They kidnapped Danielle! We've got to help her." He rushed towards me, grabbing me by the shoulders.

"*Who* kidnapped Danielle? What are you talking about?"

"A couple of guys with tattoos and a minivan, just a few minutes ago!"

"How do you know that? Did her parents call? Was it on the news? Danielle's on the other side of the planet, Seth."

"No. No, she's not. She's here in China. I was going to tell you, but..." he trailed off, his eyes wide with panic. I put one arm around him and motioned for Aaron and Nathan to go back into their rooms with my other hand.

They hesitated with inquisitive looks. Aaron mouthed, "What's going on?"

"Boys, we're creating a scene. Let me talk to Seth privately, then I'll bring you up to speed." They both shut their doors reluctantly but obediently.

By this time, more people had gathered in the hallway and were pointing and whispering.

"Sorry, folks," I said. "Family crisis."

I guided Seth by the shoulders into Hank's room.

His head was down and eyes so filled with tears that I don't think it registered to him how full the room already was. He just kept crying and repeatedly saying, "I'm so sorry."

"Son, I can't help you until I know what's going on."

He made a visible effort to gain control, lifting his head and drying the tears with the back of his hand. That's when he noticed everyone. "What's going on? Why is everyone up so late?"

"We could ask you the same thing," I said curtly. I was starting to put two and two together. I was worried about Danielle, but I was also worried about the mission. I suddenly had two major crises on my hands, and time was not on my side in either scenario.

Lauren shot me a glance that told me to show a little more compassion to our oldest, who was obviously distressed. I have a tendency to focus on the task at hand in any given situation; Lauren has the good sense to focus on the people.

She came over to Seth and put her arms around him. I stepped back. "Go ahead, Seth," she said soothingly, "tell us what happened. And take whatever time you need."

That last comment was directed at me, I was pretty sure.

"I'm not sure where to start. Remember a few weeks ago when I asked if Danielle could come to China?"

"And we said *no!*" I interjected. Lauren glared at me. I think the hypocrisy of my indignation registered with her before it did me.

"Anyway, Danielle had a passport—and she had lots of frequent flier miles from all her mission trips with our church—so she checked to see if her summer job would let her off and if her roommate would feed the cat."

"Did she check to see what her parents thought of the idea?" I asked.

"Jon, let him talk," Lauren admonished. "He'll never finish what he has to say if you keep interrupting him."

Now it was my turn to glare. She was right, of course, but I didn't like being told. Especially not in front of my colleagues.

"Go on," she coaxed Seth gently.

He took a deep breath before the tumble of words continued: "So once her boss and roommate agreed, she tried to get a flight and a hotel room. But she couldn't get just any flight with the frequent flier miles, so she had to take this off-peak flight that got to China in the middle of the night, because that was all they had available on such short notice."

I glanced around the room. Everyone was listening grimly. So far, the story did not bode well. Whenever there's a major sporting event, like the Olympics or the World Cup, there's not only an increase in tourism in the host country, but also an increase in human trafficking that goes with it. It was entirely possible that the Hong Kong traffickers had been emboldened by the increased demand in Beijing.

"She agreed to meet me here first before going on to her own hotel," Seth was explaining. "She took a taxi, and I waited out front. But when her taxi arrived it didn't come to the front of the hotel. It just dropped her off at the corner and pulled away. I saw it happen and thought it was strange even before I realized it was her, but then she waved, and I started towards her to help with her bags. And that's when it happened.

"A minivan pulled up out of nowhere and these two big Asian guys with sleeveless shirts and lots of tattoos jumped out and grabbed her from behind. She was so focused on me that she never even had a chance to react."

Seth made a sound somewhere between a sob and a wail. His eyes grew feral as he ran his hands through his hair.

We all waited patiently.

"I had only taken about ten steps towards her at that point. It all happened so quickly. I immediately ran after them. I don't know if they saw me, but they sped away before I could even get close. I chased them for a couple of blocks, but they were gone.

"I rushed back to the hotel and tried to get the clerk to call the police to report a kidnapping. But he didn't seem to understand what I was saying, so I came to get you instead. I don't know what to do. I'm scared. And I'm so sorry."

Seth's head sank down as he completed his story.

There was a moment of silence; then someone said, "I think I can help."

We all turned towards the voice. It was Chen. He repeated himself and, reaching into his backpack, pulled out a small laptop computer. He hurried towards the desk as he opened it up. Zhou moved out of his way, so he could sit down. Hank, Ranch, Zhou, and I all exchanged glances.

"What do you have in mind?" I asked.

"The city has surveillance cameras on virtually every corner. All I have to do is hack into the security department and find the feeds we want. Then we should be able to track where the van went."

"You can do that from a laptop?" Hank asked, impressed.

"Not ordinarily. I'd normally need my server and my artificial intuition software to do it, but I still have the passwords from when I hacked in earlier this week. If they haven't been changed, then I think I can help. There are two problems though.

"First, if they realize the power outage from a little while ago was the result of a hack, they may have changed the passwords already.

"And second, if I do this, I will only be able to cover our tracks temporarily—you know, make it look like the hack came from New Zealand or something. However, they will eventually track it back to here, and then we will all be in danger. Especially with someone like Steven involved."

"Who is Steven?" we all asked together.

"Steven is Director Lao's son. He's a whiz with computers, maybe even better than me. All I know is that he figured out what was going on with Jung and me and was waiting for us in the stairwell when we left the hotel."

"Hold on," Ranch blurted, "Someone knows you're gone—and that you have help? Sounds like our cover's blown already!"

Ranch liked things to go smoothly whenever he was on a mission. I think this newest bit of information was the last straw.

Jung came to Chen's defense. "Steven said he wouldn't give us away until he had to. I think he is trying to help us."

Ranch looked at her with a hint of a smirk. "That's reassuring. The son of the guy who wants to kill everyone on the planet is trying to help you? Who knows what game he's playing? I say we all get out of here, and quick. Let the police look for Danielle. Let the diplomats handle the controversy around Jung and Chen. The rest of us need to skip town and forget this whole crazy adoption thing, as well, before we all wind up dead."

"I can't do that, Ranch," I said. "I want this mission to succeed as much as you do, but I brought my family into this. Technically, Danielle isn't family yet, but she's close enough that I won't leave her behind anymore than I'd leave one of my own children. I don't think we can trust the police here, or anyone else in the Chinese government for that matter. We've got to do this ourselves."

Lauren touched my arm and smiled appreciatively at me.

Ranch looked at the wall. "So what do we do?" he asked quietly.

"We divide and conquer. You and I can go after Danielle. Grace and Hank can go on to the embassy with Jung and Chen. And Zhou can get the rest of my family out of here as soon as possible—a late night flight or something."

"I don't think there are any more flights out until morning," Zhou said.

"Slow down a second," Seth interrupted. "Missions? Embassies? Adoption? What's everyone talking about?"

"Dad's a spy," Grace told him frankly.

"*What?*" Seth looked to me for an explanation.

"I'm not a spy."

"You are a spy, Jon," Lauren corrected.

"Fine. I'm a spy, then. We still need to develop a plan and get moving. We have no idea when this Steven character is going to blow the whistle on us."

"I'm going with you, Dad," Seth said resolutely. "I got Danielle into this, and I want to help get her out."

"Seth, just stay with your mother. Ranch and I can handle this. I don't want you to get shot or something."

"I *have* to go, Dad," Seth pleaded. "I'll go crazy if I don't. *Please.* I'll do my best to stay out of the way, but I've got to go."

Lauren touched my arm again. I looked at her, and she nodded her approval.

"Alright, Seth. You can come. But bring your Crossing Guard backpack and get behind it if anyone starts shooting."

"Thank you," he said and gave me a hug.

"Alright, Chen, start looking for our kidnappers. Lauren, you'd better get the other kids up and ready. I'm not sure where you'll go, but you can't stay here."

"I think I have something," Zhou said.

"What?"

"Well, originally we thought the researcher was an adult. We planned to take him away shortly after midnight. None of this adoption stuff, right?"

"So what are you saying?"

"Well, I have a container ship lined up that leaves early in the morning from Hong Kong to Taiwan. I had originally reserved a spot inside one of the containers for our mysterious researcher. However, with a little persuasion and some extra money, I think I can convince my contact to find a way to fit your entire family inside."

"A container ship? Those don't move very fast. How long would they be locked inside? Is it safe?"

"The plan was to climb inside at two in the morning. By four, the ship would be loaded and ready to go. It's about a twenty-hour trip for most of these big ships, but this particular one does it in twelve. That would put your family in Taiwan tomorrow afternoon. It isn't perfect, but it's probably our best bet under the circumstances and should be reasonably safe. I've done this many times before with these same people and had no problems."

I looked at Lauren.

"We'll be okay, Jon. We've been through worse."

"Been through worse?"

"Sure. Don't you remember the time we all stayed in the bachelor's quarters for two weeks while you drilled with the Army? Ten people in five hundred square feet with only one tiny bathroom. This will be a cake walk."

"Alright," I said. There really wasn't a better option.

Lauren stood to her feet and gave me a hug. I prayed it wouldn't be our last. I turned to Zhou. "Take good care of her and the kids."

"I will, Dr. Gunderson. They'll be fine."

"Lauren, I'll leave it to you to explain things to the other kids. Let them know that I'm sorry I couldn't tell them in person."

"Okay, I will."

She turned to leave with Zhou.

"I've got it," Chen called out. The rest of us gathered around the computer as the door closed behind Lauren and Zhou.

Sure enough, there was a grainy picture of a girl being pushed into a minivan and the minivan pulling away. Then Seth came into view. We watched him running after the van as it disappeared into the distance.

Seth let out a low growl.

"It'll be alright, son," I said. "We'll get her. This is just the first step."

Chen hopped from camera to camera on his laptop, following the course of the minivan. The van eventually turned down an alley. The alley was poorly lit, but we could make out a large man stepping out of the shadows and opening the sliding door of the minivan from the outside. He then turned and opened a door into the building and held it.

Several bodies seemed to struggle out of the minivan and make their way inside the building. The large man shut the door behind them, closed the sliding door of the minivan, and stepped back. The minivan pulled away as the big man slid back into the shadows. The alley looked deserted once more. The whole process had taken less than thirty seconds.

"Alright, I think we know where we need to go. How long ago was that?"

Chen looked at his watch, then back at the screen. "About seven minutes."

"We'd better move out. I only wish I had a gun."

"I've got one," Ranch stated.

"How'd you get it past airport security?"

"I didn't," he answered. "Zhou gave it to me. The two of us were originally in charge of the extraction, and she thought I might need it."

"Great. Now we have a fighting chance. What about you Hank? Any weapons?"

"None," he said, giving Ranch a knowing glance. "But, I'll have Chen with me. He seems pretty good in a tight spot."

"That he is."

We all smiled at Chen, who blushed ever so slightly.

"Well, Ranch, why don't you give Hank the keys to the van so he can drive on over to the embassy with Grace and these two? You, Seth, and I can catch a taxi to the alley."

"Sounds good." Ranch handed Hank the keys as Chen folded up his laptop.

"Good luck, Dad."

"You, too, Grace, but let me give you something before you go."

I hurried across the hall and grabbed my shoes, belt, and the two ketamine injectors. When I returned, I handed one of the injectors to Grace.

"What's this?"

"It's a tranquilizer dart. If you happen to be attacked, just stab it into your assailant like this." I demonstrated the maneuver.

"You don't think I'll actually have to use that, do you?"

"I sure hope not, but better safe than sorry. It's time we get going. Hopefully, we'll have Danielle back in short order, and by tomorrow morning, I'll be a grandfather."

She and the others looked a little confused, until I pointed at Chen and Jung. Then it registered, and everybody laughed.

I checked the time as we headed out the door. *Five till one.*

A lot had happened since midnight.

CHAPTER
16

Our cab pulled up to a corner about a block from our destination, and the three of us piled out. We didn't have a lot of resources, just a vague plan. Unless the guard had changed, I wasn't sure my modified Mark I injector would be enough. One injection of ketamine could easily take out an average-sized man, but this guy was huge. He outweighed me by a hundred and fifty pounds, at least.

I found myself wishing I'd kept both the tranquilizers. Then again, I felt better knowing Grace had a way to defend herself. Besides, Ranch had the gun to back me up. Of course, it would attract a lot of unwanted attention if he had to use it. I hoped he didn't have to.

"Come on, Dad. Let's go!" Seth was chomping at the bit, and who could blame him? If it had been Lauren in danger, I'd have felt the same way.

Danielle meant everything to Seth, whether I was ready to admit it or not. She was his future; his mother and I were his past. If the two of them survived this little adventure, they would have an entire life together that didn't involve us.

Sure, we'd get the monthly phone call, the occasional visit, the obligatory Christmas card. But our role was clearly shrinking. Danielle's was growing.

We were the place Seth was coming from; Danielle was the place he was going to. In his heart, he was already there.

"We can't all go in at once. It'll spook him, and he'll sound the alarm. Seth, do you have a picture of Danielle? I've got an idea."

Seth fished a picture of Danielle out of his wallet, while I took the Mark I out of my pocket and tucked it behind my ear.

"What exactly is that thing?" he asked.

"One of your Dad's tranquilizer darts," Ranch whispered.

"Tranquilizer darts!" Seth exclaimed.

We both gave him a sharp glance and then looked around to see if anyone had overheard. No one seemed to have noticed us, and hopefully the language barrier provided some protection.

Seth lowered his voice. "I thought that's what you told Grace, but I wasn't really paying attention. Man, you really *are* a spy, aren't you?"

For the first time in years, he seemed genuinely impressed.

"Yes, I am," I mouthed back, a tiny bit of pride welling up inside of me, despite the crazy circumstances.

"Shouldn't you hide that somewhere?"

"Hide in plain sight. That's my motto."

"What does *that* mean?"

"It means," said Ranch, "that big guy's brain will ignore the tranquilizer dart when he sees it casually tucked behind your Dad's ear. If your Dad had to reach into his pocket or behind his back, the guy would instantly be on the defensive."

"Basic psychology, really," I added by way of explanation.

"That little toy is your Dad's special invention. I think the agency should issue them standard, but what do I know?"

"Alright," I told them, starting toward the next corner with the picture in my left hand and the dart behind my right ear, "give me three minutes, then walk by and check on me."

The next corner wasn't a corner in the proper sense; it was more of an entryway to a small alley for deliveries, trash pick-up, that sort of thing. I paused at the entry and examined the picture in my hand, looked around like I wasn't sure about the address, then looked back at the picture. When I glanced at the big guy midway down the alley, he was eyeing me suspiciously. I acted glad to see him and walked briskly towards him, holding out the picture face down. I hoped he thought I was looking for directions.

As I approached him, I reached up and smoothed back my hair. I handed the picture to him with an inquisitive look on my face. He took the picture and turned it over. Just as his eyes dilated with recognition, I brought the ketamine dart down hard on his left shoulder.

The muscle that covers the shoulder, the deltoid, is the best place for intramuscular injections in terms of how quickly the drug will work. The legs and buttocks are bigger targets, but the drugs take a lot longer to kick in.

Actually, if the tongue is injected, the drugs will work even faster, but people typically won't take a needle to the tongue without a fight. I was pretty sure this guy wouldn't.

Now the speed of onset with the deltoid is quick, but not instantaneous. Even intravenous drugs take thirty to sixty seconds to kick in. I knew it would be a couple of minutes before the guy was completely knocked out; in the meantime, I just needed to stay alive while he gradually succumbed. Assuming, of course, he'd gotten an adequate dose.

His left arm made a quick circular motion, knocking my hand away and sending the now empty dart skittering across the concrete alley. *Nice try, but too late*, I thought. Then I saw his huge right fist headed for my face.

The thing to remember when fighting big guys is that they have a lot of strength, but not much endurance. I should know—I'm a big guy myself. If I could keep this one moving, without letting him connect, I could eventually tire him out.

Unfortunately, to deliver the ketamine, I had already come in too close for comfort. I ducked his right-handed punch (I play ping-pong with the kids to keep my reflexes sharp), but he caught me with a left-handed uppercut to the nose (obviously not enough ping-pong).

Getting socked in the nose is both shocking and disorienting. My head popped back and my hands instinctively reached for my now bleeding appendage. He had his arms around me instantly in a monstrous bear hug intent on breaking my spine.

I boxed his ears and dropped a few elbows on the top of his ogre-like head, but he barely noticed. I think he was used to such treatment. Plus, it was impossible to get any kind of force behind my blows while pinned the way I was.

Two things saved me.

The first was my middle-age paunch. I think that extra layer of blubber around my torso actually acted as a shock absorber for the pressure being applied to my spine.

The second was that by exerting so much energy trying to crush me, this Sumo wrestler look-alike was actually increasing the blood flow to his muscles, thereby hastening the onset of the ketamine.

Gradually, his grip began to loosen, although he never did let go. He also began to wobble. We must have looked like two drunken sailors dancing in the alley. The only thing missing was some neon lights and a jukebox blaring in the background.

He eventually stumbled forward and brought us both down in a heap, despite my best efforts to stay upright. I abruptly found myself pinned to the ground beneath a nearly four hundred pound man. That is exactly how Ranch and Seth found me when they came around the corner. Blood from my nose was getting all over everything as I struggled to free myself.

"*Dad! Are you okay?*"

"Sure, I'm fine. Just get this behemoth off me."

Together they pried his arms back, tilting him just enough for me to squeeze loose. The phone in my pocket had been crushed. I cleaned up my nose with my shirttail and held pressure as best I could.

"Let's see if he has any keys," Ranch said as he began patting down the big guy's pockets. "Ah, what have we here?"

With some effort, he pulled a small pistol out of the right front pocket. It was a compact .38 special—easy to hide, but packing enough power to make it worth having. He didn't find any keys.

"Check the door. Maybe it isn't even locked," I suggested. Seth ran over.

"It's definitely locked. But it's got one of those electronic pads. See if there's an electronic key in his wallet or something."

"Good thinking."

I reached for his wallet. Sure enough, there was an employee badge with his ugly face staring out from it. "Bingo!"

Clearly, a legitimate business was fronting the illegal business going on inside. Ranch and I ran to join Seth at the door.

We left the big guy laying face down. This would allow his saliva and secretions to drain from his mouth and nose and would keep him from choking on his own enormous tongue—he looked the type to have a bad case of obstructive sleep apnea. It would also protect him somewhat if he happened to vomit—a guy that big always has something in his stomach.

"Ranch, give me that guy's gun. Seth, let me have your backpack and stay behind me. We don't know what's inside."

I waved the badge in front of the keypad and heard the click. Pocketing the badge, I nodded to the others and pulled the door open.

A long, mint-green hallway with doors coming off either side led to a central intersection roughly sixty feet away with a bank of elevators. No one was around. I held my finger to my lips, and we advanced slowly.

The first few doors were locked. We weren't exactly going to knock, so we kept on going. The third door on the left, which was the last one before the elevators, was open. It was just a janitor's closet. I shook my head, indicating there was nothing to see. Suddenly, we heard several gunshots and the sound of muffled screams.

"That's Danielle!" Seth shouted. He attempted to go around the corner, but I held him back.

"Wait," I told him before stealing a peek around the corner myself. There was nothing to see except a hallway identical to the one we were standing in. I held the backpack in front of me like a gladiator's shield with my left arm. The pistol was in my right hand, aimed straight ahead, ready to shoot any lowlife thug that moved. Hearing the gunshots and screams had put me into a primitive fight-

or-flight mode, although fleeing wasn't an option with Danielle's life at stake.

I could see a door standing open near the other end of the hall and could hear some scuffling inside. Before I could advance very far, a man stepped out of the room and into the hallway. I had the drop on him and could have given him a round or two right then, but I hesitated. He was wearing a uniform. It was complete with a flak jacket and helmet that made him look like he was on some kind of Chinese SWAT team.

He, however, didn't hesitate. He squeezed off two rounds right at my center of mass, just like soldiers are trained to do. It's a good thing he didn't aim for my head, because he probably could have taken it off. As it was, my left arm fell useless at my side and the backpack hit the floor as I jumped back around the corner.

The thing about Kevlar is that stopping a bullet is not the same thing as preventing a bullet from causing damage. Kevlar requires a lot of padding underneath for it to perform optimally—padding I didn't have.

The shock from the bullets' impact had stunned the nerves in my left arm enough to temporarily render that arm numb and useless. This was a mercy, because one of the bullets had also broken the radius bone in my left forearm near the elbow—I just didn't know it yet. I'd feel it later.

Fortunately, the proximal radius is one of the few places on the human body where you can break a bone and not need a cast. The muscles and ligaments that surround the radial head, allowing it to rotate, also act as a built-in splint while the bone heals. Nonetheless, my arm immediately started to swell.

"We've got to stop them!" Seth hissed frantically. He grabbed the gun out of my hand as I leaned against the wall to catch my breath.

"I think they may be the police. If they're here to rescue Danielle, they may think we're the bad guys," I said, attempting to decipher what had just happened.

"I don't care who they are. They have Danielle, and I want her back." Seth leaned around the corner to look. "There she is!" Before I could hold him back, he was running towards her.

"Don't shoot Danielle!" Ranch hollered after Seth, but he was gone. There was nothing for us to do but to take off after him.

We came around the corner in time to see two uniformed men, the one who had shot at me and another one, pushing Danielle into a service elevator at the end of the hall. Seth was midway between us and them. As the second guy stepped into the elevator behind Danielle, he fired a shot down the hallway. It went wide and imbedded in the wall to Seth's left.

I got to the elevator a second or two behind Seth, but it was already on its way up.

"Let's see what level they stop on, then we'll follow them up," I told him.

Seth had already pushed the button for the next elevator, and the two of us stood there panting, waiting for what seemed like eternity as the numbers blinked from one floor to the next.

"Hey!" Ranch called. He was looking into the room from which the guard had stepped moments before. Seth and I had simply run by it, intent on Danielle. "There are a couple of girls tied to chairs in here, as well as a couple of dead goons. If those guys were cops, why'd they take Danielle, but leave the others?"

"I don't know, but I think we're about to find out," I said as the second elevator door popped open. "They got off at the very top floor. Meet us up there once you set those girls free and find out what they know." We stepped onto the elevator, while Ranch stayed behind to release the other girls.

Seth had a grim and determined look on his face as we rode up. I wondered how much he blamed me for what was going on and how much he blamed himself.

"You want me to take that?" I gestured towards the gun in his hand.

"You're hurt," he said, pointing at my arm. It was discolored and starting to throb. I tried to move my fingers, but they responded sluggishly. My arm felt as if I'd slept on it funny and it was just coming back to life.

"Okay, fine. Just don't shoot Danielle, and don't get yourself shot. Whoever these guys are, they're professionals. They're probably waiting for us at the top."

"I know dad. I'll try to be more careful. I just—I don't know —I guess—"

"I understand."

The elevator door opened on the top floor. It was empty. A door directly across from the elevators read: "Exit to Roof."

We both heard the unmistakable sound of helicopter blades revving up as we ran for the door. Seth shoved through it with me on his tail. We climbed the short flight of stairs and burst onto the open rooftop.

The helicopter was just lifting off. Seth raised his gun as if to shoot, but thought better of it as he caught sight of Danielle in the open bay. "Danielle!" he screamed.

She looked back at him, her eyes wide. She tried to call out, but her mouth was gagged and the whirring blades quickly drowned out what little noise she made. Their eyes locked for a split second before the helicopter pulled away into the night sky.

Seth fell to his knees. I ran over to him and put my arm around him. He was sobbing. We'd come so close. If only I hadn't hesitated to shoot earlier.

My eyes looked out over the rooftops as the sound of the helicopter faded into the distance. It was a military helicopter. Those must have been soldiers. Something wasn't adding up.

"Come on, Seth," I said. "We have to find Ranch and get out of here. I think Danielle will be okay. I don't think they'll hurt her. I think someone wants her as a bargaining chip."

"She's not a bargaining chip!"

"I know that, son, but they don't. I'm sorry. Come on, now. We've got to go." Seth reluctantly stood to his feet and followed me back to the elevators.

CHAPTER

17

Human trafficking is the modern term for the buying and selling of slaves, a practice that is still alive and well the world over. More than eighty percent of human slaves are female. Over fifty percent are children.

They say one can tell how civilized a society is by how it treats its weakest members. As a race, we may be in trouble.

In Africa, the slaves take the form of boy soldiers who are captured and trained to be killing machines before they're even old enough to read and write, toting machine guns as tall as they are.

In India, the slaves are impoverished farmers who have worked the land for generations, living in squalor with no rights, no property, and no hope.

But in Asia, human slavery has become an art form—it knows no bounds but the human imagination. There is no limit to whom they will enslave or what they will do to them.

Human trafficking is too benign a term, too sterile. We need to come up with some new way to express this affront to human dignity, but no combination of words will ever truly capture the horror that is human slavery.

As Seth and I came back off the roof, we found Ranch standing in front of the elevators with a Chinese girl, a little older than Seth.

"Jon, Seth, this is Ling. She lived in the States briefly as an exchange student a couple of years ago. She says she wants to help us and knows a way out of here." Ranch held up a couple of name badges and two more guns, presumably from the dead thugs.

"You help me. Now I help you," Ling said with a slight bow of her head.

"Thanks, Ling. The sooner we get out of here, the better."

We all stepped back onto the elevator. Ling pushed the button for the lowest floor, just one level below the basement where we had entered the building. Ranch handed Ling and me each a gun and a name badge, but kept the one he'd gotten from Zhou. Since Seth still had the gun from the big guy in the alley, we were all armed now.

"Shouldn't we go to the police or something?" Seth asked.

"I don't think that will help. That was a military helicopter, and I'm pretty sure those were soldiers."

"Soldiers, yes," Ling confirmed. "But why they only take blonde girl?"

"I don't know for sure, but once we get out of here, I intend to find out. Where's the other girl? Weren't there two of you?"

"She was terrified and ran off as soon as I untied her," Ranch said. "I just let her go. I didn't think she'd be much help."

"Yeah, that's probably for the best."

The doors opened. The buzz of electricity was palpable. In front of us was a doorway similar to the one leading to the roof but labeled, "Danger: High Voltage Area. Authorized personnel only."

"This way," Ling said, holding up the name badge Ranch had given her.

A quick wave in front of the keypad, and we were on our way down a short flight of metal steps that doubled back upon themselves and deposited us into the bowels of the building. Pipes and giant cables ran off into the darkness. Water seeped through the concrete walls and gave everything an eerie sheen.

Ling led the way. She seemed to know where she was going. I followed behind with my gun at the ready in case we encountered any more trouble. As we rounded a corner, we nearly ran into a smartly dressed and attractive young woman. She had a startled expression on her face. No doubt, so did we.

Before anyone could say anything, shots rang out in rapid succession. The noise was close and deafening. I winced and dropped into a partial crouch, looking behind me briefly. When I turned back around, I saw that the pretty young woman was collapsed on the floor with multiple holes in her chest.

Ling had stepped forward and was straddling the body with her arms extended. I could hear her faint sobbing over the click-click-click of the trigger.

I wrapped my arms around Ling from behind and pulled her away. The gun fell from her hand and clattered to the floor. Her sobs became a moan, her chest heaving.

"It's okay," I said, trying to be as soothing as I could. "It was an accident. You were scared. I never should've let you have the gun in the first place. It's my fault, not yours."

"That's *her*," she said quietly.

"Who?" I asked, grasping her by the shoulders and turning her around to face me.

"Girl who sell me."

"What do you mean?"

180

"We meet at health club. She pretend to be my friend. She say she is fashion model. Say I can be model, too. She promise she will introduce me to her friends."

"I guess those thugs the soldiers killed were the friends she was talking about?"

"Yes, but what she say hurt me most."

"What did she say?"

"She say I am vain, foolish girl. Too ugly to be model. Tell me be grateful—my vanity not last much longer."

"Heartless," I said, letting go of Ling as she reached up and wiped her eyes.

"She say I not so special. Many girls like me. She use her looks to catch us. Everyone fall for it."

"Not anymore."

"No. Not anymore."

Ranch picked up the gun from where it had fallen and began wiping it for fingerprints. "We'd better get out of here," he said, tossing the gun onto the body. "Ling, there is nothing to link you to this woman. She and her thug friends are dead. I don't think the other girl I set free or the soldiers ever saw your face without the gag in place. If you want, I think we can—"

"My purse in her apartment. She have computer there, too. She show me I only worth five hundred dollar. Show me pretty girls worth much more."

Ranch looked to me for guidance.

"Get her keys," I said, pointing at the dead girl. "We'll get your purse back, Ling. Plus, I think we can use that computer to put a dent in the local slave trade, once all this is over."

As Ranch retrieved the keys, I looked at Seth. He had a half snarl on his lips and was staring into space. Catching his attention, I mouthed, "I'm sorry."

"I'm not," he said. "That woman was part of the slave trade that took Danielle. She got what she deserved.

We just need to get Danielle back and get out of this crazy country as soon as possible."

"Agreed," I replied. Ranch handed me the keys, and Ling led the way once more.

As we wound through the underground labyrinth, I thought of all the things I wanted to say to Seth when this was over.

I didn't want him to become bitter and cynical. I wanted him to understand that these slave traders were actually enslaved themselves —they were enslaved to an ideology that devalued human life.

I especially didn't want him to think that I took the killing of other human beings lightly—no matter how much they might "deserve it." I'd seen my share of death, and it was starting to take its toll.

I didn't want to see him go down that same road. I knew where it led.

Ling guided us onward. We arrived at a stairwell at the base of an apartment building and headed up. Once we reached the appropriate floor, I had Ranch and Seth wait while Ling and I went on. We stopped outside the apartment door to listen. Hearing no sound, we entered quietly and searched the apartment. I showed Ling how to use her shirttail like a glove when opening doors and drawers. We didn't want to leave any fingerprints.

Ling found her purse in a drawer in the bedroom. I found the computer on top of a desk in the living area. There may have been other interesting things to discover, but I wanted to get out of there as fast as possible. Ling was of the same mind.

We returned to the stairwell at the end of the hall and could hear the elevator arriving just as we shut the door behind us. Seth started to say something, but I held my finger to my lips. We could hear voices as a couple of people walked down the hallway towards the room we had just vacated. A key rattled in a lock. A door squeaked on its hinges. Footsteps receded into an apartment.

Wondering whether it was the same room, I cracked the door to the stairwell door open and looked down the hallway just in time to see the door of the slave trader's apartment snap shut. We had missed being caught by mere seconds, but we weren't in the clear yet.

Had those been soldiers we had heard, or just friends of the woman? Were they looking for her or her computer? Would they become suspicious when they found neither?

We didn't wait to find out. I held up the computer for Hank and Seth to see and then pointed at Ling's purse. We'd gotten what we'd come for. I motioned for everyone to remain quiet as we silently moved back down the stairs.

By the time we reached the bottom, we could hear angry voices from above. A door slammed. We hurriedly exited the stairwell and continued along the underground corridor away from where we had come.

We intentionally took several turns. After at least ten city blocks, we began to search for another exit. We found an elevator labeled, "Public Transportation," with an arrow pointing up. Stepping inside, we soon found ourselves standing in a plaza between buildings.

Several large modern art pieces made of a shiny metal were scattered amongst carefully manicured lawns. Ahead of us and to our left, we could see a small stand of taxis.

"Listen, I think we'd better split into two groups. It will look less suspicious. Ranch, you and Ling go first. Seth and I will wait a few minutes, then follow in a second taxi. Let's meet back up at the embassy."

"That's a good idea, but the drivers are going to call in our destination to a dispatcher. We should probably change taxis a time or two between here and there, maybe even walk the last few blocks to the embassy just to be safe," Ranch suggested.

"You're exactly right. You tell your driver you want to go to the nicest hotel in town. I'll tell mine I want to go to the cheapest. Hopefully, we'll end up at different locations and neither back where we started. Good luck."

Ranch and Ling took off across the plaza while Seth and I waited. After they were gone a few minutes, we followed suit and climbed into a second taxi.

"Take us to the cheapest hotel in town," I instructed. The driver looked at me with a puzzled expression. He said a few things in Chinese, and I realized he didn't speak English.

The taxi drivers who spoke English probably had the day shifts when all the tourists were awake. The drivers who didn't speak English worked the night shifts when it was mostly locals roaming around.

I had to chuckle to myself. I really was the world's worst spy. I hoped our taxi driver was good at playing "charades" as I began using improvised sign language to communicate where we wanted to go.

CHAPTER

18

The hallway had cleared of spectators by the time Lauren and Zhou went to gather the kids and head for the docks. Lauren gently rapped on the door of the boys' room. Nathan answered, and Lauren and Zhou went in.

"What's going on, Mom?" he cast an uncertain glance at Zhou, not knowing how to interpret her presence. "What was Seth saying about Danielle?"

"I'll explain in the van. But first we've got to gather our stuff and clear out of here."

"Seriously?"

"Yes, seriously. I'm going next door to wake the others. Will you get Joshua dressed and ready? Get Philip up, too, so he can help pack. I'll send Aaron back over in a minute to help carry our stuff downstairs. We'll need to leave right away."

"Yes, ma'am," he said and went to retrieve clean clothes from Joshua's backpack.

"Thanks, sweetie."

"No problem. We'll come to your room once we're ready."

"That'll be perfect."

"Your children are very obedient," Zhou observed as she followed Lauren back into the hall. "They would make excellent Chinese."

"Thank you." Lauren responded, taking the statement as a compliment. She tapped on the door of the adjacent room. Aaron opened it promptly, asking questions before they even got in the room.

"What in the world is happening?"

"It's too much to explain right now. We've got to get out of here."

"But—"

"No buts, Aaron. I'll do my best to answer your questions later. In the meantime, I need you to go next door and help the boys pack while Zhou and I get the girls ready."

"Okay, Mom. Sure." He turned to leave, a look of obvious bewilderment on his face.

Lauren grabbed clothes for the girls and went to wake them. As they rubbed their eyes and yawned, she turned to Zhou. "Do you mind helping these two, while I pack our things and change the baby?"

Zhou looked a little shaken at the prospect. "What do you need me to do?" she stammered. "I—I've never had children."

"You'll be fine. The girls can dress themselves, but they may need help with some of the buttons and zippers. They'll let you know."

"Is it time to get up already, Mommy?" Abigail chirped cheerfully.

"Yes, dear, I'm afraid it is."

"Can I have some ice cream?" Anna murmured in a daze, staring into space.

"No, sweetheart, no ice cream." Lauren took Anna's jaw in her hand and looked into her eyes. "I need you to wake up now and get dressed. Okay?"

"Okay," she answered as she shuffled out of bed and headed for the bathroom, eyes half-shut.

"You, too, Abigail."

"Yes, ma'am." Abigail bounced off the other side of the bed and began peeling off her pajamas.

Zhou sat down in a chair and smiled at the girls awkwardly. "You are taking all this very well, I think," she told Lauren.

"Oh, make no mistake, Zhou. This matter's far from settled in my mind." Lauren's voice faltered, "Inside, I feel like I've been hit by a ton of bricks, but—circumstances being what they are—I can't very well give in to that right now, can I? We've all got to do what we've got to do."

She turned away, scanning the room for stray clothes and hurriedly stuffing them into the backpacks. After double-checking the drawers, closets, and bathroom for missed items, she piled the packs by the door and turned her attention to the baby, who was awake now and just starting to fuss.

By the time she had changed him into fresh clothes and a dry diaper, Matthew was crying loudly. Lauren sat on the edge of the bed and tried to nurse him, but he refused to be consoled.

Fearing he could sense the inner turmoil she was striving so hard to keep hidden, she forced herself to take deep breaths and relax her own tense muscles as she rocked him gently, patting his back and stroking his soft skin. It worked. The baby calmed down and latched on. Lauren spoke quietly to the girls as she fed him.

"Anna, will you help your sister fix her hair, please?"

"Here, I can do that," Zhou offered.

Abigail looked at Anna, who shrugged, then handed a hairclip to Zhou and turned around. Zhou quickly wove Abigail's hair into a fancy arrangement with the clip neatly applied, holding everything in place.

"Wow," Anna admired. "Look what Zhou did to Abby's hair, Mom."

"Let *me* see," Abigail squealed, pushing past Zhou to look in the mirror. She smiled at her reflection, turning her head from side to side. "Cool!"

Lauren looked on approvingly as she shifted Matthew to the other side. "That looks very nice, Abigail. Did you remember to thank Zhou for helping you?"

"Thank you, Zhou. I like my hairdo. Is this how you used to fix your sister's hair?"

"I never had a sister," Zhou answered, "or a brother, either. In China there is only one child per family."

"Oh, that's right," Lauren said, shaking her head. "How strange that an entire generation doesn't know what it is like to have even a single sibling. Everyone an only child. That seems so lonely."

Zhou looked thoughtful. "It was very lonely. Of course, I had friends. When we would play together, we'd often pretend to be brothers and sisters. That was the biggest type of make-believe we could think of."

There was a light tap on the door, and the boys piled into the room with their stuff. While Zhou called for the valet to bring the minivan around, Lauren gave last-minute instructions.

"Everybody grab your backpacks and partner up. I'll get the baby. Aaron, you carry Joshua. Remember— *no* running in the hallway and *no* loud talking—we don't want to wake the other guests. Zhou, you lead the way, and the rest of us will follow."

The sober little procession snaked its way down the stairs and through a mostly deserted lobby. Although they received a couple of inquisitive looks from the hotel staff, no questions were asked, and soon everyone and everything was loaded—albeit a bit snugly—into the van and ready to go.

The trip to the docks was a relatively short one. The streets were lit up like Las Vegas with neon everywhere. True, the roads were less congested than they'd been during the daytime, but traffic was still surprisingly heavy given the hour of the night.

Zhou drove. Lauren stared out the window without seeing, watching instead a mental replay of the past hour's events.

The older boys attempted to comfort their younger siblings who were acting irritable after being awoken in the middle of the night and taken from the hotel still half-asleep.

Baby Matthew was resting peacefully again, but three-year-old Joshua whimpered sporadically through the whole ride, and Abigail and Anna, who were double-buckled, kept complaining that the other was hogging the seat. The remaining children sat wide-eyed and alert, exchanging puzzled looks, willing their mother to say something.

Finally, Aaron asked the obvious, "Mom, when are you going to tell us what's going on? Where are Dad and Seth and Grace? What happened to Danielle?"

"I wish I could tell you," Lauren answered, still facing the window. "I'm not even sure I know."

"Won't you at least tell us what you *do* know?" Nathan implored.

"Yes, I owe you that." She smiled at the kids who were all eagerly awaiting some type of explanation.

"Well, to begin with, your father has just informed me that he is a spy."

"*No way*," Aaron said.

"Dad is way too boring to be a spy. Are you sure he wasn't just joking around?" Philip asked.

"Yeah, maybe it is all part of this reality television thing. Like, they're trying to play a trick on us to see how we'll react. From what I've heard, they do that sort of thing on T.V. all the time," Nathan offered.

As a homeschooled kid, he didn't actually see much network television, but his friends kept him up to date on the latest trends. "Isn't that right, Zhou?" Nathan presumed she was in on the charade.

"You're right, but your father really is a spy, Nathan. I work with him. Besides, there aren't any cameras."

"There could be hidden cameras," Philip suggested.

"Good point," Aaron agreed.

"No hidden cameras. I promise," Zhou replied. The van got quiet.

"Well, what about Danielle then?" Aaron asked.

"She's been kidnapped."

"By other spies?" Philip asked.

"I don't really know."

"Why would spies go to a little town in East Texas and grab Danielle?"

"She wasn't kidnapped in Texas," Lauren answered. "She was kidnapped here."

"*Here?* What was Danielle doing here?" Aaron asked.

"Apparently, she came to see Seth and got herself kidnapped instead."

"Man! Seth's going to be in big trouble," Philip observed.

"More than you know," Lauren agreed. "Much more than you know."

Zhou turned into the dockyards. In the distance, they could see giant cranes lifting huge rectangular shipping containers into the air. From this vantage point, the containers looked like Lego blocks being neatly stacked on the massive cargo ships.

As they drew closer, the enormous scale hit home. Each rectangle was actually the truck bed of an eighteen-wheeler packed tight with freight. They would soon be some of that freight themselves.

"Look there, kids," Lauren pointed towards the ships. "That is our ride home—or at least to Taiwan."

"We're sneaking out of the country in a cargo ship?" Aaron asked. "We must really be in hot water. What about Dad and the others?"

"I don't think any of us are in trouble yet," she replied, "This is just a precaution that Zhou recommended. Your father and everybody else will be joining us very soon, I'm sure."

The kids looked at Zhou, who nodded.

They pulled up to a gate set in a high chain-link fence. A guard spoke to Zhou briefly and then waved them through. Driving forward into a little warehouse, they parked next to an idling eighteen-wheeler.

A man jumped down from the driver's seat as they approached. Zhou got out of the van to speak with him.

It was quickly apparent that the man did not like what she had to say. He would hold up one finger, and Zhou would hold up eight. All the while, he was shaking his head in the negative. She would demonstrate with her hand held about three feet above the ground how small the children were. Finally, he came over and looked in the van.

The youngest children had gone back to sleep, which naturally made them seem less troublesome, and Lauren smiled as kindly as she knew how.

The driver walked back over to Zhou. He reluctantly gave in, but rubbed his fingers together to show he would need more money than was originally agreed upon. Zhou quickly accepted his terms and signaled for everyone to get out of the van.

Lauren carried the baby while the older boys distributed backpacks and marshaled their younger siblings.

Opening the back of the truck, the driver indicated a narrow path between crates. Aaron jumped into the truck bed first, then gave the others a hand up while the driver boosted them from the ground. Last of all, Lauren passed the baby up before scrambling in herself.

The driver turned on an electric lantern, handed it to Lauren, and gestured for them to move on along the makeshift pathway. It was a tight squeeze, but she and the children slowly made their way, single file, into the lorry.

At about the midpoint of the cargo container, they found a small area with two cots and two chairs, several blankets, and a battery-powered fan. Lauren spotted an ice chest under one of the cots, which was found to contain several bottles of water and soda. A large paper sack behind the chest was filled with cookies, crackers, and chips—nothing particularly nutritious, but stuff that could tide the little ones over in a pinch and would keep well without being refrigerated.

"Well," Lauren announced, "we're going to be here for awhile—we may as well make ourselves comfortable. Aaron, you take that chair and hold Joshua in your lap. Matthew and I will take this one. Nathan, you share one cot with Abigail. Philip, you and Anna can have the other. We'll rotate later if we need to."

"How do we use the restroom?" Philip asked urgently. "I've really got to go."

"Just a second." Lauren looked around. Surely they had addressed that issue, but she didn't see anything obvious. Zhou came up beside her.

"Finding everything you need? I'm sorry it's so crowded, but at least it's safe. I've used these people many times before. They're very reliable."

"What about a restroom?" Lauren asked.

"It's up at the front for privacy. Just follow the path as it continues." Zhou pointed the way. "Anyway, the driver is getting some more drinks. He doesn't have another cooler, but it's better than nothing."

"Thank you—thanks for everything," Lauren said, offering her hand from underneath Matthew. "I hope we get to meet again under better circumstances."

"I hope so, too," Zhou said, gently squeezing the tips of Lauren's fingers.

Zhou's phone rang and she answered it. She nodded and said, "yes," a few times as her face became more and more concerned. Finally, she hung up.

"Is something wrong?" Lauren asked.

"I'm not sure."

"Are we still going on with the plan?"

"Yes, of course. Nothing has changed relative to your leaving the country."

"What, then?"

"Well, your husband has a friend at the CDC in the US. Apparently, he was supposed to call Jon if anything unusual happened, especially anything involving the Chinese researchers working there."

"And..."

"And one of the researchers had some kind of weird seizure yesterday and dropped over dead. He spilled a bunch of chemicals near a Bunsen burner in the process and set his lab on fire. If a co-worker hadn't witnessed it and promptly used a fire extinguisher, the whole lab might've been destroyed. The fire alarm never went off, which only adds to the mystery."

"What does Jon think about all that?"

"That's the problem. Your husband isn't answering his phone. His friend had my number as an emergency backup."

The driver banged on the door of the truck, making Lauren and Zhou jump. They turned to see him pushing some more drinks towards them along the floor, then pointing at his watch and waving for Zhou to get out.

"What now?" Lauren asked.

"You go on to Taiwan. I'll track down Jon." With that Zhou hurried down the aisle and jumped to the ground.

The driver closed the doors before either could say goodbye, and within seconds the truck lurched away.

As Lauren sat down with the kids, Anna asked, "Are we really playing Moses and Pharaoh?"

"What do you mean?"

"Aaron says we're inside a great big basket, and we're going to float away to escape from the bad guys, just like baby Moses did. Is that true?"

Lauren smiled tenderly. "Yes, honey—I suppose it is."

CHAPTER
19

The minivan was uncomfortably quiet as Hank and Grace drove toward Guangzhou with the young Chinese fugitives. Hank glanced over at Grace, but she was staring straight ahead and giving him the silent treatment for some reason.

Here he'd finally met someone he was genuinely interested in, and she wouldn't give him the time of day. Sometimes life just doesn't seem fair. There had to be some explanation. Could Grace have been burned in the past, like he had?

In his mind's eye, he could still see his ex-girlfriend's long blonde hair being tossed in the breeze that morning when they had first met on the beach. She had invited him to church and he had gone. They became inseparable—he even followed her to Bible College. Ironically, it was the faith in God to which she'd introduced him that later sustained him when she met someone else and left him shattered.

"So who was he?"

Hank directed the question at Grace, almost accusingly.

"Who was who?"

"The guy who broke your heart and made it impossible for anyone else to have half a chance?"

Grace didn't answer immediately. She studied him dubiously for a moment, then turned back to the window and said, "Nobody."

"Well he must have done a real number on you, because I've been nothing but nice, yet every time I give you a two stimulus, I get a ten response."

"A ten response? What are you talking about?"

"I thought you'd know. I heard your dad say that to Seth on the airplane."

"I know what Dad means when he says it," Grace answered, amused. "I'm just curious to know what you mean when you say it."

Hank was undaunted. "I mean that whenever I try to make casual conversation with you, you treat me with total disdain—somewhere just shy of loathing. I give you a small friendly stimulus and you give me a big unfriendly response." Hank shrugged, "It tells me you're carrying around some emotional luggage that has nothing to do with me. A two stimulus followed by a ten response means there's eight of something else underneath the surface. I'm just assuming it must have been the previous guy in your life."

"I already told you, it was nobody."

"Suit yourself. You're just proving my point, anyway."

The group traveled on in silence, until some time later when Chen called timidly from the back seat, "You will need to turn left at the next light."

"Will do," Hank answered, turning his attention to Chen and leaving Grace to stew. "Now, explain this to me again. You didn't want to arouse suspicion by consulting a map, but you also didn't want to get lost, so you *memorized* the roads for Hong Kong and all the surrounding areas off the Internet?"

"Basically, yes." Chen answered.

"So you turned yourself into a walking, talking GPS."

"What did you expect?" asked Grace. "He's a geography whiz, remember? It's really just an extension of what he'd been doing for the competition."

"I knew you'd be handy in a tight spot," Hank told Chen warmly. "I'll bet you could probably do the same thing for all the major cities in the world, couldn't you?"

"It would take some time, but probably."

"And do you actually speak all those languages you used at the geography competition?"

"Yes. Jung and I both know fifteen different languages, plus a handful of regional dialects. Technically, we are both fluent, but she is much better at languages than I am."

"No, I'm not," Jung protested.

"Yes, you are," Chen insisted. "You have a more natural rhythm and cadence when you speak. It is much more flowing and musical. I always sound so robotic."

"You don't sound robotic."

"My Russian sounds robotic, and you know it. You laugh about it sometimes."

"Everybody's Russian sounds robotic. Besides, I don't laugh. I just smile."

"I distinctly remember you laughing."

"It was your robotic German that made me laugh," Jung said with a grin, then added in a mechanical staccato, "Ich bin ein robot."

"See. I told you," Chen said, pointing good-naturedly at Jung, his eyes narrowing.

"That's enough, kids. Stop fighting in the backseat. You sound like my little brothers and sisters," Grace said.

"That or an old married couple," Hank added, looking back over his shoulder.

Suddenly embarrassed, Jung and Chen looked out their respective windows.

"Anyway," Hank changed the subject, "with your geography and language skills, Chen, you'd make a terrific agent."

The uncomfortable silence returned.

"I shouldn't have said that," Hank apologized. "I'm sorry."

"Don't be," Chen reassured him. "I have been considering that idea myself lately. I had always planned on being a computer scientist, but that's not working out very well. So, who knows? Maybe?"

Hank looked at Grace and raised his eyebrows.

"You need to take another right at the next corner," Chen said. "Do you think I could be an actual spy and travel around? I mean, I wouldn't want to just be some government-sponsored computer hacker. That's basically what they do with the brightest agents here in China. In fact, that is how I started out, until this other project came along. I've had enough of that kind of thing."

Hank slowed down for the right hand turn. "I can't say for sure, but I suspect they'd let you do whatever you want."

"Good."

Hank looked at Grace again, who now seemed lost in thought herself. "What do you think?" he asked.

"Oh, I don't know, she answered. "I just got to thinking about what a strange honeymoon this is going to be."

"*Honeymoon?* I thought the groom's supposed to think about the honeymoon, and the bride just worries about the wedding."

"Well, don't *you* think about it too much! We aren't really getting married, you know." Grace blushed ever so slightly.

Hank grinned. It was the first time he'd seen Grace get flustered. She caught herself, and then added in her usual cool manner, "Besides, our little wedding planners in the backseat have taken care of all our marriage arrangements already."

Hank kept on grinning. He was enjoying Grace's newly found discomfort. She tucked her hair behind her ear and began to brush off her clothes self-consciously.

"Anyway," she added, "People will undoubtedly ask what we are doing for our honeymoon. If we want to sound convincing, we'll need some kind of answer. I'm just trying to decide if sight-seeing is the best response."

"Sight-seeing would be reasonable," Hank said, dropping the grin and letting Grace off the hook. "It did occur to me, though, that we're probably the first couple in history with a marriage arranged by the children, instead of vice-versa."

"That's probably true—unless you think about older couples who've been widowed or something. Their kids might make the introductions later."

"Oh sure, but that's not the same thing as an arranged marriage they'd have in India or someplace. That's what I'm talking about."

"I have a hard time getting my mind around that whole concept," Grace admitted. "How can they expect you to marry someone you hardly know—maybe even someone you've never met?"

The longer she talked, the more animated she became. She seemed a little feisty, even. Hank's grin grew broader, but he did his best to suppress it as he nodded soberly in agreement.

"—and then you're supposed to spend the rest of your lives together?" she was saying. "That just seems so strange."

"We're getting close," Chen called from the backseat. "You'll need to make a final left at the light—and it's really not *that* strange."

"What?" Grace turned to face him.

"I said it's not that strange. Lots of cultures have relied on arranged marriages for centuries, and it appears to have worked fairly well."

"Maybe so—but are the couples happy?"

"Obviously, it would depend on your definition of happiness. It seems to me that in America, you define happiness as being able to do whatever you want, whenever you want. Naturally, marriage is an impediment to that kind of happiness.

"In China, however, we think of happiness as the natural outgrowth of a balanced and stable life. A spouse adds balance; a child adds stability. Happiness is merely the by-product of such a life, not its primary goal.

"However, to lead that kind of life requires putting the needs of others ahead of your own, which is not a popular concept in some cultures."

"You're one really smart kid, Chen," Grace said thoughtfully.

"After a fashion, I suppose."

"After a fashion?" Hank laughed. "I know you're trying to be humble, but you can't deny being blessed in the brains department."

"It's a matter of perspective."

"What? So you think intelligence is a curse instead of a blessing?"

Chen pondered that idea for a moment. "That isn't what I meant, but I guess one could make such an argument, in light of all that has transpired."

"What do you mean?" asked Grace.

"Obviously, it was my intelligence that resulted in my parents' death and my subsequent life as Lao's pawn.

But that's not my point. What I mean is that the type of intelligence I possess is—well, it's obsolete."

"Obsolete? How can you say that? You're a whiz at computers, you won an international geography competition, and you speak fifteen different languages. What more could you possibly ask for?"

"I'm not asking for anything more—I wouldn't know what to ask for, if I could. I don't know how to fully explain it, but basically, people tend to value the types of intelligence they can measure. But by the time we are able to measure it, it is already becoming obsolete. It's the things we cannot yet quantify—things on the horizon of our understanding—which are the true realm of genius. That's why we say someone is ahead of his time or that he was born too soon—like a caveman who can do calculus."

"You're serious, aren't you?" Hank said.

"Yes, I am," Chen assured him. "Consider my knowledge of geography. Anybody who can log onto a computer can access far more detailed information about any spot on the planet than I could hope to memorize in a lifetime. And with so many online translators available now, the same can be said about languages, as well. I'm like the strongman with a travelling show—just an interesting curiosity, nothing more."

Grace smiled, "You didn't say anything about your programming ability."

Chen grinned back. "Well, I may be a little ahead of my time in that area."

"Finally, I get you to admit something!"

"But not by much. Within a year, there will be thousands of people doing what I've done, only better."

"But you will have shown them the way. Isn't that the kind of visionary ability you're talking about?"

"Yes, perhaps it is," he agreed with a smile. "Oh, and turn into this parking area up here. We'll need to walk the last few blocks."

As Hank pulled to a stop, Grace asked a final question, "What sort of abilities do you think will be important in the future?"

"It's impossible to know for sure," Chen replied thoughtfully, "but I can think of two qualities that will always be important, precisely because we cannot quantify them."

"Which are?"

"Character and creativity," Chen answered. He let that sink in and then continued. "Obviously, with the help of high speed computers and sophisticated statistical analysis, we can solve problems and answer questions more quickly and easily than ever before. However, it is *creativity* that causes us to ask questions in the first place, and *character* that guides how we use the answers, once we find them. That may be the most important issue of all, as Director Lao has proven."

"But you've proven it, too," Grace said. "As creative as you are, it was your character that ultimately proved most important—it's what is going to save millions of lives."

"I hope so," Chen replied. He opened his door and stepped out into the crisp air of the early morning. To any onlooker, he appeared to be nothing more than an average, ordinary school kid.

CHAPTER

20

Seth and I were the last ones to make it to the embassy. We found Ranch waiting for us outside the conference room. When I asked him how Ling was doing, he simply said that she was being questioned and debriefed, and that the computer had been turned over to the information technology people at the embassy.

"Did you tell them what happened?" I whispered.

"Yeah, I did. I don't necessarily want the Chinese government to know, and I definitely don't want any underworld types to find out, but I felt like our guys needed to hear the whole story—especially if they try to use Ling as an agent one day."

"You think they'll do that?"

"I'm certain they will. She's young, well educated, has a positive view of America—and most importantly, she's highly motivated to fight human trafficking at this point in her life. Armed with the data on that computer and with Ling as an agent, we could do some real good in this little corner of the world."

"I'm glad you handled it like you did. Did you tell our little prodigies in there what happened?"

"I decided to leave them out of it. This whole thing is probably scary enough for them already."

"Good call. I'll keep my mouth shut for now, but shouldn't we be getting inside?"

"Yeah, come on in." Ranch held the door. Seth and I preceded him in.

The conference room was beautifully appointed in the British style with lots of dark wood, heavy picture frame molding, and the like. Someone with exquisite taste must have done the decorating way back when.

Seated were Hank, Grace, Chen, and Jung, as well as a thin, pale man I didn't know. Standing in the corner was a young blonde woman with her hair in a bun. She was wearing stylish, plastic-framed glasses that made her look about ten years older than she probably was.

Grace stood up as soon as she caught sight of us. "I'm so sorry, Seth," she said, reaching to hug her brother's neck. "We'll get her back. These guys know what they're doing."

Seth nodded silently as tears welled up in his eyes, but managed to keep his composure otherwise. I gave them both a pat on the back.

The slender pale man stood to his feet, extending his hand. He was taller than I expected, actually a couple inches taller than I am, but thin to the point of frailness. He had the look of Ichabod Crane about him. His name badge identified him as the embassy librarian.

"Hello, Dr. Gunderson. I'm Grant Simpson," he introduced himself. "I shall be coordinating your departure from China."

"But—you're the librarian, not the travel agent," I said, pointing to his name badge with a smile.

"Ah, yes—the librarian," he glanced at the badge and returned my smile, "amongst other things." He left what those other things might be to our imagination and continued, "I would offer you a seat, but my assistant must first take some quick measurements."

"Measurements?"

"Yes, measurements, Dr. Gunderson. As I believe you Texans are fond of saying, this is not our *first rodeo*. We have a system in place to deal with such contingencies, and that system begins with the taking of measurements. So, if you please...." He gestured towards his assistant. Seth and I walked over to her.

She went to work like a seasoned tailor, although her name badge indicated she was the embassy's assistant librarian.

"An assistant librarian *and* a seamstress? There sure is a lot of multitasking that goes on around here."

"Indeed," said Mr. Simpson. His assistant merely smiled and slipped out of the room once she had what she needed.

"Now then, let us proceed. I will tell you my understanding of the situation as best I apprehend it. You may correct me as I go, and then I will tell you what we are going to do to get you quickly, quietly, and safely out of China."

Everyone nodded in agreement.

"Our present situation began when the two young people seated here, Chen and Jung, contacted the United States Government in a clever and convincing way, asking for asylum. They were allegedly being forced to work on some brand of new biological weapon and no longer wished to do so. Is that correct?" he regarded our prodigies with the stern look of a Puritan minister.

"Yes, sir," they answered, glancing at one another.

His austere manner and the use of the word "allegedly" was the first time anyone had shown skepticism of any sort regarding the kids' story. I must admit—it gave me pause. Yet, it would all have been such an elaborate hoax, and to what end, if it weren't true? We moved on.

"Dr. Gunderson was then contacted as an experienced agent in unusual assignments. He agreed to come to China with his family as a cover for Dr. Richter

205

and Mr. Sanders. They were to be responsible for the extraction, along with a local by the name of Zhou Li, with whom this office, incidentally, has done business in the past." We all nodded.

"Contact was made at an international geography competition where a time and place were arranged for the desired extraction. Things were going swimmingly up until that point. However, two things transpired at that time that brought about our present predicament. First, Chen and Jung requested formal adoption in order to make their escape legal, which is primarily why you are here now. Second, local ruffians kidnapped an associate of the Gunderson family, a Miss Danielle Jones."

Everyone instinctively looked at Seth, who was staring at Mr. Simpson unflinchingly, obviously trying to keep his emotions in check. We all followed his gaze back to Mr. Simpson.

"It is my understanding that an attempt was made by Dr. Richter, Dr. Gunderson, and Dr. Gunderson's oldest son, Seth, to rescue said associate, but without success. They were thwarted by what appeared to be Chinese soldiers, who carried Miss Jones away in a helicopter. At that point, our search and rescue team decided to abandon the chase in favor of making their way here, which was accomplished with the assistance of a local woman, who is being questioned even as we speak."

I don't know what came over me, but hearing the events of the last few hours laid out so succinctly somehow caused me to think, then to say aloud, "If only *Danielle* hadn't come to China!"

I immediately regretted having said it. Everyone glared at me and cast furtive glances at Seth—but before I could apologize for my thoughtless remark, Seth replied coldly, "I wish *none of us* had come to China."

"Me, too," added Grace.

"I'm sorry, Seth—that was out of line. I guess I'm just frustrated. Things would have been a lot simpler if you two had only been honest with us."

The unintended irony of that comment was lost on nobody but me. Seth bristled when I said it.

"No, Dad. Things would have been a lot simpler if *you* had been honest with *us*." His eyes flashed. "You're the one who's been leading a double life for years, dragging us all over the world and putting our lives in danger without ever breathing a word. You'd better take a good look in the mirror before you start blaming me or Danielle for what's going on."

The room was as silent as a crypt. I stared at the table. I knew Seth was right and couldn't look him in the eye.

"I'm sorry," I said quietly.

I was rescued from the awkward silence when the Assistant Librarian returned with several uniforms. "If I might have everyone's attention," she announced, "it's time to play dress up."

Her voice, reminiscent of a Civil War era Southern Belle, caught me off guard. For some reason, I had expected a Boston accent—or at least something from the Northeast. It was a welcome surprise to hear the voice of a fellow Southerner and an even more welcome distraction from the current discussion.

"Now, if y'all will kindly stand up, I think I can get a good idea whether or not this is going to work."

After first holding selected sizes up to each person's shoulders and checking the length, she handed out what appeared to be some kind of medical uniform. Chen, Jung, and I were the only ones not to receive one.

"I'm sorry, Dr. Gunderson, but we didn't have a uniform that would fit you. I'm afraid you'll have to pretend to be the victim in this little charade. And kids, I didn't have anything in your sizes either, but y'all are a little young to make believable ambulance drivers, anyway."

"So that's how you're going to do it? Dress us up as ambulance personnel and whisk us away to the airport or something?"

"Yes, sir—except that you'll be wearing your normal clothes, Dr. Gunderson, and playing like you're the patient. The kids can hide in the storage compartments. Of course, you're all going to get new IDs, in case you're stopped." She reached into her pocket and began distributing passports.

"Now, the restrooms are right through those doors. If y'all will just try on those outfits and take a little time to review your new identities, I think my work here will be done."

As the others went through the doors to change, Mr. Simpson's phone rang. He answered it quietly, stepped to the corner of the room, and continued speaking in hushed tones. It reminded me that my own phone was broken, so I asked his assistant whether she could get me another.

"I'm working on it, Dr. Gunderson. Dr. Richter told us about it first thing."

I thanked her and looked down at my passport. "*Thor?*" I exclaimed. "You made my fake name *Thor*? Give me a break."

"Well, you won't have any trouble remembering it now, will you, Dr. Gunderson? Besides, if you'll notice, you're supposed to be Norwegian, not American—and Thor's a fairly common name in Norway."

"But I don't know a word of Norwegian. What if someone tries to talk to me and blows my cover?"

"Don't worry about that. Nobody else in China speaks Norwegian, either."

"We do," Jung and Chen corrected her in unison.

"I mean, besides y'all," replied the assistant. She got a mischievous look on her face and glanced over at her boss, who was still on the phone. Seeing that he wasn't paying attention she whispered loud enough for me to hear, "What languages do y'all speak? I've heard it's a lot."

The kids listed all the common European languages, plus a variety of languages like Punjabi and Urdu that most Westerners wouldn't even think about. The assistant seemed to be adding on her fingers as they listed them.

"I see y'all primarily focused on the most widely spoken languages—that was smart."

"It seemed most efficient to do so," Chen said.

Jung nodded.

"Well, if my calculations are correct, y'all should be able to communicate with well over half the six billion people on the planet without needing an interpreter. That's quite an accomplishment."

"Thank you," they said together.

"Don't tell me you're a linguist in addition to being an assistant librarian and a seamstress," I said.

"I do a lot of things, Dr. Gunderson. It goes with the territory when you serve in a diplomatic capacity. I don't know whether I could properly be called a linguist, but I did have the privilege of studying linguistics at MIT under some of the best professors in the world. I speak eleven languages fluently, plus a smattering of others less well."

She glanced at her boss, who was still preoccupied, then back at the kids.

"What I'm curious about, though, is how long it takes y'all to learn a new language?"

Chen looked at Jung. "About three or four weeks, if we can work on it exclusively. Longer when we're busy with our research."

"It's not that difficult," Jung added. "It's just a matter of fitting it in."

"Sidis could do it in a day," the assistant said almost wistfully. "It takes me an average of two months, if I can really focus—but finding that kind of time is nearly impossible these days. Of course, the tonal languages take awhile longer, since they're not native to me—but that wouldn't be a problem for y'all now, would it?" she said, smiling at the kids.

"You can learn an entire language in a couple of months?" I blurted out and then more quietly, "And these kids can do it in three or four weeks?"

"Sidis could do it in a day," Chen said, echoing the assistant's previous comment.

"Who is Sidis?" I asked, looking back and forth between them. Apparently, it was someone a linguist would know about, but not an ordinary mortal like me.

"William James Sidis was probably the smartest person who ever lived," Chen said.

"I thought Einstein was the smartest person that ever lived," I answered, displaying my ignorance and thereby eliminating myself from the running for that illustrious title.

"Einstein was the most *famous* smart person who ever lived, not the smartest," Jung said. "They're two completely different things."

"Some people argue that Goethe was the smartest, but it's hard to prove since he lived a couple hundred years before we really started measuring such things. I'd have to agree with Chen and put my money on Sidis. The guy wrote a book at four, passed the entrance exam for MIT at eight, and could speak over two hundred languages, translating back and forth between any two. That was nearly every known language at the time. Of course, we know now that there's over sixty-nine hundred languages," the assistant added, "but in all fairness, most of those are small tribal languages in places like Papua New Guinea and sub-Saharan Africa."

"I see you are all getting better acquainted," Mr. Simpson announced. We hadn't noticed him get off the phone, and it was a bit startling to have him suddenly join the conversation again. Before I could formulate a pithy answer to reestablish my intellectual worth, the others returned to the room wearing their paramedic disguises.

"It looks like you found some perfect fits," I said.

The assistant made everyone turn around so she could inspect her work, and then she took her leave.

"I'll be back with your phone in just a minute, Dr. Gunderson," she called to me from the doorway.

"I enjoyed talking to you," Chen told her, somewhat awkwardly. She gave him a kind smile and disappeared. He glanced shyly at Jung, who acted as if she hadn't noticed a thing.

"Attention, please. If everyone would please take a seat, I'll put Agent Smith on the speaker phone so that we can all discuss our next move."

Mr. Simpson pushed a button, and we could all hear Eric Smith on the line. "Jon? Jon—are you there?"

"I'm here."

"Listen, before we go any further, I just want to say that Zhou has always been one hundred percent reliable in the past. She must've gotten spooked and decided to lie low, possibly with the rest of your family somewhere. I'm sure she'll check in with us as soon as it's safe for her to—.

Smith's tone, even more than his words, frightened and confused me. "What—what are you saying, Eric?" I stammered.

"Jon, we're not sure why, but we've lost contact with Zhou. We don't know what's happened, but she—and your family—may be in jeopardy."

CHAPTER
21

I was speechless. Lauren and the kids—in jeopardy? Now it was my turn to wish none of us had come to China.

"Well, what's being done to locate them?" I demanded.

"We've got people working on it, Jon. But I'm telling you, Zhou is one of our best agents. She probably has good reasons for doing what she's doing, and we can't afford to blow her cover by being too aggressive here."

"Practically my entire family's missing, and you're worried about being too aggressive?"

"Don't forget about Danielle," Seth chimed in. "She's still missing, too!"

"Slow down, Jon," Smith backpedaled. "All I mean to say is that I trust Zhou. I think she's hiding your family somewhere. If we're not careful in the way we go about looking for them, we might end up leading whoever they're hiding from right to them. Now, the last person to speak with Zhou was Joel Rothstein—just a few hours ago. He was trying to reach you to tell you about a death at the CDC yesterday, but he got Zhou instead. He said he could hear an echo like she was in a small room somewhere. I really think they're just hiding out."

"Maybe Zhou went with them on the container ship. That would explain the echo, and they'd naturally lose phone reception once they were out to sea," I suggested hopefully.

"Accompanying your family wasn't the plan, but parts of that scenario would certainly fit the situation. Unfortunately, it will be nine or ten hours before we can confirm or deny that hypothesis. No one but Zhou knows which container or which ship they left in, assuming they made it that far. I'm not trying to frighten you, Jon. I just want you to have all the information that I do. I owe you that much."

"Maybe Zhou is a double agent."

It was Jung who had spoken. We all turned towards her. "I'm sorry, Mr. Gunderson, but I think we should consider that a possibility, even if it is painful to do so."

The assistant returned at just that moment. She immediately sensed the tension in the room and quietly slid the phone across the table to me. She then handed two Barbie dolls holding Chinese babies to Grace, who picked the dolls up inquisitively.

The assistant whispered, "*Going Home* dolls from the White Swan Hotel," and gave a quick smile to Chen, who was staring adoringly at her. She eased out of the room again.

"What prompts you to suggest such a thing?" Mr. Simpson asked Jung.

"Wouldn't it make sense?" she asked defensively, "Mr. Gunderson's family missing, and Zhou cannot be reached. Isn't that a strange coincidence? And how is it that soldiers got to Danielle before Mr. Gunderson could? Maybe Zhou tipped them off. How else would they know exactly where to go?"

"Jung, I told you I thought it was Steven who did that," Chen said.

"But you covered your electronic tracks. It would have taken Steven hours to trace your computer hack back to the hotel."

"But I'm not talking about tracing it back to the hotel. All he had to know was that someone was hacking into the city's computers, then check to see what they were looking for. It is entirely possible he learned of Danielle's whereabouts at the same instant we did. At that point, he probably guessed she was someone important and reported it to Lao. Steven warned us not to do anything dumb. From a hacking standpoint, what we did was dumb—although clearly necessary," Chen said, glancing first at Seth and then me.

"Who is Steven?" Smith's voice blared over the speakerphone.

"Steven Lao is one of China's top computer hackers and is the son of our boss," Jung answered.

"Ex-boss," Chen corrected.

"Yes. Ex-boss, thankfully," Jung echoed, smiling at Chen and giving his hand a quick pat.

"Ah, Steven Lao, the petite bourgeoisie. He claims to be an anarchist, but functions more like a capitalist, selling his computer services to the highest bidder. This office is quite familiar with young Steven Lao," Mr. Simpson said. "I suppose he might even be willing to work for his estranged father, if the price were right."

"Steven is definitely working for his father, so the price must be right. He was at a meeting Director Lao and I had recently with several top Army Generals who wanted to discuss the military implications of my artificial intuition program. What's strange, though, is that Steven caught Jung and me escaping last night, but immediately let us go. That's when he told us not to do anything stupid, because he'd be watching. Why would he do that?"

"Because he's a bit of a wild card," Mr. Simpson answered, "not unlike others from the second generation of the Prodigy Project—including the two of you,"

"You know about the Prodigy Project?" Chen asked, surprised.

"I know about a lot of things, Mr. Shih."

"Then why have you done nothing to stop it? It's evil!" Chen was more animated than I'd ever seen him. He was nearly shouting, and his ears had a touch of red to them.

"Why do you assume I've done nothing to stop it? You're here, aren't you?"

"Yes, but I contacted you."

"Then, wouldn't it be logical to assume that others, comparably gifted, would also contact us seeking asylum? I told you this wasn't our first rodeo. We obviously haven't time to discuss this in detail now, but please let me assure you that many of the exceptional children identified by the Prodigy Project have found their way to America and Europe and are now leading very happy and satisfying lives."

Clearly embarrassed, Chen hung his head and looked down at the floor. "I apologize for my reaction. The more I discover about this horrid project, the more upset I become. But you said Steven was from the second generation. What does that mean?" he asked, raising his head as he addressed Mr. Simpson.

"Again, details are for another time, but I'll attempt a brief summary: As you doubtlessly know, all of China's intellectuals were either shot or driven underground during the Cultural Revolution—doctors, lawyers, artists, schoolteachers, everyone. The only safe jobs were farmer or Communist party boss, and even those were not entirely free from danger. Not surprisingly, the new leadership found it impossible to run an entire country with nothing but farmers and political flunkies, so the search began for

215

promising youth who could be trained up to replace the old intellectuals, but with the correct political ideology, of course. Most of the prodigies from that first generation were sent to France for schooling, including your Director Lao. Despite his shortcomings, he and others like him have rebuilt the intellectual infrastructure of China, literally from the ground up."

"And the second generation?"

"The program was so successful that the leadership decided to continue it indefinitely. However, with the new infrastructure in place, it was no longer necessary to send the children away to school; they could be trained right here in China. Unfortunately, having them so close to home meant that parents were around and tended to get in the way of what the leadership was trying to achieve. Eventually, the parents just started disappearing or having unusual accidents. The blessing of a bright child quickly became the ultimate curse."

"That's *horrible*," Grace said, glancing at Chen and Jung who were both looking very solemn. Chen's lip began to quiver and tears formed at the edges of his eyes.

Mr. Simpson continued, "If there is any justice in this terrible tale, it is this: The killing of parents has backfired on the Prodigy Project. Without parents to provide encouragement and emotional stability, the children have grown much more rebellious and unreliable. Many now in leadership want to scrap the project altogether. They've exerted great pressure on Director Lao to show some results, or else. It's a difficult assignment, especially considering the fact that his own son has rebelled against the system. I believe you two were his last hope. Your artificial intuition program was the only thing keeping Lao afloat with the other leaders, Chen. I suspect your leaving China will shut down the program for good and will save the lives of countless parents."

"Then it sounds like our first priority is getting these kids out of China as soon as possible," Smith said over the speakerphone.

"And finding my family," I was quick to remind him.

"And Danielle," Seth added.

"Yes, of course. But we'll be in a much better position to do that once Chen and Jung are safely on American soil—or at least in Taiwan. Now, if everybody is ready, we can probably have you all to Taiwan within an hour or two. It's nearly five-thirty in the morning your time, so we should be able to have you in the air and on your way before the commercial airline traffic really gets rolling."

"Spot on, then. Everyone follow me," said Mr. Simpson.

There was the noise of multiple chairs scooting back all at once—the classic sound of a meeting coming to an end. Mr. Simpson held the door as the others filed into the hallway.

"Smith, are you still there?" I asked.

"Still here."

"Who died at the CDC?"

"One of the Chinese microbiologists Joel was keeping an eye on. Even more concerning, the guy had a bunch of stuff about endogenous retroviruses on his computer. Oh, and guess who wrote one of his reference letters?"

"Lao?"

"You got it. That's another reason I want those kids in America as soon as possible. They'll have a better understanding of what we're up against. Apparently, they weren't the only ones working on this project. It may be further along than even they know."

"How'd the guy die? I mean, what happened exactly?"

"Again, very strange. It's a fairly young guy we're talking about, late twenties at the most. He died quite suddenly while at work. One witness says he let out some guttural animal sounds, then started thrashing about and knocking stuff over before collapsing to the ground and dying. He even upset a Bunsen burner and started a small fire in the process. We're guessing he had a massive stroke, but we'll have to get permission from the Chinese government to do an autopsy. They're dragging their feet and intimating they want to do the autopsy themselves. That little gesture, of course, makes me even more nervous about the endogenous retrovirus angle, but it really isn't too unusual for them. After all, the Chinese don't trust us either."

"So, at this point, you have no idea how this researcher died?" I pressed.

"Well, we did manage to get some blood work, including a toxicology screening—not much, but it's better than nothing. We're still waiting for the results. We held on to an extra blood sample, in case the kids know any tests we can run. And we've stalled on sending the body back to China for now."

Mr. Simpson, still at the door, nodded for me to come on.

"Alright, Smith. Just keep me in the loop, okay?"

"You got it."

I passed through the door, which Mr. Simpson closed behind me. The others were waiting at the end of the hallway. Mr. Simpson edged around them to lead the way. We made a few turns, then took an elevator to an underground parking garage. There we found two ambulances parked side by side, one a newer, shinier version of the other.

"Well, this is where we say our goodbyes, and I go back to my duties as a librarian," Mr. Simpson told us with only the tiniest hint of sarcasm.

He pulled a key from his pocket and unlocked the door to the older ambulance.

"Ranch, I believe you are the most familiar with this area—other than the kids, of course—so I'll put you in charge of driving. There is an old-fashioned map on the front seat, on which my assistant has carefully marked your route to the airport. Our new ambulance is equipped with all the latest technology, including GPS, but we felt it would be prudent to hold on to this older model, for situations such as yours."

Ranch shook Mr. Simpson's hand before sliding in behind the steering wheel. He then unfolded the map and began to look it over.

"Dr. Gunderson—or should I say, Thor—I believe you are to serve as the patient. I hope you will not find the gurney too uncomfortable."

He opened the back of the ambulance and gestured inside. I climbed into position. It was actually very comfortable, especially with so little sleep, but it left me with an odd sense of vulnerability, lying on my back and staring up at the ceiling.

"Now, Chen and Jung, we have several storage compartments to choose from, but none of them are very spacious, I'm afraid. You should count yourselves lucky that the drive to the airport is so short."

Mr. Simpson climbed inside and opened several cleverly hidden panels. The kids picked a couple and climbed in, and he closed the panels behind them.

"The rest of you may take your seats, either up front or in the back, but at least one of you will need to attend the patient."

"I'm up front," Seth announced and disappeared around the side of the ambulance.

Grace watched him go, then looked at me. "I'll look after Dad," she told Mr. Simpson.

"Mind if I join you?" Hank asked.

219

"Not at all," Grace answered sweetly. "After all, we're married now—we even have kids." They grinned broadly at one another, then looked at me.

I rolled my eyes. Obviously, the paperwork had been completed while Seth and I were en route. I wondered if there had been a ceremony. Hank helped Grace into the ambulance before jumping in behind her, then Mr. Simpson shut the doors.

"Good luck," he called as he rapped on the steel door. Ranch fired up the engine, and we were on our way.

We hadn't gone far when we heard a knocking from inside one of the storage bins. Hank managed to open it, and Chen stuck out his head.

"Getting claustrophobic?" I asked, peering down at him over the edge of the stretcher.

"No, I'm fine. I just wanted to tell you something. It may or may not be useful, but you have put your entire family at risk to help me, and I wanted to offer whatever help I could."

"What do you mean?" I asked.

"Well, about a week or two before we escaped, I began systematically sabotaging our work at the institute by adding miniature viruses to the computers and carcinogens to the biological samples. I wanted to lure the other researchers down as many false trails as possible. You know, let them think they had this terrible new bio-weapon, when it was really just a dud. I kept a log of all the changes I made to the computer program, which I stored on a thumb drive and hid."

Now there came a knocking from the overhead bin. Hank reached up and opened that panel. Jung's head popped out.

"Chen, did you add something to the samples in my lab?"

"Yes, to several of them."

"Oh, good," Jung sighed with relief. "I was so excited to actually see positive results that I pulled the lid off one of the leaded containers and examined the sample without first turning off the radiation emitter. I've been afraid I was going to get some kind of weird tumor ever since."

"I can't believe you never mentioned it. Does Lao know?"

"He knows about the positive results, I'm sure. I discussed them in my daily progress reports. I never mentioned my exposure. I was too embarrassed."

"I still can't believe you didn't tell me."

"We were plotting an escape. I didn't want you to worry."

"Well, now you don't have to worry, either."

"Thankfully."

"So why are you telling me all this now, Chen?" I asked.

"I figured I could use the thumb drive as a bargaining chip if we got caught escaping—maybe trade its location for our freedom. Now that we're safe, but your family may not be, I wanted you to be able to use it in the same manner, if you can."

"Thank you," I said, pondering the offer. "Chen, here is the thing. Suppose they have my family. They won't release them until we tell them where the thumb drive is located, but once they know its location, they won't feel obligated to release my family either. It's a Catch-22. However, if I had the thumb drive in my possession, I could arrange a swap in a public location or something."

"Like at the Olympics," Grace said.

"Exactly," I said, smiling at her. "My only other concern is that by giving Lao the information on the thumb drive, he'll be that much closer to his goal. In a sense, I would be exchanging the lives of my family for the lives of millions around the world. My heart wants to do it, but my mind knows there must be a better way."

"Mr. Gunderson, I don't expect the information will matter that much. With Jung and myself gone, I sincerely believe this project will collapse."

"You see, Dad," Grace began. "Technology alone is insufficient. You've got to be creative enough to ask the right questions, to look beyond the horizon of our current understanding."

She grinned at Chen. Hank and Jung smiled, too. Apparently, I was not privy to some inside joke.

"What are you talking about?" I questioned.

"Oh, just a little conversation we had on the way to the embassy," Hank explained. "It basically means that, without these kids, the project is doomed to fail."

"You really believe that, Chen?"

"Yes, sir. I do."

"Alright, then tell me where the chip is."

"Inside the right ear of the terra cotta horse pulling the chariot in the visitor center in Xian. It's the lead horse on your left when you are facing the horses. It was the easiest for me to reach. We went to Xian last weekend to meet with the Generals, and I hid it during a specially guided tour."

"Oh, boy. Isn't Xian up in northern China? I was hoping you'd hidden it somewhere close by in Hong Kong. How in the world did you get it inside the horse's ear? Don't they have those things roped off or something?"

"They do, but they sometimes let special guests get a little closer. You know, journalists, photographers— people like that. In our case, it was a bunch of computer programmers and soldiers."

"Too bad we don't have Hank's camera equipment. We could pretend to be journalists doing a piece on the Terra Cotta Warriors for a Norwegian newspaper."

"I've got my digital camera," Grace offered. She rummaged around in her purse and produced a small stainless steel Casio camera.

"Oh, that would never work," I said.

Grace shrugged her shoulders and started to put it back.

"On second thought, let me have it."

She handed it over.

"You aren't going after it yourself—are you, Dr. Gunderson?" Hank asked.

The ambulance pulled to a stop. I heard the engine die. I could see through the small window that we were at the airport.

"Yeah," I said, unfastening the straps that held me to the stretcher. "I am. I've got a fake passport, a money belt full of cash, and an international airport just across the parking lot."

Ranch opened the door, and I quickly climbed out.

"Hey, where are you going?" Ranch asked. "The medical evacuation plane is this way. The pilot's on our team. Simpson's taken care of everything."

"I've got a different plane to catch—a commercial flight. Hank can explain. Just don't try to follow me in those ridiculous outfits," I called back over my shoulder. "You'll blow my cover."

I left Ranch still holding the door, looking down at his uniform self-consciously as I took off at a jog across the asphalt.

CHAPTER

22

I'd made it about three-quarters of the way across the parking lot when I felt my new phone vibrating in my pocket. I stopped and fumbled around for a second or two before managing to answer it.

"Hello?" I said tentatively.

Who would be calling me, especially on a phone I had just received? I didn't even know the number myself, yet.

"What are you doing?"

It was Ranch. I turned around. He waved at me, and I waved back.

"I told you to get Hank to explain."

"He did."

"But I haven't even made it to the fence yet!" I protested.

"I guess you're not as fast as you used to be," Ranch stated matter-of-factly. I couldn't help but laugh, despite the situation.

"Then you already know what I'm doing," I said. "How'd you get this number?"

"Simpson's assistant gave it to me back at the embassy. I guess what I'm asking is, why are you going after the chip instead of letting someone else handle it?"

"Because—it's my family on the line."

"First of all, I don't think they have your family. But even if they did, we both know you can't be objective in this business once it becomes personal."

"Well, it *is* personal—which is why I have to do this myself and not leave it to someone else. It's just like Seth wanting to help find Danielle earlier. You understood that."

"I understand this, too," he assured me. "But that doesn't mean it's a good idea."

"I'm not pretending it's a good idea. It's just something I've got to do."

"Okay, fine. At least I'll be able to tell your widow I tried to talk you out of it."

"Thanks for the encouragement."

"Any time. Just be careful—and stay in touch. I'll keep you abreast of developments on this end."

"Will do—and, Ranch?"

"Yeah?"

"Thanks."

We both hung up with a wave, then I turned back towards the airport. My arm was starting to throb again, but the swelling was going down. I reached up to feel my nose. It was still a little sore, but didn't seem to be broken. I guess injuries are like enemies; they tend to accumulate over time.

I made my way inside, through a checkpoint, and over to a ticket counter. I knew the others would probably be airborne soon. Part of me wished I'd waited to see them take off before coming inside, but it was probably for the best that I hadn't. Loitering around in a communist country tends to raise suspicions.

Like the time our family visited Prague on another assignment. It was a miserably cold morning when our train pulled into the station at five thirty and deposited us right in front of a little pastry shop that opened at six. We could see the proprietor bustling about inside the shop, stocking the display cases with piping hot kolaches fresh from the oven.

The prospect of a warm breakfast seemed wonderful after an all-night train ride, so I had my wife and children sit at some tables in front of the shop while I stepped up to the counter to wait the final few minutes until the shop opened and I could place our order. Upon spotting my family seated in the chairs, however, the owner became apoplectic and rushed out of the shop exclaiming that the seats were "for paying customers only." I tried to explain that we would be paying customers as soon as the shop opened.

"After shop open, you buy, you sit. Not before," he ranted, forcing us all—even the sleepy-headed toddlers—to stand to our feet while he turned every last chair upside down. It was only two minutes till six when he finally finished and stormed back behind the counter. We left in disgust.

Fortunately, the Chinese were catching on to the idea of free enterprise more quickly than the Czechs. The girl behind the ticket counter greeted me with a big smile and took my passport, typed a few things into her computer, then recited in a cheerful voice, "God morgen."

I had no idea what she was saying, but knew it didn't sound like Chinese. She repeated the phrase. Seeing my confusion, she added in crisp, clear English, "It means 'good morning' in Norwegian. Our computer provides a native greeting to share with international travelers."

"Oh, yes—of course," I said. "It's just that your accent threw me off. Norwegian is like French—very subtle and difficult to master. But I appreciate the effort. So thank you—and *god morgen* to you, too," I said, changing the pronunciation ever so slightly. She smiled and went back to her typing.

"Where will you be travelling today?"

"Xian."

"Going to see the Terra Cotta Warriors?"

"Yes."

"They're a great national treasure and also one of the most popular tourist attractions in China. Did you want one way or round trip?"

"One way."

"We have a special on round trip travel."

"No, thanks. I'm one of those tourists who likes to take one day at a time—spontaneous in my traveling, you might say."

"That's the best way," she smiled. "What time would you like to depart?"

"The earliest flight you have."

"Seven-thirty?"

"Perfect."

"Any luggage to check?"

"No. I also believe in travelling light."

"Very light. How will you be paying?"

"Cash," I said, reaching for my wallet. That's when I remembered: All my cash was in my money belt, which I proceeded to take off right there in front of the counter. I unfolded the carefully creased bills and handed them, one by one, to the girl whose eyes were full of laughter by that point. I really am the world's worst spy, as I believe I've noted before.

"Here is your ticket, sir," she said with a grin. "Your terminal is just around the corner and down the long passageway. Good luck and enjoy."

I thanked her and made my way to the terminal. Once I got my boarding pass, I sank into a cozy little chair in the corner of the waiting area and fought to stay awake so I wouldn't miss the boarding call.

I picked up a discarded newspaper and thumbed through it. The lead article was on the Olympics—I could

227

tell that much from the front-page photos—but the text was in Chinese, so it did little to distract me from my thoughts.

Naturally, I was worried about my family and about Danielle. Everyone seemed convinced Zhou was on the up and up, but that was no guarantee. Spy work is like the stock market—past performance is no predictor of future results. All I could do was hope they were right.

The Danielle situation was a conundrum. Chen's explanation was plausible, but seemed a bit of a stretch. It was true that he had just shut down power to a big chunk of the city, literally moments before we began looking for Danielle on the city's computers. They might have been watching the city's computers fairly closely at that point. Maybe—but it still didn't feel right.

The other explanation was a mole—but who? Not my family, obviously. Not Ranch or Smith—I'd known those guys far too long to believe that. Zhou? It's possible. That, or Hank. But Zhou had my family, and Hank just married my daughter. Neither of those options were very comforting.

The boarding call came, and I found my seat. Next to a window over the wing. Once we were in the air, I figured it would be relatively safe for me to sleep for a few hours. I turned my phone off and was soon dead to the world.

The next thing I knew, we had landed, and a flight attendant was shaking me awake. Disoriented, I smacked my lips a few times. There was a terrible taste in my mouth, and I had one of those dehydration headaches—*possibly from the drooling alone*, I thought, judging by the puddle that had accumulated on my left shoulder.

I shuffled off the plane feeling gross and sticky and headed straight to the men's room to freshen up. That's when I noticed the bloodstains all over the front of my shirt. Fortunately, the shirt was dark and they had dried long ago, so they didn't stand out too much. I guess that's why no one bothered to point them out to me. I ended up buying a souvenir T-shirt and tossing my soiled one.

Once I felt semi-human again, I located a shuttle to take me to see the Terra Cotta Warriors. The traffic was stop-and-go, as throngs of other tourists were bound for the same destination. We pulled into the museum parking lot behind a long line of busses. Passengers poured out through their bi-fold doors and flocked toward the entrance.

I felt like I was on some giant human conveyor belt, being moved along passively. It reminded me of running in one of those big city marathons and getting swept along with the crowd. It's impossible to stop or slow down. I don't know what touring Xian is like ordinarily, but that is how it felt that day. Other than my height, I was able to blend into the crowd of tourists fairly well.

The problem was getting close enough to the exhibits. I found the horse Chen had described easily enough, but there was no getting near it without drawing attention.

I approached one of the docents and told him I needed to take some pictures for a story I was working on. He wanted to see my press pass and asked where my camera was. I showed him my little digital camera and explained that there had been some last minute changes in my itinerary resulting in my video camera and other identification papers winding up in Taiwan instead of with me in Xian. Technically, it was the truth, but he still seemed skeptical. Finally, he relented, but told me I'd have to wait until after hours.

That old Tom Petty song was soon running through my head, "The waiting is the hardest part!" But that's just what I did—waited and waited. I worked my way through the exhibit hall, examining every statue, reading every plaque, inspecting every artifact. Then I roamed around in the gift shop and bought a book about the Terra Cotta

Warriors. I read all about the making of them, how they had originally been constructed using one of the earliest known assembly lines in history. I read about their fairly recent discovery in the 1970's and about the tedious care with which they were restored. Eventually, I took the tour again, even more slowly, looking carefully for all the hidden details described in the book.

I found myself playing a little game, trying to travel back in time and make medical diagnoses based on what I could see displayed on the Terra Cotta Warrior's faces. Having practiced medicine as long as I have, I find that I can often make a diagnosis from across the room. Naturally, I run the appropriate tests, but I quickly learned that I don't actually need the labs to spot the guy with emphysema, renal failure, or cirrhosis. The labs merely confirm what I already know. The Germans call it Augenblick, which literally means making a diagnosis in the blink of an eye.

I don't know whether it's possible to do the same thing with character or not, but I know I do get a vibe from people—sometimes almost immediately.

When we lived in California briefly, I worked with an organization called "Idle Hands." The premise was that many young movie stars and rock stars get into trouble simply because they have too much time on their hands—not to mention endless amounts of money to fund their mischief.

Anyway, by getting them to volunteer at places like the hospital where I worked, they could contribute their time and their talents to the needy. In the process, they stayed out of trouble themselves. Thus, we turned sinners into saints, through the magic of community service. Everyone was a winner.

If only it had actually worked out that neatly. For some, it did. For many, unfortunately, it didn't.

I won't go into the sordid details, but I will say that the experience convinced me of two things: First was that I could usually tell who was going to make it and who wasn't within a few minutes of meeting them—something about the look in their eyes. Second was that only God can turn sinners into saints.

So there I stood, staring closely at the terra cotta faces, trying to pick out the healthy from the sick and the sinners from the saints from across the centuries.

But what would they see if they could return the stare somehow? What message was written on my face? Could they see the dead woman from Iraq or maybe the one from last night reflected in my eyes? Could they hear the half truths and compromises that rattled around in my head, gnawing at my conscience?

Would they judge my current predicament as a simple matter of my bad deeds finally catching up with me?

If so, then nearly every religious system in the world would agree with them. Hindus and Buddhists call it karma. Muslims speak of the great scales that weigh the good and bad deeds of your life against each other. Even Catholics demand penance.

You get back what you put in. GIGO—Garbage in, Garbage out. Someone has to pay the piper, eventually.

The problem was that I didn't really *want* what I deserved. Who does? What I wanted was mercy—mercy for me and for my family.

I wanted us to be rescued from this terrible situation, plain and simple. A little dose of divine intervention would be just fine with me. I yearned for some good, old-fashioned, Christian grace. Unmerited favor they call it.

As I stood pondering these things silently, I felt a light tap on my shoulder. It was the docent.

"We will be closing soon," he said quietly. "Then you may take those close-up pictures you wanted."

True to his word, the announcement for closing time came, and the crowds were hustled out. Everyone except me.

Once we were alone, the docent took me to the horses like I had asked. I snapped a few pictures and, when his back was turned, I stuck my fingers into the horse's left ear. All I felt was the bottom of the ear. There was no thumb drive that I could find.

Not willing to give up, I turned to the docent and asked if the exhibit had a lost and found. He said they did and led me to it. I rummaged through old sweaters, books, cell phones, and what not, but didn't see anything that resembled a thumb drive.

"Are you looking for something in particular?" he wanted to know.

When I described the thumb drive, he got that look like a light bulb had just come on. He held up a finger to indicate just a moment and left the room. I continued to nose about in the piles of forgotten paraphernalia until I heard someone clearing his throat behind me.

I turned, expecting to see the docent, but found a thin, impeccably dressed, middle-aged Chinese man, instead. He casually held up a small thumb drive and asked, "Are you looking for this, Dr. Gunderson?"

My happiness at finding the thumb drive was quickly replaced by a sense of foreboding when I realized he had just used my real name. Smiling at my obvious consternation, he stepped to the side of the doorway.

Several armed soldiers rushed into the room. There was definitely a mole in our camp.

So much for mercy and grace.

CHAPTER
23

Chen leaned back in his seat. He was able to relax for the first time in probably months. They were halfway to Taiwan, which meant he was outside of China for the first time in his life. He could hardly believe it had all worked out. If he had been caught at any point along the way, the consequences would have undoubtedly been dire.

With a shudder, he looked over at Jung. She had come with him. It made his escape feel complete. Without her, it wouldn't have been the same—a part of him would have been left behind.

Jung was looking out the window at the ocean, unaware that Chen was watching her. This was her first time to leave China, too, and she seemed preoccupied by her own thoughts, perhaps even a little nervous.

Chen smiled to himself and began eavesdropping on the conversation going on between Seth and Hank.

"So your Dad just cooks up all these inventions and gets you kids to test the prototypes?" Hank was saying.

"Pretty much," Seth answered, his leg bouncing up and down with nervous energy.

Hank examined with admiration the Kevlar insert Seth had handed him. "That's awesome," he said. "This little bulletproof shield is brilliant. I wouldn't mind having one of these myself."

"Just keep that one."

"You sure?"

"Absolutely. We've got loads more at home—rectangular ones for briefcases, these egg-shaped ones for backpacks. I'm sure my dad would want you to have one."

"Fantastic. I'll go put it with my stuff. Thanks, Seth."

"No problem."

Hank moved towards the back of the plane as it started to descend. Before long, it landed at a small airstrip in Taiwan and they unloaded their things. The pilot said his goodbyes and was quickly in the air again, flying back to China.

"Now what?" Grace asked.

"Now we find a hotel and lay low until this afternoon," Ranch answered. "Then we'll all fly to LA. From there, some of us will go on to the CDC on a private plane, the rest will head home via commercial flights."

"Why not head for Los Angeles now?" Hank asked.

"Because we have to pick up the rest of the Gunderson family at the docks first."

"I thought we'd lost contact with the Gundersons."

"We did, but that's because they're in the middle of the ocean with no phone, just as Jon pointed out. Zhou actually called me with their pickup location and the name of her local contact right after she spoke with Joel at the CDC, but she asked me to keep it confidential until we were all safely in Taiwan. She's worried about a mole just like we are. Once we find the Gundersons, we'll all go to the States together. It should only be a thirteen hour flight from here to Los Angeles."

"What about Dad and Danielle?" Seth wanted to know.

"Hopefully, your dad will have found the chip and traded it for Danielle by now. They'll join us as soon as they can, I'm sure."

"But what about Zhou?" Jung asked.

"I'm sure Zhou can take care of herself."

Ranch hailed a minivan taxi, and they all piled in. With Chen acting as interpreter, the driver took them directly to a nearby hotel and deposited them on the doorstep. They quickly checked in at the front desk and were soon resting comfortably, overcome with exhaustion from the night's adventure.

A few short hours later, the brilliant afternoon sun was glaring into the small room. Ranch pulled open the drapes and shook his companions awake.

"Get up. It's time to go," he told them. "While you were napping, I found a shuttle bus that will take us to the docks and then on to the airport."

"A shuttle?" Grace asked blearily.

"It seemed the easiest thing to do. We are going to have a really big group once we get the rest of your family," Ranch explained.

The dockyards were an endless sprawl. If Zhou hadn't given Ranch detailed directions, finding the correct container would've been as hard as finding a needle in a haystack.

The shuttle waited as Ranch and the others located Zhou's contact. Once they found him and gave him the instructions, he took them to the precise container they needed. The entire group leaned forward in anticipation as he opened the heavy doors to the container.

"Mom?" Grace called out tentatively.

"We're here honey. We're okay."

Before anyone could say anything else, Zhou's contact shouted in English, "Everyone inside! Now!"

The man had stepped back behind them, a gun in his hand. He gestured with it, trying to wave them all into the container.

"Everyone inside," he repeated.

"What is this?" Ranch asked.

"Sometimes it pay to catch the fish. Sometimes it pay to throw the fish back," he shrugged.

"Zhou isn't going to like this," Ranch warned him.

"Zhou is only one customer," he shrugged. "Now go. No more talk, or I shoot."

As he gestured again with the gun, Hank lunged at him. The gun fired twice, point-blank, before Hank even reached him, then a third time as they both fell to the ground. Blood could be seen seeping through Hank's shirt as the man rolled on top of him. They fought for control of the gun, Hank struggling to keep the man's arms over his head, his assailant twisting and turning in his attempt to take aim again.

Grace scrambled frantically through her purse, then tossed it aside as she jumped suddenly forward and hit the man in the middle of the back with what looked like a large, ballpoint pen. The man turned and looked at her with a strange expression on his face before collapsing, unconscious, on top of Hank.

"Help me—get him off," she grunted, tugging at the limp body of their assailant. "I need—to check Hank's wounds."

The others hurried forward and helped roll the man away, who was now snoring loudly. The ketamine had worked quickly, as intended.

Grace gingerly lifted Hank's shirt as he groaned in pain. There, duct-taped to his chest, was Seth's bulletproof shield. Grace gave a cry of relief and laughed when she saw it. Two bullets were compressed against it, but the third had gone to the side and nicked his skin. Although he was bleeding, it was clearly a superficial wound, to which she promptly applied pressure.

"We've got to get out of here," Ranch commanded. "Grace, you help Hank. Seth and I will help your mom with the kids. Someone's sure to investigate those gunshots, and I don't want to be around when they do."

Grace retrieved the ketamine injector, and everybody moved out quickly. They made it back to the shuttle bus without further incident. Their driver was all smiles. He'd been listening to the radio and apparently hadn't heard the shots.

The group was soon on its way back to the airport. Lauren sat next to Ranch, grilling him about Jon. Seth recounted for his brothers his failed attempt to rescue Danielle. Anna and Abigail sat quietly side by side, staring wide-eyed at Jung, who smiled uneasily then avoided eye contact.

Chen wondered vaguely what the other dock workers would think when they found their co-worker passed out, gun in hand, after hearing several shots fired. *Drunk, maybe?*

Grace had rolled up Hank's shirt and was inspecting his gunshot wound again. "It's really not that bad," she said. "The bullet only grazed you."

"That isn't what's hurting," Hank groaned. "I didn't have any padding under this thing your Dad made. I think I've got some broken ribs, or at least they're bruised really badly."

"Let me look," Grace said.

Chen watched as she pulled at the duct tape. He could hear the hair on Hank's chest ripping loose.

"Stop! Stop!" Hank begged.

"I've got to get this thing off to see. Don't be such a baby."

"I just took three bullets to the chest, and you're calling me a baby?"

"Only because you're acting like one."

"Fine, but pull it off quickly," Hank said. He looked away, gritting his teeth. Grace removed the tape with a few rapid movements. Hank winced, but didn't make a sound.

Two large bruises were visible on Hank's chest. Grace immediately started pushing on them. Hank winced and looked down at Grace's probing fingers. "Are you just trying to torture me or what?"

"No. I'm just trying to see if the ribs are broken underneath. They feel intact as best I can tell, but you'll probably need an X-ray to know for sure." Grace lowered Hank's shirt and leaned back against her seat.

"I'm sorry," he told her. "I guess I *am* being a baby. It just hurts quite a bit. I didn't mean to snap at you."

"That's okay. I didn't mean to hurt you, but I needed to see how badly you were injured. What you did back there was really brave, Hank. Thank you."

"I don't know whether it was brave or just foolish—but you're welcome."

"It was undeniably brave," Lauren called from the front.

Grace and Hank looked up, surprised to discover everyone was watching them. Even the driver was casting furtive glances in his rearview mirror, while baby Matthew strained to look over the seat and see what was going on.

"I'm glad to have you as my son-in-law. I'm assuming you two did get married and adopt Chen and Jung as planned?"

"We sure did," Hank said, looking admiringly at Grace.

This time, Grace didn't blush or object. She just took Hank's hand and smiled. Then turning to her mother, she added, "Marrying me was Hank's biggest act of bravery yet."

CHAPTER
24

The soldiers handcuffed me and led me out of the room. The docent was waiting at the entrance to the exhibit with a set of keys. He seemed a bit embarrassed as he unlocked the door and held it open for us. Looking back over my shoulder, I could see one of the soldiers giving him some money.

Judas, I thought.

But realistically, what choice did the man have, especially in a country like China? Besides, it wasn't as if I were his close friend or something. If anything, I'd given him plenty of reason to be suspicious of me. He probably thought I was some sort of criminal and that he was actually doing a good deed. I couldn't blame him. There was really no one to blame but myself. Ranch had tried to warn me.

The soldiers led me to a long, black Mercedes limousine flanked front and back by army Jeeps. One of the soldiers held a door open as another shoved me roughly inside. I whacked my shoulder and scraped my back on the doorframe, but managed not to hit my head. It's fairly awkward getting into a car with your arms behind the back, especially at my size.

Mr. GQ climbed in through the other door and sat in the seat next to mine. He carefully straightened his tie, folded his hands, and turned to face me.

"I suppose I should introduce myself," he sniffed.

"Let me guess—Director Lao?"

"Ah, so you are not as inept as I was beginning to believe. Good—that will save us both some time. We can go straight to discussing my business proposal."

"We're not conducting any business until you tell me what you've done with my family."

"What *I* have done with your family?" He laughed derisively as I glared at him. "The better question is, what have *you* done with your family? Whatever possessed you to bring them to China in the first place, to risk entangling them in such a messy affair as this one? My source tells me this isn't the first adventure in which your family has become unwittingly involved. It seems to me that you have a bad habit of playing fast and loose with your loved ones' lives, Dr. Gunderson. You should save your anger for yourself."

What could I say? He was right. Hadn't Seth said basically the same thing earlier this morning? I broke off my stare and looked out the window. The night was clear, except for a few wispy clouds drifting across the face of the full moon. My head was throbbing, my stomach in knots. "Where are they?" I insisted.

"If you must know, then I will tell you: I have no idea. It seems your newfound friend, Zhou, has double-crossed you and disappeared with them. I thought you were aware of that fact. But not to worry, I am sure they will all fetch good prices on the black market—especially those pretty little girls of yours."

I lunged at him in a rage. I intended to head-butt him, but managed only to flop, face-first, into his lap. I'm embarrassed to admit it, but I was in the process of biting his leg when Lao grabbed my head and slowly pushed me back upright.

He pulled a silk handkerchief from his coat pocket and wiped his hands on it in obvious distaste.

"Dr. Gunderson, please! This behavior is hardly fitting for a man of your stature. I remind you, I am not the one who entrusted your family to a complete stranger. I am merely the messenger. The sole blame lies with you. Your venom is entirely misdirected."

It may sound odd, but I suddenly had the sensation of being conspicuously underdressed. Like showing up for a meeting in jeans when everyone else is wearing a suit. Or running to the store for a quick item when I am filthy from yard work, and bumping into someone I know—or even worse, someone I don't like.

That's how I felt in Lao's presence at that instant. I became instantly and inexplicably self-conscious of my bad breath, my body odor, my silly souvenir T-shirt. How very foolish I felt next to this crisply pressed man with his cool demeanor and refined manners. Perhaps my venom *was* misdirected.

"What do you want?" I finally asked.

"I want your help," he replied coolly. "You see, I sent Jung to America with a computer virus to upload at the Centers for Disease Control. Naturally, it will take a while for the virus to jump from one government computer to the next; however, the virus will eventually find its way to the Pentagon and shut down your entire missile defense system. Six degrees of separation, as they say, is true for computer systems as well as people. I only needed a back door to circumvent your government's elaborate firewall."

"*Jung?* Wait a second. Jung's carrying a computer virus? The Jung we just rescued?"

"Yes, Dr. Gunderson. Unless I'm mistaken, she's the only *Jung* we both know. You see, your rescue cast her in the role of victim, which allowed her to gain your trust. Soon, fear of my new biological weapon will also gain her access to the CDC's computers. It is a simple ruse, if you think about it—but Jung's youth is what made it all work."

"I don't believe it."

"Believe it, Dr. Gunderson. And believe this, also: America without a missile defense system is just the opportunity North Korea has been waiting for. Naturally, China will apply diplomatic pressure on North Korea in an attempt to avoid disaster, but—alas—to no avail. Everyone knows how... *unpredictable* Kim Jong Il can be. So North Korea fires a few rockets at America, and China suddenly becomes the world's last remaining superpower."

"You're insane. I'll never help you."

"I believe you will, Dr. Gunderson. You see, everyone has a pressure point—a point of weakness, so to speak. It's just a simple matter of finding yours. In fact, I think I already have."

"Is that how you forced Jung to help you? Found her pressure point?"

"No pressure was necessary, Dr. Gunderson. She volunteered. You would be amazed what a daughter will do for her father."

"Her father? You're Jung's father? Chen said you killed her parents."

"Half true, half true. Her mother was my mistress after my wife died. But wives and mistresses both have a way of becoming burdensome over time, of outliving their usefulness, so to speak. It was the same with my wife, Steven's mother. I simply had to unburden myself of them both."

I looked at him aghast. "You really *are* sick. Have you no shame? You seem almost proud of your evil deeds."

"Ah, you Americans and your primitive ideals of good and evil. You whine incessantly about the millions killed by Hitler, Stalin, and Mao, but completely overlook the genius of their actions. They did what was necessary to drive forward the evolution of mankind."

I stiffened in my seat, enraged by his choice of role models. *The evolution of mankind!* As if such cold-hearted monsters were more advanced, more civilized, than the innocents they slaughtered? That is madness.

As if he could read my thoughts, Lao uttered a deep sigh and examined his fingernails in the moonlight before continuing calmly, "Survival of the fittest means the weak must be cleared aside to make room for the strong, Dr. Gunderson. The work I do now is simply a continuation of the work those men began decades ago. It is a fulfillment of their combined vision to purify the planet of the unfit. And know this: There is nothing I won't do to push forward the ultimate evolution of man. An evolution that finds China restored to her rightful place—at the top."

"You'll never get away with it, Lao. Not the computer virus, not the endogenous retroviruses, none of it."

"That remains to be seen," he brushed aside my opinion as one might shoo a fly. "It cost me a fortune to hire Steven to develop the computer virus on such short notice, but it will be worth it in the end. Who would have guessed that both my children would play such important roles in seeing my dreams come to life?"

Clearly I was dealing with an egomaniacal madman.

"What about Chen? What's his role in all this? Is he another of your children, as well?"

"Brilliant dupe. Nothing more. When I realized he would not help me with my endogenous retrovirus project and had actually contacted you Americans, I was furious. I would have killed him myself had Jung not intervened. The idea of planting a computer virus at the CDC was hers, and is the only thing that spared Chen's life."

The limousine pulled to a stop at the entrance of what appeared to be a military base. The guards conferred with the driver of the lead army jeep that was escorting us, then quickly waved the whole entourage through. After making several turns, we parked outside a large warehouse. My door popped open, and a couple of armed soldiers wrenched me from my seat and prodded me inside the building.

The warehouse was barren, except for a single empty chair that stood in the middle of the room facing away from the door. Fifteen feet beyond the chair stood a heavy metal desk. A bespectacled young man with a crew cut and civilian clothes sat at it, working intently at a laptop computer. As we approached, Lao tossed the thumb drive to the young man, who promptly plugged it into the laptop.

"Have a seat," Lao commanded me, indicating the chair with a nod of his head.

"Now tie him up," he ordered the soldiers. My arms and legs were secured tightly. Lao stepped around in front of me to inspect my bonds, then fixed me with a flinty stare.

"Hard way or easy way?" he asked in a calculated voice.

"Hard or easy way what? I don't even know what you want yet."

"I'll take that to mean the hard way."

Lao signaled to someone behind me. The lights immediately shut off, plunging the warehouse into total darkness. I could see nothing momentarily but the young man at the desk, his pale face illumined by the laptop, the computer screen reflected in his eyeglasses.

Then suddenly, a large spotlight beamed down from above, creating a six-foot diameter circle of light with me in the center. I could now distinguish Lao standing just on the edge of the circle of light.

"Your theatrics don't scare me, Lao," I said. He didn't respond but moved further away from me so that I could just make out the whiteness of his face and hands.

A door opened behind me. It sounded as if something metal were being knocked about and dragged towards me, scraping the concrete. I followed Lao's gaze towards the source of the sound on my left. It ended with an abrupt clang as a big metal cylinder similar to a scuba tank was heaved to the edge of the spotlight, where I could see it dimly. A man wearing a welder's mask and gloves stepped up beside it and stood perfectly still.

"Torture, is it? Well, it won't work," I said, feigning bravery. I still had no idea what Lao wanted from me.

I heard the door open again and several pairs of footsteps entered the warehouse. They circled around and came up between Lao and the welder, but stopped before I could see to whom they belonged. Then one, a woman, was shoved into the spotlight, her hands and feet bound and her mouth gagged. She fell to the floor and looked up at me.

It was Danielle.

Before I could say anything, the welder's torch sprang to life with an unmistakable whoosh. Danielle's head whipped around. Upon seeing the flame, she quickly scooted over beside me, as if I could protect her somehow.

"I repeat, Dr. Gunderson, hard way or easy way?" Lao said contemptuously.

"Easy! Easy!" I shouted. "Just leave her out of it and tell me what you want."

"As I mentioned earlier, Dr. Gunderson, I've delivered a fairly nasty computer virus to the Americans. It appears that Chen has returned the favor and infected his artificial intuition program with something as well. Steven is back in Beijing working on it, but it will take time—time I may not have." Lao's eyes cut to the man at the computer desk as he said it.

"Jung informs me that the storage device you came to retrieve contains a record of all the viruses Chen used.

What she cannot tell me, however, is the password needed to unlock that storage device. But I believe you can."

He produced a miniature hourglass from his pocket and turned it over on his palm.

"Sixty seconds, Dr. Gunderson. Give me the password, or you will have some very unpleasant things to explain to your son when you tell him what happened to his foolish young girlfriend. Wrong answers will not buy you time. They will only buy the girl more pain."

I looked at Danielle, who was staring back at me pleadingly. The grains of sand were slipping quickly away.

"Why don't we just call Chen?" I suggested. "I have a phone in my pocket."

"That does not sound like a password to me," Lao answered coldly. "I repeat, wrong answers will only buy the girl more pain." He was intentionally being obtuse, perhaps looking forward to torturing her.

"No, I'm just asking—couldn't we call?"

"Time is running out, Dr. Gunderson."

I wracked by brain. What would Chen use— something about endogenous retroviruses or geography, maybe? As the last grains of sand slid through, I recalled the passwords from the GeoBee. "Try Kissinger or Nixon," I blurted out in desperation.

Lao nodded to the man with the computer. Except for the tapping of his fingers on the keyboard, the room was deathly silent.

I couldn't see what happened, but at a signal from Lao, the lights turned back on. The welder slouched away dragging his cylinder behind him, his shoulders hunched like a disappointed kid. The computer guy pulled the thumb drive loose, snapped the laptop shut, and headed for the door. Two soldiers came over and stood by Danielle and me. A third grabbed the chair from the desk and brought it over. They lifted Danielle into it and secured her arms and legs just as they had done to me earlier.

"Now that was *easy*, wasn't it?" Lao asked in a patronizing tone. "And to think that only a few minutes ago, you said you would never help me...."

He turned to the guards. "You can remove her gag. It doesn't matter if they talk. And get the phone out of his pocket—you shouldn't have missed it earlier. Have your fun, but do not rough them up too much, just in case. And don't kill them unless you absolutely have to. They are my insurance policy to get Jung back. If at any point they cease to be *useful*, however, I will let you know."

Lao gave me one last knowing look before leaving the warehouse, his footsteps echoing in our ears. One of the guards came over and fumbled for the phone in my pocket. He tucked it into his own pocket, gave me a broad grin, then punched me square in the face, knocking over my chair and breaking my already sore nose.

CHAPTER

25

The combination of my large upper body and the small chair created just the right mismatch so that when the guard slugged me in the face, the chair tipped over backwards. Since I was tied down, there wasn't much I could do to stop it. I just tucked in my chin as I fell, to prevent my head from smacking the concrete when I landed. The soldiers found this highly amusing. The one who hit me stood over me, pointing and laughing.

He called the others over, and they all took turns setting me up and knocking me down again, laughing hysterically each time. It was a morbid game of ten pins. When I saw the blow coming, I tried to turn my face away. This maneuver resulted in a broken left cheekbone, but did spare my broken nose additional pain.

Another right hook sent blood and a piece of tooth spewing from my mouth. Instinctively running my tongue along the edge of my teeth, I could tell my upper left canine had broken in half and was partially missing. The soldiers were all right-handed, so my left side was taking the brunt of the beating. It became difficult to anticipate the timing of their punches, because I could no longer look to the left without getting double vision.

I suppose I should be grateful that Lao told them to go easy on me. No telling what they'd have done otherwise. I still ended up with my eyes nearly swollen shut, several loose teeth, and split, puffy lips in addition to the broken nose and cheekbone. Fortunately, my jaw stayed intact, and I never lost consciousness.

They say in the early days of boxing, before the big padded gloves, the fighters usually looked terrible, but rarely sustained brain damage. Their faces absorbed all the punishment. I can testify to that firsthand now.

I was twice the size of the men who were working me over. Maybe that's why they took such pleasure in it. They were finally getting to live out the fantasy of taking on the big guy and winning.

Perhaps there was a little anti-American sentiment tossed in, as well. It's human nature to hate what we envy—the rich businessman, the pretty girl, the talented jock, or the powerful politician. For most of the world, that basically means hating America. As a rule of thumb, I think other nations despise America to the degree they want to *be* America.

Then again, they may have simply enjoyed the novelty of watching me fall over.

Whatever the case, the game made them forget about Danielle for a while. Eventually, though, they got bored, or their hands started hurting, because they quit hitting me and began eyeing her. They elbowed one another and spoke amongst themselves in Chinese. I tried insulting them to draw their attention away again, but to no avail. Except for an occasional backhand, to try and shut me up, they mostly ignored my comments.

After a short debate, one of the soldiers swaggered over to where Danielle was sitting. Egged on by his comrades, he grabbed a handful of her hair and jerked her head back, forcing her to look up into his face. She shut her eyes tightly. I could see the tears streaming freely down her cheeks as her lips moved in silent supplication.

I strained against my bonds, uttering fragmented prayers of my own on her behalf. The guard leaned menacingly close to her, breathing on her neck and whispering incomprehensible threats in her ear.

I don't know exactly what he had planned, but before he could carry it out, we heard angry voices and a loud bang behind us as the door to the warehouse burst open.

Embarrassed, the guards hurriedly straightened their disheveled clothing and snapped to attention. Three smartly dressed soldiers came over—two men and one woman. The woman appeared to be in charge. She gave the original guards an earful, after which they sheepishly gathered their things and left with only the mildest of protests.

Once they were gone, our new guards immediately came over and began to untie us, presumably to move us to another location. I looked into the face of the woman before me through hazy eyes and blinked a few times to see her better.

It was Zhou. Quick thinking and her father's old contacts had paid off, but I didn't know that yet.

"*You*," I hissed. "What have you done with my family?"

"Your family is fine. Ranch and the others met them in Taiwan this afternoon. By now, they're halfway to America. I'm here to rescue you, but we've got to hurry."

"They're alright?" I said uncertainly. I tried to smile, though it hurt to do so.

"Yes, they're alright, all of them. I promise," Zhou assured me, loosening the last of my bonds and setting me free.

That's when the tears started—bloody, messy tears. I sat there sobbing, unable to do anything else. I was so relieved. I didn't really care what happened to me at that point, but to know that they were safe was everything.

"But how—" I began.

"I'll explain on the way to the airplane. We have only a few hours before the real guards show up. I told those soldiers that Lao sent us early because he didn't trust them and it was obvious why. I threatened to call Lao and report them, but they begged me not to."

"What if—"

"I've confined them to their quarters. They're probably too scared to enjoy the extra sleep, but I don't think they will be bothering us again tonight."

"Where'd you get the uniforms?"

"A good spy, like a good reporter, does not reveal her sources. Come," she said trying to pull me to my feet. Danielle rushed over.

"Dr. Gunderson, I'm so sorry. This is all my fault. I should never have—" and she began to cry.

"It's alright, Danielle. And it's not your fault—it's mine."

I stood up and put my arm around her shoulders. One of the new soldiers slid my chair out of the way as I guided Danielle towards the door. There was an old Buick sedan waiting for us in the dark. I didn't ask how a classic American car wound up in the middle of rural China; I just got in. Danielle sat between Zhou and me in the back seat. The two soldiers sat up front, one of them driving.

We made it through the checkpoint without any trouble. There was a brief discussion in Chinese, a flashlight was shone in our faces, and then we were on our way.

"Did they hurt you?" I asked Danielle tentatively.

"I have a few bruises from being shoved around, but no one hit me or anything. They just kept moving me from one place to the next, and the whole time, no one ever spoke to me. They'd stand there talking *about* me, gesturing towards me as if I were a piece of furniture or something. It was weird."

"That is basically how women are viewed in China, I'm afraid—like pieces of furniture," Zhou commented. "At least you weren't hurt. That's the main thing. I'm sure you were very scared, but you are safe now."

"Thanks—but who are you?"

"I'm sorry. My name is Zhou. I work with Dr. Gunderson."

"I don't understand. What's going on."

"Danielle," I said, "I work for the government. I—I'm a spy. Those men were using you to get at me."

"So—this really isn't my fault?"

"Well, not entirely. I mean, it's mostly my fault—like I said. But it *was* your decision to follow us to China without telling anyone."

I know I should have held my tongue, but now that we were relatively safe, I just couldn't help myself.

"I did tell Seth."

I had already opened my mouth to say more when I noticed Zhou giving me a quick shake of her head. I inhaled slowly and willed myself to smile. "That's right," I agreed. "You did tell Seth."

There was a moment of strained silence, and then I asked, "So how did you find us, Zhou? What happened with my family? Tell me everything."

"Well, after Chen helped us locate Danielle using the city's traffic cameras and you and Seth went to rescue her—"

"I *thought* I saw you and Seth on that rooftop, but it was dark and the helicopter was shaking, so I wasn't sure," said Danielle.

"It was definitely us".

"Wow."

"Anyway," Zhou continued, "I took your family to the container ship as we had discussed. Then I got a call from a friend of yours at the CDC—"

"Joel Rothstein?"

"Yes, but he said he couldn't reach you. That worried me, so I called Ranch—he was in Hong Kong, waiting for a taxi somewhere."

"That must've been after we split up."

"He told me soldiers had gotten to Danielle before you could and that he was afraid the mission had been compromised. We thought maybe Hank was a mole, since none of us had worked with him before. Unfortunately, Hank was alone with Grace and the kids by that time, so Ranch wanted me to start looking for them, in case they didn't show up at the embassy for the adoption."

"Grace and the kids? Adoption?" Danielle echoed.

"I'll explain later," I promised.

"Naturally, we were relieved when they arrived safe and sound, but Ranch was still concerned that Hank might be a mole and decided it would be best if I kept a low profile. When you decided to head for Xian, he told me to follow you. Based on the fact that Lao was already waiting for you, I think it's safe to assume that Hank is indeed a double agent. We'll need to let Ranch know as soon as possible."

"Hank isn't a double agent," I said as we pulled up to a small barn just off the country road we'd been travelling along.

"Then who is? Hank's the only one that makes sense."

"It's Jung."

"*Jung?* No. The little girl? You can't be serious."

"Jung is Lao's daughter. She has some kind of computer virus she plans to plant at the Centers for Disease Control. Eventually, it will find its way to the Pentagon and shut down our missile defenses. The bio-weapons thing was an elaborate ruse to gain access to our government computers. We've got to get word to Ranch immediately. I just hope it isn't too late."

The two soldiers climbed out of the front seat and headed straight for the barn. They quickly threw open its doors, revealing a small plane softly illuminated by an old fashioned lantern.

A withered old man in the traditional pajamas and beret of the Mao era hobbled over from a dark corner and greeted the soldiers. I took him to be a farmer, perhaps hiding the plane for a little extra income. When he climbed into the cockpit, I realized he must be the pilot, as well.

The soldiers removed the blocks from around the plane's wheels and began pushing it towards the narrow lane we'd just left.

"Where's the runway?" I asked.

Zhou was dialing on her phone. "Just a second," she signaled as she pressed it to her ear. The plane was now square in the middle of the road, and the soldiers were waving us over. I looked at Zhou.

"Runway?" I mouthed. Zhou snapped her phone shut in obvious frustration.

"I can't get a signal—there aren't many towers out in this farmland," she said, scanning the horizon.

She ran over and spoke to the farmer, then came back. "The nearest phone is about fifteen minutes away. It's probably that far to pick up a decent signal, as well."

"What do you want to do?"

"I don't think we can spare the thirty minutes getting there and back, but the flight to Shanghai will take several hours—we can't afford to wait until we land there to call, either. Jung and Chen are already well on their way to America. I've got to try and warn someone before she has a chance to upload that virus."

Zhou stood thinking for a moment, then reached up to pat me on the shoulder. "You'll have to go on alone.

The pilot will take care of you, but I've got to make that phone call. I'll catch up with you later, if I can."

She didn't give me time to respond. She ran back to the car and fired up the engine. The soldiers hustled us into the plane, but didn't board themselves—they rejoined Zhou in the car.

We strapped into the jump seats lining the sides of the plane as we watched the car pull away. The old man smiled and gave us the thumbs up, then started the plane. Zhou never did explain about the runway, she just waved and drove back down the road that we had arrived on.

I understood soon enough, however. The plane taxied down the country road following the path of the Buick, slowly at first, then with mounting speed: The road *was* the runway. The Buick was lighting our way in the dark. We lifted into the air and actually flew over the old automobile. I thought I saw one of the soldiers lean out and wave. We lost sight of them as we banked to the right and headed for Shanghai.

I tried to think through our situation as the plane rattled and shook. I gave Danielle a crooked smile, but she seemed as nervous and airsick as I was beginning to feel.

Clearly, the old man was some sort of smuggler. If he could make it to Shanghai in three hours and return in the same time frame, then he would actually be home with the first rays of sunlight. The entire trip would be in the dark and, by flying low, he could avoid any radar. I suspected that this wasn't *his* first rodeo, either.

"You alright?" I asked Danielle above the engine noise.

She nodded, but didn't say anything.

"I'm really sorry you got mixed up in this whole thing," I apologized, trying to get both her mind and mine off the turbulence.

She just nodded again. It might've only been the green lights from the plane's instrument panel reflecting off her skin in the dark, but she was starting to look a little nauseous. Casting about for a bucket or bag, I spotted a half empty sack of birdseed near me. I couldn't reach it with my hands because of the straps, but managed to kick it towards Danielle just in the knick of time.

Fumbling to get it opened, she vomited violently inside, then wiped her chin and nodded her thanks. The smell, however, started me retching, so I snatched the sack away from her and used it myself. We passed it back and forth until our stomachs were empty.

My nose was on fire from the acid and the fresh injuries. I felt a little guilty about ruining the birdseed, but at least we didn't soil the plane. I would have loved to toss the sack out the window to be rid of the smell, but thought better of the idea and just pushed it as far away as I could with my foot.

That's when I noticed the wooden crates full of sleeping white ducks. Apparently, the seed was for them.

"Sorry," I whispered to the ducks.

"I'm not," said Danielle.

"What?"

"I'm not sorry."

"About the birdseed?"

"No. About getting mixed up in this whole spy thing."

"What makes you say that?"

"Well, it's just that I believe things happen for a reason—even bad things. The bad things may actually be necessary for even better things to happen."

"How so?"

"Well, if I hadn't followed Seth to China and gotten kidnapped, you would never have met Lao. Then that girl—Jung, did you say?—would've gotten away with the whole computer virus thing, and nobody would've known about it until it was too late."

"She may still get away with it."

"Maybe so, but we have a better chance of stopping her now that we know the truth, right?"

"That's true," I nodded thoughtfully.

"Even now, as I look at your beat up face, I know you prefer it that way. You didn't want those guards to do something even worse to me. Isn't that why you kept taunting them whenever you saw them looking at me? To keep them distracted?"

"You bet it is," I admitted, a fresh wave of relief washing over me that the ploy had worked as long as it had.

"That's the kind of thing I'm talking about. Something bad—your being beaten—led to something good—my protection. Does that make any sense? I'm sad about your injuries, but grateful at the same time. So, thank you. I really appreciate what you did."

I looked out the window. I'll admit I had always thought of Danielle as an aggravation, even before we came to China. But now I was seeing her in a whole new light— seeing her as a person, not just an idea.

I was seeing Danielle as *Danielle*, not just as Seth's girlfriend.

"I do understand, and you're welcome. It was the least I could do," I said. "I would never have forgiven myself if something worse had happened."

We were silent for a while. I thought about all the crazy adventures I'd been involved in over the years, including that first one in Iraq. And I thought of the many regrets I'd accumulated along the way.

But then I remembered Smith's steadfast advice to focus on the good being achieved, not on the shortcomings along the way. Maybe he had been right all along.

"I can think of several other things that fit into your idea of bad things being a necessity for even better things happening," I said.

She smiled. "Like what?"

"Like vaccines."

"Eww! I hate needles."

"Me, too. But there are even bigger things—like democracy, capitalism, and free will—that also fit the pattern.

"Take democracy, for instance: It's a known fact that crime is much higher in democratic states than non-democratic ones, but it's a trade-off. In a democracy, a few people get their rights or property trampled on by crime, but the alternative is that everyone has their rights and property trampled on by an oppressive government.

"It's the same way with Capitalism: A certain percentage of the population inevitably gets left behind, but history has shown that the majority of people do very well. In a communist state, virtually everyone gets left behind—except for a handful of cunning politicians."

Danielle nodded solemnly. She looked at the back of the pilot's head, then flashed a smile back at me.

"Capitalism at work in a communist state," she mused, tilting her head towards the old man.

"Yeah," I chuckled. "You would never guess it to look at him, would you?"

"Not at all. But what were you saying about free will? I've studied democracy and capitalism in school, but not free will. What do you mean by that?"

"Oh, it's just another one of those things. If human beings are simply a bunch of automatons doing what they're programmed to do, then they can't really do anything evil. They are just following their programming or following their instincts like animals do, and are therefore completely innocent. On the other hand, if we are just robots, we can't do anything good, either. Helping the poor or caring for the sick would just be part of our programming, as well.

"It's our ability to *choose*—our free will—that not only defines us as humans, but also provides meaning to the concept of good and evil. It is only when we allow for the possibility of *evil* that *good* truly becomes good, don't you see?"

"That makes a lot of sense," she said thoughtfully.

By this point, the plane had begun to bounce around again. I heard raindrops pelting against the metal hull. I closed my eyes and attempted to steady myself against the side of the plane.

After a little while, things settled down. I could still hear the rain, but the turbulence let up somehow. As it turns out, flying through the rain often decreases turbulence. Once you're in the middle of it, it's actually a uniform and stable weather pattern. It seems counterintuitive, but sometimes the middle of the storm is where things are the smoothest.

I was enjoying this calm when the engine started to sputter. The old pilot began to methodically flip and jiggle control switches, but the engine died anyway, and the plane began to fall.

Gripping the edge of my seat, I sent up silent prayers and braced myself for a crash landing in the middle of China, in the middle of the night, in the middle of a rainstorm, in the middle of a mission that had gone terribly awry. I wondered if any good could possibly come of this, as the earth loomed large beneath us.

CHAPTER
26

It was late, and Grant Simpson was half-heartedly packing boxes as he awaited news of the day's events. It would be a few months before he retired as the embassy "librarian," but he had been there many years and had accumulated a lot of things—and a lot of secrets. By packing early, he could ensure nothing was overlooked or left behind in some last minute rush. The US government would be grateful for his meticulous nature and his discretion. They always had been.

He heard a knock at his door, and looked up to see his assistant enter the room.

"I see you're still up, as well," he said.

"You know I want to find out what's on that computer just as much as you do. I talked to the guys downstairs—they said it won't be much longer."

"Excellent. I can't tolerate these late nights any more. Getting old, I suppose," he said with a wry smile.

"Is that why you're going to retire?"

"Partly. I just can't see myself starting over somewhere else. I've been in China too long. How about you? How are your plans coming along?"

"Pretty good. I've been offered a research position in Africa, but I'd like to hear more about the opening in

Papua New Guinea before I commit. I'd prefer to go there, if possible."

"So you're getting out of the intelligence business for good?" he asked.

"I don't know about 'for good,' but at least for a while. I'm trying to think of it as an extended sabbatical."

"Running around in the tropics, living with natives, and sleeping in tents doesn't sound like much of a sabbatical to me. Remind me again what you call this research you'll be doing?"

"It's a variation of linguistic anthropology. I'll be looking at the language divergence between people groups and then comparing it to DNA data for those same groups. The goal is to piece together a more complete history than either data set could provide alone. It's really more interesting than it sounds."

Simpson gave his assistant a dubious look as his phone began to ring.

"They must have finally gotten the data off the computer," the assistant said.

"That's odd," Simpson said, reaching for the phone. "It isn't the computer department. It looks like it's Zhou calling."

"I wonder where she is? She wasn't with the Gundersons earlier today," the assistant said.

"I have no idea," Simpson said, picking up the receiver.

"Hello?"

There was pause and then he hung up.

"Well?" the assistant asked.

"I'm not sure. The line went dead just as I picked up."

Before either could wonder further what it might mean, the door burst open. The guys from the computer department were standing there looking excited.

"You're not going to believe what we found on this computer," one of them said, holding up the laptop from the slave trader's apartment.

CHAPTER

27

The plane hopped along like a smooth, flat stone being skipped across a pond, spinning around, bouncing at ever-shortening intervals until it finally and thankfully came to a stop. The bouncing was real, but the spinning was just in my head due to the broken cheekbone that had left me cross-eyed.

We hadn't crashed per se, but we'd landed hard and in a hurry. I suspect the storm had caught our pilot by surprise—he'd set us down as quickly as he could once we lost power, which basically meant landing on another two-lane country road. Thankfully, we hadn't hit anything. I suppose weather reports with Doppler radar aren't as commonplace in rural China as they are in the rest of the world.

Our ancient but friendly pilot turned around with a big grin. Perhaps he was glad to be alive; perhaps he just enjoyed seeing us scared to death. I don't think this was the first time he had done this particular stunt; I was grateful to think it hadn't been the last.

When he urged us to get out, we obliged, and then followed him back down the road we had just traversed. With the wind blowing in little gusts and the rain coming down at a moderate tempo, we hadn't gone far before I was wishing for the shelter of the plane again.

That's when I noticed the overturned truck on the side of the road. It was one of those big two-and-a-half ton types that the military uses to transport troops. We always used the term deuce-and-a-half in the Army, but I have no idea what they're called in China.

The truck had an open top and a fence-like railing made of wood and metal around the sides. Lying on its side like that, with its tires in the air, it resembled a giant, overturned turtle.

The thing had apparently gone off the road onto a downward sloping embankment and flipped over. The scene looked so fresh, it occurred to me we might have forced them off the road when we crash-landed. I could imagine the driver looking into his rearview mirror, seeing the small plane bearing down on him, and trying to dodge quickly out of the way.

Whatever its former contents had been, the truck bed was empty now. Amazingly, the driver was still seat-belted into place when we ran over to check on him. He was struggling to get loose as we came up, but together we managed to open his door.

"Are you alright?" I asked.

He answered back in English and without pause, "Yes, yes, just help me check on the others."

There was no one else in the cab and the bed was empty, but I could now hear wailing from down the hill and could make out a few dark shapes like little gray mounds scattered here and there. A small flash of lightening briefly illuminated the slope. There were maybe twenty or twenty-five bodies sprawled about.

"Do you have a flashlight? I'm a doctor and could help those people, if I could see to do it."

"Just a moment," he said and began rummaging under the seat. As he looked, I realized that even with the flashlight, I'd have a hard time assessing and triaging the injuries quickly under the circumstances. Then I recalled a trick a Special Forces friend of mine had used in a similar situation in Afghanistan.

"Listen," I said, "Can you shout something for me in Chinese so that everyone can hear it?"

"Of course," he replied, handing me the flashlight.

"Alright, then explain that I'm a doctor. Tell them if they're hurt badly to come up here quickly so I can look at them."

He translated the instructions into Chinese. I felt a little guilty as most of the mounds began to scramble towards us. Obviously, anyone capable of hearing the instructions and working their way up the hill couldn't be too seriously injured. I'd wait to examine those. It was the mounds that didn't move that I was most concerned about.

Another flash of lightening revealed three remaining bodies. One was about half the size of the other two—I assumed it to be a child. "Listen, Danielle, you check on the person over there to the right. Do you see him?"

"I'm on it." She sprinted off.

"And you," I said to the driver, "take the person in the middle. I want to look at the little one on the left."

"What about all these others?" he asked.

"Tell them I'll be right back, but there's an unconscious child I need to check on first."

Suddenly understanding what I'd done, he explained the situation to the others. There was a little grumbling, but most of the people quietly gave their consent. I even saw a few heads nod in agreement.

As I headed down the embankment, I felt someone tugging on the tail of my shirt and following me. I glanced back and saw a young Chinese girl of maybe nineteen or twenty and very petite. She was holding on tightly, trotting barefoot behind me.

The young mother, perhaps?

When we arrived at the child's side, there was no doubt. She let out a wail and tried to lift her unconscious son into her arms. It was all I could do to stop her, especially since I didn't speak Chinese.

The boy was young, maybe three, lying on his back with arms and legs sprawled. Blood was pouring from a scalp wound just at the hairline, and he didn't seem to be breathing. I held pressure on the wound with my bare hand and lifted his chin with my flashlight hand ever so slightly, trying not to manipulate his neck more than was necessary. He still wasn't breathing, so I gave two gentle breaths that went in easily.

Handing the flashlight to the mother, I checked for a pulse. It was still strong and steady at about a hundred and twenty beats per minute, which isn't too bad for a kid that age. I gave the mother a reassuring smile and noticed her hair was tied back with a scarf or bandanna.

I motioned for her to give me the piece of cloth to use as a bandage. As she untied it, I gave the boy two more breaths. After the second, he gasped slightly and began to breathe on his own. I continued to support his chin to prevent his tongue from occluding his airway.

Lifting my left hand off the wound, I reached to take the bandanna while the mother shone the flashlight on the face of the child. I could hear the sound of running water over the gentle patter of the rain and quickly looked back at the wound, which was still bleeding, but not enough to make the sound I was hearing. As I applied the cloth and held pressure again, the sound increased to a steady stream.

I looked around in a bit of a panic, my left eye going haywire and the nausea returning. I realized it wasn't blood I was hearing, but rather the mother releasing her bladder. The terror of the moment and the gore of seeing her child's wound had overwhelmed her to the point of losing continence.

I pretended not to notice and kept working, my heart going out to her. For me, dealing with injuries of this sort had become commonplace, but for her it was uniquely horrifying, especially since it was her own flesh and blood, and very likely the only child she would ever have.

I got her to hold pressure on the wound and to hold the chin up while I tied the bandana around the back of the child's head and cinched it tight. The scalp has a lot of blood vessels, and a person can bleed to death pretty quickly if not properly attended. Fortunately, the skull beneath is nice and hard, so the blood vessels can be compressed with relative ease.

I did a secondary survey of the child, looking for other injuries now that the ABC's of Airway, Breathing, and Circulation had been addressed. The skull seemed intact with no obvious fractures and the spine felt aligned as best as I could tell.

The chest sounded clear when I put my ear to each side—like most kids, he had such a thin chest wall that I could actually hear pretty well, even without a stethoscope.

The long bones in his legs and arms all felt intact, but one of his fingers was dislocated, so I popped it back in place. The child groaned and started to rouse, which was a good sign.

I quickly finished up by feeling the abdomen, which was soft, and seeing if the pelvis was intact by pushing on the hipbones. The only other thing I found was a broken clavicle, which felt crunchy when I pushed on it, but those usually heal up quickly in kids—three to four weeks at most.

Danielle and the driver rejoined us, along with a couple of passengers who were drawn to the flashlight.

"How are the other two doing?" I asked.

"Mine seems fine," Danielle answered, "just a little stunned. He's young and has a fairly good knot on his head, but acts okay otherwise."

"Mine was dead," said the driver. "An old woman with no family. Her neck was broken. People from her village will make sure she is buried."

"I'm sorry. I hope we didn't push you off the road when we landed."

"Push us off? No. We just hit a large hole in the road. It twisted the wheel and threw us over just a few minutes before you arrived to help."

"So you didn't see the plane land?"

"What plane?"

"We just landed a plane on that road you were on. Apparently, the pothole you hit saved all our lives, except for the old woman, of course," Danielle commented.

"And possibly this boy," I added, then asked the driver if he had a board and some straps or tape I could use. "I need to secure this boy to a hard surface before he wakes up fully. We'll need to stabilize his spine until we can get some X-rays."

The rain continued to subside as the remainder of passengers gathered around. The driver sent a few of them in the direction of the old woman with some instructions. He also sent a couple of them to get the board and duct tape, which they returned with promptly.

About the time I finished securing the boy's head, torso, and legs to the board with the duct tape, his eyes popped open. He looked around calmly at first, as if he were assessing the situation. When he realized something wasn't right, he began to scream and flail his arms around. I got his mother to hold his arms to his sides as she spoke to him reassuringly.

Eventually, he calmed down. He lay there looking up at his mother with little tears running down either side of his face and his lower lip quivering. He didn't make another peep the rest of the trip. His mother just quietly sang a lullaby to him in Chinese over and over.

"We need to figure out how to get this kid to the nearest hospital," I said.

The driver spoke to the mother. After some conversation back and forth, he relayed what she had said: "She insists on going to Beijing. That is where she and her husband work. It is also the location of the hospital they have been told to use."

"Isn't there anything closer? That seems a long way to travel with an injured child."

"Beijing is about three or four hours from here. There's a closer facility two hours away, but in the opposite direction and not as good. However, all these people were on their way to Beijing for work in the morning, so if we want their help to get the truck going again, we will do well to head in that direction. In the meantime, you should keep your promise and start looking at the other injuries before people get restless," the driver suggested.

"Alright," I agreed, surveying the faces of the crowd. "Tell them to line up on the road, and I'll examine each one with the flashlight."

"Good," said the driver. "Send all the healthy ones to me, so we can get the truck up."

I took one end of the board with the child on it, Danielle grabbed the other, and we made our way back up to the road. The mother walked alongside us, aiming the flashlight towards her son and continuing to sing.

We set the boy down on the roadside, and his mother handed me the flashlight. The crowd parted to allow a middle-aged man with a broken wrist to come forward. I retrieved a small board from the truck railing and splinted his arm using the duct tape and some rags for padding.

The remaining passengers had minor scrapes and bruises and were promptly sent to help with the truck. The driver coordinated the effort. Having attached ropes to one side of the truck, he had half the people pull and the other

269

half push. Danielle and I joined in on the pulling side. I didn't want to be underneath if things went awry.

Once the truck was righted, we used the remaining boards to provide traction to get it back on the road. I'd never dealt with an overturned truck before, but the Chinese acted as if this were something that happened all the time. Maybe it was.

"Everyone seems used to doing this sort of thing," I said to the driver as the others loaded up.

"Oh, yes. In China, the roads are bad and the vehicles are not much better, so we are used to it."

"You speak very good English," I commented.

"Yes, the nuns taught us well. I am originally from the Philippines, but I was sent here to help with the very poor who live out in the countryside. I am taking most of these to jobs in the city. They like to come home to see their families on the weekends, but most cannot afford transportation, so I help provide it."

"That's very kind of you."

"Just one beggar helping another beggar, really," he said dismissively.

"That describes all of us, I suppose," I replied with a smile.

"True, but not everyone sees it."

The last few men to board tossed some shovels into the truck with a clatter and climbed inside. The driver and I both turned at the noise.

"What about the old woman with the snapped neck?" I asked him, suddenly suspicious about the shovels.

"Those men just finished burying her."

"Just like that—on the side of the road? No funeral or anything?"

"Much too poor for that. Just beggars, like I said."

I nodded. Although I'd been thinking figuratively, he was speaking literally. I'd lived in the West so long that words like *beggar* and *poverty* had lost their true meaning for me. They were words from a fairy tale—long ago and far away. Sadly, for these people, they were their entire existence; they were life itself.

Our pilot began speaking to the driver, gesturing towards the back of the truck and pointing at us. Finally, the driver explained in English that the pilot had asked him to take us on to Beijing. When the weather cleared, the pilot needed to fix his plane and get home as quickly as possible, so he couldn't finish the trip to Shanghai as originally planned.

"Is that alright with you?" I asked the driver.

"Sure. I'm going that way anyway. If you'll keep an eye on the little boy, I won't even charge you," he said with a wink.

"It's a deal."

"What about Zhou?" Danielle asked as we climbed into the truck behind the others.

"We can phone her from the consulate in Beijing to let her know we've had a change in plans."

CHAPTER
28

Zhou held the steering wheel with her left hand and her cell phone with her right. She was driving as fast as the antiquated Buick would go, but was about to enter a winding patch of road. Her eyes shifted to the phone briefly. Still no signal. She let off the gas slightly and tossed the phone to the soldier beside her.

"Let me know when we pick up a tower," she said. Her companion caught the phone and grunted his acknowledgement.

Zhou began to wind her way along the wooded lane. She had to slow down further as her tires began to squeal with the progressively tighter turns. Her associate cast her a sidelong glance as the other soldier in the back seat held on tightly to keep from being tossed about.

Zhou knew she was rushing partly from necessity and partly from anger. She was angry with Jung for betraying their trust. She was angry with the Lao for putting kids like Jung in such impossible situations. Mostly, she was angry with herself for believing this assignment was different from any other.

It had been the first time in a long time, maybe ever, that she had felt good about her work. The good guys were good, and the bad guys were bad—none of the usual amorphous shades of gray to sift through. Now Jung had relieved Zhou of that illusion, and it was making her mad. She could feel her foot mashing down on the pedal again when her partner suddenly held the phone towards her.

"We have a signal, but it's weak," he said, showing her the display screen.

She let off the gas and took the phone. She began carefully dialing the number for Ranch. Busy. She slowed down further and tried to remember the number for Grant Simpson. The signal was getting stronger. She dialed the number. The phone rang.

"Look out!" her companion shouted.

She looked up just in time to see a roadblock ahead and slam on the brakes. The phone rang again as she threw the ancient car in reverse. As she attempted to spin the car around, she spotted a shoulder-mounted rocket launcher in her headlights.

"Get out!" she screamed, reaching for the door handle just as the rocket fired.

The phone rang one last time.

CHAPTER
29

We had been travelling for a couple of hours, and I could barely keep my eyes open. The fatigue was finally catching up with me. Across the truck bed, I could see Danielle sitting next to the young Chinese mother with her injured son. The mother held one end of the board in such a way that the boy's head rested in her lap. She continued to sing softly to him, although he appeared to have fallen asleep. His breathing seemed rhythmic and stable, which put me at ease.

The other end of the board rested in Danielle's lap. I looked up at her face and smiled. She seemed to be preoccupied, her lips moving silently. At first I thought she might be singing along with the mother, but as I looked closer, I realized she was counting. When she came out of her trance, she seemed embarrassed to find me looking so intently at her.

"Sorry," I apologized. "I didn't mean to stare, but it looked like you were counting something."

"Oh, it's nothing. Kind of silly, really."

"What's silly?"

"Well, have you ever heard that proverb, *Teach us to number our days that we might apply our hearts to wisdom?*"

"Sure. Lauren cross-stitched that verse to hang on our wall at home."

"Of course. That's where I've seen it—in your living room next to the computer, right?"

"Yeah. She did that to remind us not to waste too much time playing video games or surfing the web. The Gunderson boys seem to be prone to those particular weaknesses."

"Well," Danielle began, "when I was being held captive and didn't know if I would live or die, my mind kept going back to that verse. It was like, suddenly, every moment was precious, each minute a gift. I found myself saying things like, *Thank you, God, for this breath*, or *Thank you for giving me another hour.*"

I nodded in understanding.

"Anyway," she continued, "I prayed that, if I were spared, God would help me remember that sense of urgency. I wanted to remember how important even the smallest snippets of time really are, so that I'd never squander another second."

"So, now you're counting how many days you have left on earth?" I asked.

"In a way. I was actually counting specific days, like Christmases and birthdays, especially as they relate to the important people in my life."

"How so?"

"Well, take my Dad, for instance. He's just a little older than you are—he's fifty."

"That's a lot older than me, I'll have you know." Defending my age helped wake me up.

"Sorry—I didn't mean it that way. But suppose he lives to be eighty. In that case, he and I will have roughly thirty more Christmases together. However, if I get married anytime soon—"

She hesitated, clearly embarrassed.

"Then?" I smiled.

"Then I'd probably need to split holidays with my husband's family. That knocks it down to just fifteen more Christmases with my dad. That's not very many."

"What a sad thought."

"I don't mean it to be sad, but I do want it to be sobering. I want it to motivate me to make my days count—not to take them for granted, but to spend them wisely, just like the proverb says."

"That's an unusually mature attitude for someone your age," I observed.

"I've been through some unusually trying circumstances over the last few days. I guess you could say it's forced me to think of things in a more grown-up way."

"So you're doing this for every holiday and every person in your life?"

"More or less. You try—it's actually kind of fun."

"Okay. Christmases with my wife should be about forty more, if I live to be eighty. That's not too bad. The kids should be roughly the same—unless their spouses make them split holidays," I teased.

She returned my smile, and may have blushed slightly, although it was still a little dark to be sure.

"Ooh," I said, "but my dad is nearly seventy, and we do split holidays with Lauren's folks. That only leaves me five Christmases with him, based on the averages we're using. That's scary. Five's hardly any at all."

"But aren't you glad you thought of that now and not ten years from now? At least this way, you have a chance to make those five Christmases count. See how it works?"

As my mind became embroiled in calculating how many summers and weekends and birthdays I had with each of my children before they left for college, the sun broke over the horizon. In the early morning light, I could see the other travelers better. In the place of phantoms, real, live, flesh-and-blood people began to appear.

They could obviously see me better now, as well. Several of them were openly staring at my bloodied face and discussing it in hushed tones. One man actually pointed and asked me something, but I couldn't understand him, so I just shrugged.

The roads had gradually gotten better and the traffic heavier. We came to some kind of factory with dark smoke oozing into the air from two giant smokestacks. The truck stopped. Several of the workers scrambled out in an obvious hurry. Apparently the wreck had set the usual routine far behind schedule. The driver came around to reassure us that the hospital would be our next stop.

When we arrived at the hospital half an hour later, the man with the splinted arm climbed out of the truck and went inside, followed by a couple of other passengers who apparently worked there. I helped the driver unload the little boy and his mother.

"Are you coming?" he asked me.

"No," I told him. "The boy will be fine now, and I can get my face looked at later. We need to get to the consulate as soon as possible."

The driver helped the young mother carry her son inside. He returned after some time, and we continued on. When the truck bed eventually emptied, he invited us to sit up front with him.

"We don't mind riding back here," I assured him.

"It's okay now that the others are gone," he replied.

"Oh, would they have protested our sitting up front?"

"No, they would never have said a thing. But their opinion of you would have fallen. They consider it rude to partake in something that others can't share in. Therefore, none of them would dare ride up front as long as there were others in the back. Your riding in the back with them was almost as important in terms of their respect for you as your helping the little boy or setting the man's broken arm. It confirmed your status as a friend—someone they could trust."

"Just one beggar helping another beggar?"

"Exactly."

We climbed into the cab of the truck and were soon fighting our way through gridlocked traffic on our way to the consulate. Danielle took the center seat, so I was able to use the side mirror to examine my face. It looked much worse than it felt. All the swelling and bruising made me more or less unrecognizable. The dried blood and mucous only added to the hideousness. I began to laugh.

"Why are you laughing?" Danielle asked.

The driver gave me an odd look—he was probably wondering if I had brain trauma to go along with the smashed face.

"I just saw how horrific I look. Those poor people who were riding in the truck with us must have been scared out of their wits when the sun came up. No wonder they were pointing and staring. I look like Frankenstein."

I turned my head from side to side trying to get a better look, but only succeeded in making myself dizzy.

"Or Dr. Jekyll and Mr. Hyde," Danielle suggested.

"Jekyll and Hyde?" I prickled. "Why do you say that?"

"Well, maybe this is what your alter ego really looks like."

"My alter ego?"

"Sure. You're a doctor with dual identities. One leads a quiet peaceful life, and the other gets into situations like this one—just like in the book. Have you ever read it? It's quite good."

"I read it in school many years ago. It didn't end very well, if I remember correctly…"

Danielle grew quiet. We both knew this adventure wasn't completely over. I looked at myself in the mirror again. Was she right? Was this my alter ego I was seeing, finally brought to the light of day?

"I'd say you look more like *The Portrait of Dorian Gray*."

Danielle and I both looked at the driver who had spoken. He shrugged.

"That's a book I had to read in school. Dorian Gray did all manner of terrible things, but none of it showed on his face, only on a portrait he kept hidden away. Then one day he was forced to confront the portrait."

He looked back at the road, his smile fading into a look of concern. "I think that story ended badly, too..."

"First of all, neither of you are making me feel any better. Second, I haven't done a bunch of terrible things; I've actually done a lot of good things. And last, as soon as we get to the consulate, we are going to get new passports, get on a plane, and head for home. We'll rejoin my family and live happily ever after. No bad endings—alright?"

I said it with more conviction than I actually felt. No one answered. We travelled on in silence as I pondered our plight.

Finally, the driver spoke up. "When you came upon my overturned truck earlier today, you did not ask me if I was driving drunk or driving too fast. You only did what was needed. You helped; you did not judge. Likewise, it is not my place to ask questions or to judge—only to help."

With those words he pulled into a parking spot. We had finally arrived at the consulate well past mid-day.

We went inside and found it surprisingly quiet. With the Olympics going on, I had expected to find the place crawling with people. The clerk looked aghast upon seeing me and rushed over.

"Please, sir, sit down. I'll call for an ambulance right away," she said.

"That really won't be necessary. I'm a doctor, and I'm not hurt as badly as it looks. But listen, the men who attacked us took our passports. Could you call the embassy in Guangzhou? We were just there yesterday, and they can approve new ones for us. That way, we can get back to the US as soon as possible and have my injuries looked at there."

"Sir, please. That's such a long flight. You should really be examined here in China before you leave. We have special arrangements in place for the Olympics."

"I'll tell you what. You get hold of the embassy and ask for Grant Simpson. Let me talk to him first, then I'll consider going to the hospital after that. Alright?"

"Okay. Give me just a second." She walked over and picked up one of the phones and dialed a number.

There's an old adage that says that *a doctor who treats himself has both a fool for a patient and a fool for a doctor.* I probably should have listened to her, but there was the risk of being recaptured by Lao. So, who knows?

After saying a few words into the phone, she signaled for us to come over. She handed me the phone and mouthed, "Just a second."

"Hello?" It was Grant Simpson's voice.

"Grant? It's me, Jon—"

He immediately cut me off.

"I'm sorry. This is a horrid connection. Let me call you back on another line. I cannot seem to hear you on this one."

The phone instantly went to a busy signal, so I clicked it off and handed it back to the clerk.

"What's the matter?" she asked.

"He said the connection was bad, and he'd have to call me back on another line," I answered.

"That connection sounded fine to me. Besides, we don't have another line," she stated.

She thought for a moment, gave me a suspicious look, and then turned towards a door off to her right.

Looking back at me with narrowed eyes, she said, "Follow me."

We moved a few steps to the door as she fumbled with some keys in her pocket. She opened the door to a small, windowless office. A phone was already ringing loudly inside. After hurrying us inside and shutting the door behind her, she answered the phone.

"Soundproof," she explained, handing me the receiver.

Grant Simpson was on the other end.

"Jon—thank God you're alive. I apologize for being so abrupt a moment ago, but I'm afraid that other line is being monitored. When we didn't hear from you and couldn't reach Zhou either, we feared the worst."

"What do you mean you couldn't reach Zhou? She should've called you yesterday—"

"She tried to call, but the line went dead, and she never answered her phone afterwards. We have people looking at satellite images from the last known location of the phone, but we are still waiting on the report."

"So you don't know about the computer virus?"

"What computer virus?"

"The one Jung's planning to upload at the CDC— she's trying to shut down our missile defense system."

"Jung? Are you certain?"

"Yes. Zhou was supposed to call you yesterday and fill you in before Jung had a chance to get inside the CDC. We were totally set up—and now it may be too late."

"I'd better telephone them right away."

"Grant, before you do—is my family really okay?"

"Yes, yes. Your family's safe and sound. Ranch located the container ship in Taiwan and got them all back to the States. Most of your children headed home with your wife, but I think Grace and Hank went on to the CDC with your little prodigies. As their adoptive parents, they're technically responsible for Chen and Jung until other arrangements can be made."

"Oh, thank goodness. You'd better call the CDC and explain what's going on—but will you call us right back afterwards? We're going to need your help getting out of here."

"No problem. My assistant will take down your information while I call the CDC from the other room. Just hold the line and pass the phone back to the clerk."

CHAPTER

30

The limousine seemed unnaturally quiet. It had been insulated against road noise, and no one was talking. Chen could hear himself chewing, which made him even more self-conscious, especially since he was the only one to order food at the drive-through window.

At least Hank and Grace had gotten drinks— probably to make him feel better. But he couldn't help it. There had been no food on the government plane that had brought them straight from Los Angeles to Atlanta, and he felt like he was about to starve. How could the rest of them not be hungry?

Chen glanced at Grace on his right. She was staring out the window, lost in her own thoughts. His eyes shifted to Jung on his left. She, too, was looking out her window, watching the streets drift by, while absently twirling a metallic pen in her fingers.

Hank sat across from Chen, gazing into a cup of coffee as though it were some swirling oracle. The Olympic rings were printed across the face of the paper cup. It seemed ironic that he had fled one Olympic city, Beijing, to come to another, Atlanta.

The only person who didn't seem distracted by his own thoughts was Eric Smith. Smith was sitting next to Hank, across from Chen, watching him eat.

"How's the food?" he asked.

"It's very good. Thank you for buying it for me."

"It's the least I could do for a kid who's helping to save the world," he said with a smile.

"I still feel bad. I know everyone is in a hurry for us to look at those computer files."

Jung stopped playing with her pen and glanced at Chen, then at Smith.

"Don't worry about it. It only took a couple of minutes, and we're almost to the CDC anyway," Smith assured him. "Besides, we can't expect you to concentrate on an empty stomach, now—can we?"

Chen swallowed his last bite of chicken sandwich before answering. "Probably not," he agreed.

"So will we be looking at the computer files first, as soon as we arrive?" Jung asked, joining the conversation.

"I think that's the most logical place to start. I've made all the arrangements—gotten security clearance for both of you. A friend of mine, Joel Rothstein, will show you around."

Jung nodded her agreement and went back to fingering her pen uneasily while gazing out the window.

CHAPTER

31

I was examining my wounds in the mirror. My reflection didn't look quite so bad this time. All the dried blood had been carefully removed. The swelling I couldn't do much about, but Danielle had used some make-up to help cover the bruising.

I wondered how many battered wives went through this same routine each morning, carefully hiding their pain and sorrow.

I pulled back my hair and slowly lifted a razor to the side of my head. The truck driver had purchased the razor and make-up along with a few other items we'd sent him to retrieve.

"Why can't I just shave the whole thing?" I shouted through the bathroom door.

"You saw the picture, Dr. Gunderson—or should I say, *Rocky*? Just try to make the Mohawk match," the consulate clerk called from the other side of the door. "You're supposed to be a Greek boxer who washed out in the preliminary rounds."

"I feel ridiculous," I said. "Besides, I thought Rocky was supposed to be Italian."

"That's the movies, Dr. Gunderson. This is China, and we want to get you out of here in one piece, so please do as Mr. Simpson instructed."

"Alright," I grumbled, lifting the razor to my head. With a few smooth strokes I had a fairly decent Mohawk.

I tried on my oversized sunglasses and stepped back to take in the whole image. A baggy Olympic sweatsuit completed the picture. I looked like a cross between a gangster rapper and a punk rocker—in other words, I'd pass for a boxer.

Could this be the alter ego Danielle had referred to earlier?

I stepped out into the hall. "Well, how do I look?" I asked self-consciously.

"Scary," the clerk observed as Danielle walked up.

"Agreed," said Danielle, looking me over. "But I think that's the whole idea, isn't it? We don't want anyone to even *think* about messing with us."

"Let's hope they don't. I'm starting to hurt all over. When I bent over to shave my head, I realized they must've kicked me in the ribs at the warehouse. Boy, am I sore on the right side. When I take a deep breath, I feel pain in my ribs and over my sternum."

"Could they be broken?" Danielle asked.

"I doubt it. They're probably just bruised a little."

In retrospect, I should have listened to her, but at that particular moment, I was intent on getting out of China and still a bit revved up on adrenaline, so I changed the subject.

"Hey, I like the short black hair, Danielle. It looks very becoming on you."

"What can I say? I'm supposed to be your Greek girlfriend," she laughed. In addition to the new hairstyle, she was sporting a loose-fitting sweatsuit that matched the one I had on.

"Here are your new passports and plane tickets," the clerk offered. "Are you sure you don't want me to call a taxi?"

"No, that isn't necessary. Our truck driver friend out there would be disappointed, I think. But thanks for everything. You've been a great help."

"I'm glad we could be of service. We're really just a temporary spillover site for the main consulate, but we haven't been nearly as busy with the Olympics as we thought we would. I'm surprised your friend even knew about us."

"Our friend is actually a pretty surprising person in general," I said.

"Actually, he's an angel," Danielle said smiling.

"That he is," I nodded.

The clerk looked at me strangely.

"His name—it's Angelo," I explained. "But he's undoubtedly on his way to sainthood anyway. Take a good look at him. One day, you may be able to tell your grandchildren you met the Mother Teresa of China."

The clerk leaned around the corner and looked at Angelo, who was sitting in the lobby flipping through a news magazine. She seemed unconvinced. That's the funny thing about saints, especially future ones—you can't always tell, just by looking.

"We'd better be going," I said. "We have a plane to catch."

The ride to the airport was painful. Each jolt of the truck made my ribs ache a little more. My face actually felt much better, which in hindsight was probably not a good sign. The swelling was gradually damaging the nerves and making my face go numb. To this day, I still have numb spots on the left side of my face, although I don't really notice them unless Lauren tries to caress my cheek and I can't feel her hand. That's always a little unnerving, no pun intended.

We said our goodbyes to Angelo at the airport terminal.

"May God bless you and protect you," he said sincerely—exactly what you'd expect to hear from a future saint.

"I think He already has."

"Very true, very true—but do we ever stop needing His blessings or protection as long as we draw breath on this earth?"

"No, I guess we don't."

"Every breath is a gift," Danielle added, waving good-bye.

Angelo nodded in agreement.

We had no luggage, no one hassled us, and we were soon in the air on our way to Hawaii. There's an Army hospital there, and I thought I might swing by and get my face looked at during the layover. My ribs didn't even register as a concern at that point.

But they should have.

As it turns out, a broken rib can puncture a lung, causing it to leak air into the space between the lung and the chest wall, a life-threatening condition known in medical terms as a pneumothorax. A small pneumothorax will usually resolve on its own, assuming you don't do anything stupid—doing something stupid being defined as climbing into an airplane and going to altitude when you have a small pneumothorax. Because of the change in air pressure, a small pneumothorax can quickly expand and become a large one. Apparently, I had sustained a small pneumothorax without realizing it, although I should have suspected, especially when it hurt to breathe after getting kicked in the ribs. We'd never gotten very high in the farmer's plane, so the change in air pressure was minimal on that flight. Not so with a commercial jet.

At a typical cruising altitude, an air bubble can expand to over four times its original size. The fact the cabins are pressurized usually offsets this phenomenon. How much my pneumothorax grew once we were initially airborne, I don't know. I may have felt a twinge of pain at the time, but I had a lot of twinges of pain. I was also bone-tired and ended up falling asleep for most of the ten-hour flight.

The plane had just entered the first stages of its descent when a sharp pain in my side awakened me. My breathing had become much more shallow and labored than it had been before.

Another side effect of a pneumothorax is a sense of panic or impending doom—I was definitely feeling that. The tiny bit of air between my lung and chest wall had been slowly growing while I slept and had now reached some critical size that could no longer be ignored.

I looked over at Danielle and saw her rubbing the sleep from her eyes. She'd been as exhausted as I was.

"Danielle," I whispered, afraid to exert myself or breathe too deeply.

"Uh-huh?" she answered drowsily.

"I think I have a collapsed lung."

Her eyes popped open, and she looked at me in alarm.

"You were right about the broken ribs. I'm having trouble breathing. Call the flight attendant. They'll need to have an ambulance waiting when we arrive."

Danielle pushed the call button, and our attendant came over. I temporarily forgot how crazy I looked, but the expression of disdain on her face quickly reminded me.

I didn't figure telling her I'm doctor would go over very well, so I simply explained that an opponent had broken my ribs and the ribs had punctured my lung. Could she ask if there was a doctor on the plane?

She agreed, then walked quickly to the front of the cabin and put out the request for a doctor, which made everyone on the plane begin to stir and look around. She returned after a few minutes with a young man who looked like a teenager but claimed to be a physician.

"Where'd you go to medical school?" I asked, pulling off my shades to look at him.

"Harvard, sir."

"What's your specialty?" I winced from the pain as I shifted in my seat to get a better look at him.

"Ophthalmology."

"Eye doctor, huh? What year are you?"

"I'm just an intern. I landed a spot in Hawaii for a year, but then I'll go on to Johns Hopkins for my residency," he answered.

"Well, thanks for coming over," I said between breaths. "A lot of doctors would try to keep a low profile after hearing that kind of announcement on a plane."

"I try to do the right thing when I can, sir," he said.

"Did the attendant tell you I've got a collapsed lung?"

"Yes, sir. She did."

"You ever put in a chest tube before?"

"No, but I doubt they carry chest tubes on the plane, anyway, sir."

"Well, we may have to improvise," I said, then looked up at the attendant. "How much time before we land?"

"It will be another hour. I've arranged to have an ambulance standing by. Can I do anything else for you?"

"Can you loan me a scalpel—or a knife of some sort?"

Her distrust meter was noticeably going through the roof. I guess I shouldn't blame her, considering how I looked with the Mohawk and bruises. She very curtly informed me that, no, they did not keep any sharp objects on planes these days.

"Naturally not," I smiled weakly. "Well, can you bring me a Dr. Pepper then—while we wait?"

"Certainly," she answered, turning on her heel and heading back down the aisle.

"You seem to have some medical knowledge," the intern observed.

"Just a bit," I told him. "I spent some time in the military." I looked at Danielle, who grinned at my vague response.

The attendant soon returned with a can of Dr. Pepper and a cup of ice.

"Thanks," I said, grimacing as I reached for the can and felt the pain intensify.

"Just use the light if you need anything else," the attendant said before disappearing down the aisle again.

Once she was gone, I turned to Danielle. "Will you drink this, and hurry?" I asked.

"Aren't you thirsty?" she said.

"A little—but I mostly need the can."

"The can? For what?"

"You'll see." I could feel my breathing getting worse.

Danielle finished the soda quickly, then handed me the empty can.

"Now, you move over there—" I jerked my head toward an empty seat across the aisle, "and let the doctor have your spot. I'll need him on my right side."

"Sure," she said, puzzled as to what I might be up to.

As the intern changed seats, I asked if he had a pen I could borrow. He produced a beautiful black Mont Blanc pen. I felt guilty accepting it, but with its metal ink cartridge and sharp point, it was actually perfect for what I had to do.

"Listen," I said, looking him in the eyes. "If my condition gets much worse, I'll likely pass out and die. Can I assume, if it reaches that point, you won't know how to help me—since you've never put in a chest tube, and you have no tools to work with?"

He nodded.

"That being the case, something's got to be done before we reach that point—and I'll need your help to do it."

He nodded, watching curiously as I took his pen apart.

"I'll pay you back for the pen," I said by way of apology. "I know they're expensive."

"Don't worry about it," he said. "Just explain to me what you're planning to do. Is this something like a boy scout doing a tracheotomy with a ballpoint pen?"

"Yeah. But you'll need to make the cut just under my armpit, at the level of my nipple, not in my throat."

"Fourth intercostal space?"

"Glad to see you paid attention in class."

"What precisely did you do in the military—if I may ask?"

"Don't ask—you wouldn't believe me, anyway."

I knew the stereotype of the image I was projecting was too strong. It would only make him think I was lying if I tried to tell him the truth. Better to let him wonder, than to make him think me a liar. Besides, it would be impossible to explain the full story in my present condition and in the short time we had.

"Okay," he said. "But how do you expect me to make the incision without a knife? And wouldn't things get a little messy, if I did have one?"

"Good thinking," I said and paused to slowly inhale and exhale as best I could. "Danielle? Will you get some paper towels from the restroom? And ask our attendant for some disposable gloves? Try not to make a scene."

As she left, I took the sharp tip of the pen and poked a few holes into the aluminum can. Then, twisting the top and bottom of the can in opposite directions, I tore at the weak spots I'd created. "Ever cut yourself on one of these cans?" I asked.

"Sure."

"Me, too. Made me curious. How deep could it cut? Ever wonder that?"

He shook his head slowly, a slight hint of concern forming on his face.

"Right through a chicken breast—no trouble," I said with a laugh that sent me into a painful coughing fit.

The intern must have felt a little vulnerable, being pinned against the window next to some beat up guy who was methodically folding an aluminum can into a homemade knife. He mastered whatever misgivings were rising inside him and remained cool and collected.

"Everything okay over here?" asked the attendant who had returned to check on us.

"Everything's just fine," I said, covering the blade.

Danielle returned just as the attendant moved on. She gave me the towels and gloves, which I quickly handed to the intern along with the makeshift blade.

"You ready?" I asked.

"I think so—but what am I supposed to do, exactly?" he asked, slipping on the gloves.

"Three things," I answered.

I gingerly pulled off my jacket and rolled up my shirttail on the side facing him. The movement started me coughing again. I felt extremely light-headed, and it was getting harder to breathe.

Danielle turned sideways in her seat to watch. I looked up and down the aisle and then whispered my instructions, so as not to alarm those in front of us or behind us.

"First, you'll need to use this homemade scalpel here to cut through my skin."

"But, it isn't sterile—"

"We can't worry about that at this point—just hold pressure with the paper towels once you're through."

"Then what?"

"Then poke a hole between my ribs. Use the sharp end of the ink cartridge."

"Isn't that risky? I might accidentally puncture a vital organ and make things worse."

"You won't. My heart's on the left—and the air has pushed my lung out of the way. We're good to go, so just drive it straight in."

The intern looked a little queasy.

"You *are* a doctor—right?" I asked.

"Yes, but we didn't get a whole lot of hands-on experience during school."

"Then think of this as catch-up day."

He nodded.

"Alright. Once you're in, you'll feel a pop. Air will rush out—and blood will spray everywhere, so keep the paper towels handy. You'll need to go a little deeper. Rotate the ink cartridge around—that'll open up the hole and allow more air to escape. Understand?"

"Yes."

"Can you do it?"

"I think so."

"Now, if I pass out from the pain, don't panic. Just do what I said. Once the air's released, I should come back around. I'm counting on you—and so are my kids."

"You have kids?"

"A bunch of them, so let's get to work. I'll look away. You just do what I said, alright?"

"Okay."

I have got to give him credit—he handled the blade with authority, cutting right on through the skin and the tissue beneath. I think he underestimated how sharp the thing was, because he never had to use the ink cartridge at all. There was a stab of pain, then a sudden sense of release accompanied by the sound of a balloon deflating.

The good doctor quickly pressed the paper towels to the wound. As we both watched the whiteness turn bright red, he slumped over in his seat.

He had passed out, not me.

His hand fell loosely to his side. I took the paper towels and alternately held pressure to staunch the bleeding and released pressure to let more air escape from the hole.

The intern came around quickly. He was just awake enough to be embarrassed when the captain announced our final descent.

CHAPTER

32

Joel Rothstein took a long, careful drag on his cigarette. His eyes were half closed in anticipation, his physical need almost palpable. The embers glowed for a moment, then he let his hand fall to his side. He slowly blew the smoke out the side of his mouth as he opened his eyes and looked at Chen.

"Don't ever get hooked on these things. They're terrible for you."

"I know."

"Ah, that's right—you two kids were doing cancer research over in China, weren't you? You want to hear something ironic? I've actually written a couple of papers on the dangers of smoking myself."

"I know."

"You do?"

"Yes. I read several of your articles about cigarettes and the vasoconstriction of small blood vessels. The decreased blood flow due to the vasoconstriction causes a buildup of waste products in the tissues. The waste products in turn interfere with normal healing, which leads to cancer and a whole host of other problems. Your research was well documented."

"Thanks, kid, but despite all that, I'm still addicted to these stupid things."

Joel held up the cigarette and took one last drag, then dropped the butt onto the concrete and rubbed it out with his loafer.

"Memorizing the diet book won't make you skinny."

"Exactly," Joel laughed. "Now come on. I've got one more addiction to deal with, then we can take Jung the can of soda she asked for."

Chen looked questioningly at Joel.

"*Coffee,*" Joel smirked. He opened the dingy gray door that separated the smoking area from the rest of the massive building.

Chen followed as Joel wound his way through the complex. Joel would wave his identification badge, and the doors would whisk open before them, just like they did for Chen in China. They finally found themselves in a small break room where Joel went straight for the coffee pot.

"You want any? I can put cream and sugar in it."

"No, thanks. I'll just get a soda."

"You got money?"

"Yes. Grace gave us some to spend on lunch and snacks."

"Didn't take her very long to get this mom-thing down pat, did it now?"

"She has a bunch of little brothers and sisters at home."

"Ah, that's right. No doubt that helps."

Chen got a couple of sodas and retrieved his change. He popped one open and turned around. Joel was leaning against the counter, sipping his coffee and waiting. Chen smiled and took a sip of his soda.

"Don't know if they told you," Joel said, "but the lab work came back on that researcher who died."

"It did?"

"Yeah. The guy turned up positive for coca-ethylene."

"What's coca-ethylene?" Chen asked.

"Ah! So there *is* something you don't already know!"

"There are lots of things I don't know."

"That may be, but this is the first that *I've* discovered."

"I'm sure you'll find plenty more, don't worry. But what is coca—?" Chen persisted.

"Just a byproduct you get from ingesting cocaine and alcohol at the same time, kid," Joel explained smugly. "Much more powerful than either one alone. Tends to cause heart attacks and strokes in otherwise healthy young people. That's what happened here—the researcher had a massive stroke. Tragic, for sure, but at least it wasn't something weird with those endogenous retroviruses everyone's so worried about."

"Just another addiction gone wrong, I suppose."

"No doubt," Joel agreed.

He had just lifted the coffee cup to his lips when his phone began to ring, causing him to jump. The ringtone was Wagner's *Ride of the Valkyrie*. He held up the phone for Chen to see. "Cool, huh? My daughter set that up for me. Knows it's one of my favorites."

He flipped the phone open and put it to his ear. "Ah, Eric. Good to hear from you."

Joel listened for a moment before responding, "Chen's right here with me...no, we're just grabbing something to drink... Jung? Upstairs in my office... Take it easy, she's just looking over those files on endogenous retroviruses."

Chen took another swig of his soda and watched as a look of concern passed over Joel's face.

"Course, she's alone... It's a secure government facility, Eric, no one's gonna bother her here."

Joel tilted his cup to take another sip of coffee. *"What?"* he spluttered, nearly choking on it. "I'm on my way now!"

He snapped the phone shut, tossed his coffee in the sink, and took off running.

"Come on, kid. Follow me."

He raced up the stairs, taking two at a time, with Chen on his heels. By the time they reached the top, Joel was completely winded. He paused to catch his breath.

"What's the matter?" Chen asked.

Joel ignored the question as he fumbled for his keys and hurried down the hallway towards his office. Finding it locked, he pounded his fist on the door.

Chen was behind him holding the two sodas. "Is something wrong?"

"I'm locked out of my own office, that's what's wrong!" Joel hissed furiously as he searched for the correct key and forced open the door.

Jung was sitting innocently at the computer smiling up at them when Joel barged in, accompanied by a mystified Chen.

"Why was this door locked? What are you up to in here?" Joel demanded, trying to catch his breath.

"Nothing," Jung answered, wide-eyed. "I was only looking at those files you wanted us to review, when the screen went dead for no reason. Maybe there was a power surge or something."

"The CDC doesn't get power surges, young lady," Joel snapped.

He tapped testily at the keyboard. No response. He punched the power button and waited as the machine warmed up.

The screen showed that the computer had been shut down improperly. Joel quickly restored it as Chen looked over his shoulder and read the ominous words: Download Complete.

299

"Come with me, you two. Right now."

He stepped into the hallway. Chen handed Jung one of the sodas before following after him. "What's going on?" he asked looking back and forth between Joel and Jung.

"Just come on," Joel snapped. He led them to a conference room at the end of the hall. "Take a seat," he instructed and then picked up a phone in the corner. "Get me the IT department. Quick."

Joel stood there waiting on hold and glaring at Jung. Chen glanced over at her, but she just shrugged her shoulders.

When Joel finally got through, his words came in a rush, "Listen, this is an emergency—you've got to send me your best programmer right away—no, no, I can't—my computer's infected with some horrible virus, and every minute counts—yeah, that's right—okay, thanks."

He hung up after a brief discussion, just as Eric Smith walked into the conference room.

"What's our status?" Smith asked.

Joel frowned.

"Too late, huh?"

Smith looked sadly to where Jung was sitting at the end of the table. "Listen, Jung," he told her, "we know all about your father and brother and the computer virus they created and sent you to plant. It's not too late to help us. You're safe here in America. Your father can't hurt you here."

"I don't know what you're talking about," Jung lied.

"Neither do I," Chen said in alarm. "Her father? Jung is an orphan, just like me. We have the documentation to prove it. We've been adopted. You helped arrange it."

"I'm sorry, Chen," Smith said kindly. "I know it's a lot to swallow all at once, but unfortunately, Jung isn't an orphan. Her father is Director Lao, and Steven Lao is her brother. They have been using and manipulating you in more ways than any of us ever suspected."

"That can't be," Chen insisted, springing to his feet. "How dare you say such things about Jung? Jung, tell them it isn't true!"

He reached for her hand, but she pulled it away wordlessly and turned to face the opposite direction.

Hank and Grace hurried into the room.

"We came as quickly as we could," Grace apologized.

"What's going on?" Hank asked.

"You better ask your daughter, Sanders," Smith answered.

"*Jung?*" Hank looked confused. Jung continued to stare at the wall.

"Tell them it isn't true," Chen pleaded.

"What isn't true?" Grace asked, her level of concern obviously rising.

"That Lao is Jung's father and sent her here with a computer virus to shut down our missile defenses," Smith answered. "She's been playing us all for fools, including Chen."

"You're kidding!"

Grace sank into a chair at the foot of the table, distraught. Hank locked eyes with Smith, who seemed to be weighing their options. Joel looked ready to vomit. Chen felt as if his entire world were falling apart, and tears began to well up in his eyes.

Smith continued. "Grace, the reason I called you here is to search Jung. I'd practically need a court order to do it myself, as she's an adolescent female. Unfortunately, we don't have that much time. Since you are technically her mother, I need you to frisk her. She's probably got some kind of computer memory device to store the virus and a cell phone to contact Lao."

Grace moved towards Jung. Without taking her eyes off the wall, Jung reached into her pocket and pulled out what appeared to be a metallic ballpoint pen. She tossed it casually onto the table. When she made no further move, Joel asked, "How about a cell phone and a thumb drive?" Jung pointed at the pen. Joel picked it up and inspected it, then handed it to Smith. There were little slits at the top and bottom for the speaker and microphone, but no obvious buttons.

"Voice activated?" Smith asked. Jung didn't respond. He pulled the cap off the pen and found a USB connection underneath.

"Why? Why would you do this, Jung?" Chen said, tears streaming down his face.

Turning on him suddenly, Jung retorted, "To save you, Chen. To save *you*!"

"But that doesn't make any sense," Chen said, wiping away his tears and regaining control. "How—"

"You were asking too many questions. You were hacking into government computers and discovering things that my father didn't want discovered."

Chen could not hide the surprise on his face. He thought he had covered his tracks fairly well.

"Yes, Chen, he knew about it all along," Jung was saying. "I knew he wouldn't tolerate it much longer. That's why I suggested this plan. Not only would it humble America, which was my father's obsession, but it would also save you."

"But shutting down America's missile defenses could start World War III, Jung. *Millions* could die. My life isn't worth that. You should have just let him kill me."

"No one's going to die, Chen. My father promised me that. He said it was all just a big political game—fear and greed. He tried to explain that to you the other day. He doesn't want to hurt anybody. He just wants to level the playing field."

"Leveling cities would be more my guess," Smith said. "Look, Jung, you just admitted Lao might've killed Chen if you hadn't intervened, and we already suspect he killed Chen's parents. What's to stop him from killing total strangers halfway around the globe?"

"Chen's parents really were an accident—I asked my father about that specifically. And I never said I was trying to save Chen from being killed. I was trying to keep him from being sold."

"*Sold?*" Chen was on his feet again. Everyone looked at Jung aghast.

"It's not as bad as it sounds. My father said he didn't have the heart to kill you, Chen, although sterner men probably would have done so, considering all the trouble you'd caused."

Smith let out a snort.

Jung glanced at him and continued. "My father told me he had some wealthy contacts who would be able to benefit from your talents, even though he no longer could. He said he's done similar things in the past, and it has worked out well for everyone."

"For everyone but the slave," Grace replied in disgust, glaring at Jung. "There's no telling what really happens to them once they're sold, Jung."

"I was concerned about that," Jung admitted, looking thoughtful. "Even if my father's intentions were good, I couldn't be certain about the buyer. That's why I decided that doing this was the better way."

Everybody sat in stunned silence for a moment. Before anyone else could speak, a disheveled man in his thirties appeared in the doorway. He had thick tangles of blonde hair and coke bottle glasses. His shirt was only half tucked in, and one shoe was untied.

"Hey, guys." He tossed his head as if to get the hair out of his eyes, but it stubbornly refused to budge. "Did somebody call for IT?"

CHAPTER

33

"Thank goodness you came quickly," Smith said, surveying the unkempt programmer who had just entered the room. "We've had a severe breach in security. Joel Rothstein's computer has been infected with a virus designed to shut down our nation's missile defense system. Joel will take you to his office and bring you up to speed while you work. Let us know if you can figure something out."

"Sounds like a challenge. Awesome!" he said, nodding his shaggy head. Joel led the programmer out of the room and down the hall.

"Now, I think it's time we call your father and make a deal," Smith told Jung. He set her pen down and reached for the phone sitting near him on the desk.

Jung stretched a slim arm across the table, plucked up her pen, and squeezed the central portion. "Call Director..." she began, speaking into the pen, but Smith promptly cut her off.

"Use our phone. I want this to be a conference call."

Jung stared at Smith defiantly, squeezed her pen again, and tossed it on the table. Smith picked up the regular phone and dialed a number.

"Get me a secure line and patch me in to the big man. He'll want to hear this."

After a moment or two, he pushed the phone towards Jung. "Dial Lao's number, and don't forget the international extension," he instructed.

Jung dialed the number without hesitation. Everyone could hear the phone ringing over the speaker.

After a few rings, someone answered in Chinese. Jung immediately began speaking in rapid-fire Chinese herself.

"English, please!" Smith interrupted. The phone went deathly silent, as did Jung.

"She has already warned him about what is going on," Chen said.

"Well, then I guess we can jump right into the negotiation. Director Lao, this is Agent Smith. Can you hear me?"

"I can hear you quite well," came the stiff reply. "Unfortunately, I do not know who you are, except that you seem to have kidnapped my daughter and one of her co-workers, though to what purpose, I cannot imagine. Is it money you want? Perhaps we can work something out. I have been sick with worry these last few days. I am so relieved to know she is alive. What kind of ransom are you demanding?"

"Don't be coy, Director Lao. I haven't kidnapped anyone. Both Jung and Chen are in America legally and by their own choice, as I'm sure you know."

"Legality, Agent Smith, is often a matter of opinion. The law—especially international law—can be very flexible. Politics often plays a major role. I suspect world opinion would be heavily in my favor, since you are currently holding my daughter against her will," Lao retorted. "You might report that to whatever agency you work for, and return her to me immediately. It will save an international scandal for yourself and your country."

"That is exactly why we called, Director Lao. We want to safely return your daughter to you and avoid a scandal for either of our countries. Unfortunately, your daughter broke a number of our laws when she infected a United States government computer with a virus developed by your son, Steven."

"I am shocked to hear this, Agent Smith, although I will admit that my estranged son, whom you mentioned, was known to associate with members of the international hacker community. How he managed to involve my daughter, I cannot guess, but I am sure Jung is quite innocent."

Everyone in the room, with the exception of Jung, rolled their eyes at Lao's glaring duplicity.

Smith continued. "Jung's innocence or guilt is less relevant to me right now than finding a fix for this virus. Since Steven is the one who developed it, I suspect he can also send us the cure, and the sooner the better. The minute we confirm the virus has been neutralized, your daughter will be on a plane back home, no questions asked."

"Ah, my daughter's life for a little bit of computer code? Is that the arrangement? The answer seems so obvious—who could resist such an easy bargain? Unfortunately, my son Steven was found dead from a drug overdose just this very morning. I am still trying to overcome the grief. Although we had our differences, I had no idea how confused he truly was. A father always mourns his children, even the rebellious ones."

The room grew quiet as all listeners processed this new revelation, their eyes downcast and unblinking. It was obvious that Lao had eliminated Steven, likely out of fear that he might change sides, if the price were right. That may have been Steven's intention all along. If so, it backfired on him, and now he wasn't around to help stop the virus at all. Smith looked at Jung. Some of the defiance had left her face, and her eyes were moist.

"Agent Smith, can you hear me?" Lao asked, echoing Smith's earlier question. "It has suddenly grown very quiet. I hope I've not lost the connection."

Smith shook his head.

"I can hear you, Lao." He stared at the phone for a moment then added, "Surely Steven left something behind that could help us undo this virus. Since you are the only one with access to Steven's things, I guess the new question is, what is *your* price? Obviously, your daughter's life is not sufficient incentive."

"My daughter's life is quite safe. That is the one thing of which I am absolutely certain. You Americans have always placed a high value on individual human lives. It is a peculiar obsession of yours—one not shared by most of the world. It is like some vestigial appendage, some archaic remnant of your Judeo-Christian heritage that you cannot seem to shake, even though it leaves you weak and vulnerable.

"Whatever the case, seeing America humbled has no price tag, Agent Smith. This is an historic moment; it transcends you, me, my daughter, my son, and many other things. America, the great bully of the twenty-first century, will finally be brought to justice. That, Agent Smith, is priceless."

With that, the phone line went dead. Lao had hung up.

Those gathered in the room looked around at each other, alternating expressions of shock, anger, or bewilderment on their faces. Eventually, all eyes came to rest on Jung. Her face was like stone, eyes staring straight ahead as a single tear spilled over and ran down her cheek.

"Steven didn't take drugs," she said resolutely. "He hated them as much or more than he hated oppressive governments. He viewed them as the ultimate enemy to human freedom, another form of slavery to be resisted at all costs. He was adamant about that point. There is no way he overdosed."

The room was quiet for a long moment, then Joel and the shaggy programmer returned.

"Well, it's a virus alright," the programmer began. "But it's different from anything I've ever seen before. It's broken into two parts. The first part helps it infect other computers. Instead of running sophisticated algorithms, it simply makes what appear to be educated guesses about weak points in the system it is attacking and then refines its attacks based on the results. You could almost say the program is learning as it goes. The second part seems to delete any data that the first part deems irrelevant—clearing away the clutter, you might say. It's fascinating, really—"

"Steven used my program!" Chen interrupted. Everyone looked at him.

"Your program?" Smith asked.

"He must have copied it. Perhaps that was his final slap at his father. He had to know I'd be able to undo it once I realized what was going on. Maybe he anticipated Lao double-crossing him."

"You can fix this thing?" Grace asked.

"I think so. I developed the program myself and have been using it to hack into databases all over the world. Steven may have modified it, but it is definitely mine. Just get me to a computer terminal, and I'll do my best."

"Well, let's go then," Smith said. "All of you, to Joel's office now. Grace, you bring Jung, and keep a close eye on her. I want everyone together."

They all crowded through the door and headed down the hallway. Grace put a hand on Jung's arm. "Are you okay?"

Jung nodded, wiping another tear from her cheek.

Grace stopped in the hallway just outside the door, holding Jung back while everyone else clustered around the computer terminal. "We don't get to pick our parents, you know?"

"I know," Jung said looking up at Grace and offering a faint smile.

Grace continued, "I have a friend who was really good at sports and whose father had been an Olympic athlete. One day I made a comment about how lucky she was to get those great Olympian genes. But do you know what she told me?"

Jung shook her head.

"She said she may be lucky in that regard, but her father was also manic-depressive, and she inherited that gene, too. Physically, she was the picture of health—but emotionally, her life was a roller coaster. Whenever she competed in a race, she usually won. But more often than not, she couldn't even make herself crawl out of bed to get to the starting line."

"What are you trying to say?" Jung asked with interest.

"Well, I'm just saying that we inherit things from our parents, both good and bad. Obviously, your father is an intelligent man, and he passed that on to you. Politics, however, aren't hardwired into our genes. Your father grew up in a different era, an era of strife and conflict. Hopefully, our generation will do better than his. I know you want to please your father—it's only natural—but I think you are starting to see what kind of person he has become. You aren't that person, Jung. Despite what you have done, you are not your father."

Jung looked at the floor, her tears flowing freely. It was a lot to process for such a young girl, even a brilliant one. Grace put her arm around Jung's shoulders and gave a gentle squeeze.

Jung looked up at Grace and said, "Thanks, Mom," with a grin. Both Jung and Grace started laughing, then realized it had suddenly gotten quiet. They looked up to see the others watching them through the doorway.

"I'm sorry," Grace apologized. She felt a little foolish, but was still happy to see the change in Jung.

Back in Joel's office, all eyes returned to the computer screen in front of Chen.

"As I was saying," Chen continued, "this is definitely my programming. It should be an easy matter to stop it, depending on how much it has been modified. Steven was very capable, but he was not given much time, and this type of programming was new to him. I'll know in just a minute."

Chen kept typing while the others watched. He let out an occasional exclamation like "okay" or "good, good," but then he said what no one wanted to hear: "uh-oh!"

"*Uh-oh?*" Smith repeated, "That can't be good. What does *uh-oh*, mean?"

"Well, I've disabled the virus on *this* system…" Chen began hesitantly.

"But?" Smith tilted his head forward in anticipation of the bad part.

"But unfortunately, it looks like the virus has already jumped." Chen finished.

"*Jumped?* Jumped *where?*"

"Jumped to another system—and not just one, either. It seems to have gotten into the Civil Service system through an accounting backdoor, and into the National Institutes of Health through a shared research backdoor. I can shut down one or the other pathway before it spreads further, but I may not have time to stop both."

"Can I help?" offered the programmer. "I've seen what you're doing. I can shout out questions from the terminal across the hall, and we can work in tandem."

"It's worth a try," Chen said. "I'll start on the Civil Service branch. You work on the National Institutes of Health pathway."

Before the programmer could even get out the door, Chen let out another, "Uh-oh!"

"Now what?" Smith looked back at Chen, afraid to ask.

"The virus just split again within the Civil Service software. It seems to be following two branches, one for non-military civil servants like postal workers, and another for those affiliated with the military like the Veteran's Administration. I'd better work on the military side and have you work on the non-military side. We'll have to ignore the National Institutes of Health for now and hope for the best. Too bad we don't have a third programmer familiar with my software."

"What if I help?" offered a quiet voice.

Everyone turned and looked. It was Jung who had spoken.

CHAPTER
34

An ambulance was waiting for us on the ground. The intern was kind enough to stay with me until the paramedics could take over. He waved goodbye as I was rolled away on the stretcher, Danielle walking by my side.

In the back of the ambulance, the paramedic started an IV infusion of normal saline in my right hand while I held pressure on my chest with my left.

"Your ribs must be awfully sore by the way you're holding them," he observed.

"It's more like a pressure-release valve to keep my lung expanded."

"A what?" He gave me a strange look.

I pulled up my shirt to show him the incision we had surreptitiously made on the plane.

"I was developing a tension pneumothorax on the plane and had to improvise," I explained.

I was kind of proud of my quick thinking, but he didn't seem impressed. He reached for something beside him. I wasn't at a good angle to see what it was. Then he pushed a button and spoke into an intercom system to the driver.

"Jim, I've got a penetrating chest wound back here, and I've got to secure the airway. Let the ER know about the change in status."

I started to protest, but felt a burning sensation in my right arm and heard my words slurring as they came out. I knew that "securing the airway," meant he was going to knock me out and put a breathing tube down my throat.

This seemed like an overreaction, but I didn't get a vote.

When I woke up, I actually felt pretty good. Most of my pain had subsided, and I was overcome by a general sense of wellbeing.

"Mmm, the wonders of narcotics," I thought as I slowly opened my eyes. Someone was just a few inches away, looking intently into my face.

"Here he comes," she announced. "You're just waking up, Dr. Gunderson. Take a few deep breaths."

I wanted to say, "Every breath is a gift," echoing Danielle, but nothing came out—there was something stuck in my throat. I turned my head from side to side and felt something lodged in my nose. The sense of wellbeing quickly turned to panic as I began instinctively whipping my head back and forth.

"Hold on, Dr. Gunderson. We're going to get that tube out of there."

I heard a sucking sound and felt something sliding out of my throat and through my nose, which made me cough like crazy for a little bit.

Once I quit coughing, I tried to speak again, but my mouth wouldn't open. Apparently, my jaw was wired shut. I made a grunting sound and pointed at my mouth.

"Your jaw is wired shut, Dr. Gunderson. It was a special request from your wife," said the nurse with a wry smile.

She looked like a native Hawaiian except there were streaks of blonde hair mixed in with the black, and she had unnaturally bright blue eyes. I thought I might be hallucinating and blinked a few times before I realized she was wearing colored contacts. She laughed at my look of confusion, thinking it was a response to her joke.

"I'm only teasing, Dr. Gunderson. You've had a big operation and are just waking up. Dr. Hollander is finishing up his dictation, but I know he'll want to talk to you now that you're awake. Let me go grab him."

She disappeared for a few seconds, giving me time to get my bearings a little better. Obviously, I was in a recovery room somewhere, and they must have repaired my cheekbone. As I reached up to feel it, the nurse returned with the surgeon.

"Good morning, Dr. Gunderson. I'm Dr. Hollander, the oral maxillofacial surgeon. You'll meet Dr. Norman, your thoracic surgeon, later on. But I can give you a quick synopsis of what we both did, if you'd like."

I nodded and stuck out my hand.

"Nice to meet you," is what I tried to say, but it just came out as a series of grunts.

"I'll take that as a *yes*," he said, shaking my hand. "Your daughter-in-law told us about the improvised knife you made on the plane."

I tried to explain that she wasn't my daughter-in-law, just my son's girlfriend, but eventually gave up. I realized that I would need a chalkboard or some paper if I were going to communicate. The grunts weren't working, no matter how emphatic.

"That knife probably saved your life, but it also nicked an intercostal vein. Luckily, it wasn't the artery. You still lost a lot of blood, all the same. Dr. Norman found at least a unit or two inside your chest when he looked in there with his scope. He was able to cauterize everything and control the bleeding then repair the hole.

He also inserted a chest tube in the rib space just below the wound to keep your lung expanded—it will need to stay there for a few days before we can take it out."

I nodded my understanding. I was becoming more alert and also beginning to feel some of my aches and pains again. I felt for the chest tube and found it. It was a big rubber hose coming out of the right side of my body—hard to miss.

"My portion of the surgery took a bit longer," Dr. Hollander resumed. "It wasn't life threatening, but it was a little more tedious. You had a whole lot of little fractures all along your left zygoma and maxilla. I was able to put a plate across most everything, but I decided to go ahead and wire you together to help maintain your alignment until you can heal some. You'll have to eat through a straw in the meantime. Sorry about that."

I nodded again and said, "Thank you," well enough for him to understand.

"No problem, just glad to be able to help. Oh, and I shaved off your Mohawk while we were back in the operating room. Your daughter-in-law asked us to, but I did get a few pictures in case you wanted them."

I reached up and felt my smooth head and smiled.

"Well, I'd better go get your wife and daughter-in-law. I told them they could see you as soon as you woke up."

"Wife?" I thought, but he'd disappeared.

He returned promptly with Lauren and left with a wave. "I'll let you guys visit," he said softly, pulling the curtain closed.

"Jon?" Lauren touched my leg gently.

I held out both my arms for a hug and gave her a big smile, which I'm sure looked like some hideous grimace, but she hugged me anyway.

"Oh, Jon—I'm so glad you're alive," she cried, clinging tightly to me. Tears welled up in her eyes as she pulled back to get a better look at me.

"They really worked you over," she said, gently stroking my clean-shaven head. "Danielle told me what happened."

I nodded and signaled that I needed something to write on, so she asked the nurse for some paper and a pen. As the nurse left to get it, Ranch came up behind Lauren and gave me a nod.

"Hey, Gunderson. I see you've gotten a haircut just like your son-in-law."

I smiled.

"Don't know if in-flight surgery counts as an extreme sport, but in this case, it probably should. Looks like you and Sanders have a lot more in common than we all realized."

I started to laugh at his joke, but ended up in a coughing fit instead.

"Sorry, buddy, no more jokes," Ranch apologized, looking me over. "Glad to see you in one piece though. Those docs did great work. You'll be able to body-double for Shrek in no time."

I grinned, but had the good sense to suppress any laughter. The nurse returned and handed me the paper and a ballpoint pen.

"I thought you said no more jokes," I scribbled across the top of the paper.

"Who's joking?" he asked. We all laughed, but I managed to cough a little less the second time around.

Then I wrote down a few questions. "How did you all get here so quickly? How long have I been out? Where's Danielle? Where are the kids? Did they stop the computer virus?"

"Whoa, now—one thing at a time," Ranch said when he saw the list. He nodded at Lauren. "Why don't you field the first four questions, and I'll tell him about the virus?"

"Sure thing," she agreed, then looked at me. "First, your friend Grant Simpson got word to us that you were injured and would be flying to Hawaii before you ever left. That gave us time to head this way ourselves—Ranch arranged a special flight out of Barksdale Air Force Base near Shreveport. I've been here with the baby for several hours while you were in surgery—that's how Danielle was able to fill me in on everything that has happened to you. As best I can tell, you've been asleep for roughly eight hours—two for the chest repair and another six for the facial reconstruction."

That sounded about right. I nodded.

"As for the kids," she smiled. "Danielle has the baby out in the waiting room—they won't let children come into recovery. The rest of the kids are at home with Seth, but my parents are helping him. They drove over from Dallas as soon as I phoned. I didn't give them many details, but they'll need some sort of explanation when we get back—assuming the kids haven't already told them everything."

I figured I had a lot of explaining to do to a lot of family members before it was all said and done. I looked at Ranch.

"My turn now?" he asked. "Well, unfortunately Jung had already planted the virus by the time your message got through to us. It had begun to spread to other government computers outside the CDC by the time we got through to them. Things were touch-and-go for a while, and it required a lot of teamwork between Chen, Jung, and one of the CDC programmers to contain it all, but they were eventually able to stop it. Luckily, Jung's brother Steven had used Chen's artificial intuition software to build the virus, so Chen knew exactly what to do. All he needed was a couple extra pairs of hands so he could do it quickly."

I frowned and wrote, "Jung helped? I thought she was the bad guy."

"Well, yes and no. I think she was confused and was trying to please her father. In the end, she finally seemed to realize what a scumbag Lao is—especially after he had his own son Steven killed."

I looked surprised and wrote, "Killed?"

"You heard me right. He murdered his own son, Jung's half-brother. Once he got the thumb drive from you, he didn't need Steven's help anymore. He probably also feared Steven would change sides and help us out, given the chance. That was all it took for Lao to bump him off. It really opened Jung's eyes."

I just shook my head.

"Oh, and there's one more thing. You remember that computer we picked up in the girl's apartment who was doing all the human trafficking? Guess who's name was all over the place in her files?"

I shrugged my shoulders.

"Director Lao's. He would use all these smart kids to do his research, then, when he got tired of them or they got too sassy for his taste, he'd *sell them!* Just like that. Einstein on the auction block. He found a niche market and was probably one of the top suppliers of human slaves for all of China."

"And Zhou?" I wrote.

Ranch shook his head soberly. "Dead, we think. Remember the guards she tricked while rescuing you and Danielle? Evidently, they did report the situation. Zhou ran into a military roadblock while trying to make that phone call. Best we can tell from the satellite photos, her car was pretty much vaporized. You barely got away yourself—and had you made it to Shanghai, as planned, there would've been an ambush waiting for you. Good thing your plane went down in that storm, huh?"

"In more ways than one," I thought, nodding. I laid my head back on my pillow and closed my eyes to process it all.

EPILOGUE

I ran my hand across the top of my head. My hair was long enough now that it looked somewhat normal again and felt soft to the touch. I was glad to have it back, since the weather was just starting to turn cool.

The final days of summer had brought a lot of rain, so the grass and shrubs were still green, even though the leaves had begun to fall from some of our trees.

I reached over and felt my ribs with my left hand. My wounds had been healed up for a while now, but I'd still get a twinge of pain sometimes when I turned suddenly or coughed too hard.

Lauren had recently informed me that she was expecting again, which meant we would be having our tenth child sometime next summer. We had decided not to announce it yet, with everything else that was going on, but I was having a hard time keeping the secret. Now that I'd come clean to my family about so many other things, it just didn't seem natural to hide stuff anymore.

"You okay, Dad?" Grace asked. She gave my right arm a squeeze with the hand she had wrapped around it.

I was grateful it wasn't my left arm. Although the fracture from the bullet had healed, my arm was still tender to pressure and would throb whenever the weather was cold.

"Just nervous, I guess."

"There's nothing to be nervous about," she assured me. "Hank and I have already been married for over three months now, anyway."

"*They* don't know that," I said, gesturing to the three hundred guests who had gathered in our backyard.

"*Some* of them do," she smiled.

"Some of them do, indeed," I conceded, then stepped back a little to look her over.

"You look every bit as beautiful as your mother did when she wore that dress—but don't tell her I said that."

"I won't," she promised, "but Mom wouldn't mind anyway. She put a lot of work into making this dress. I'm just glad we didn't have to alter it too much." Grace smoothed out the front of the wedding gown as she said it.

"Over four hundred hours and twelve thousand sequins and pearls," I said. "And you know it won—"

"First place at the Texas State Fair?" Grace finished the sentence for me.

"You've heard that story before?"

"Just a few times," she smiled.

Before I could think of a snappy come back, the wedding music began. Instead of traditional wedding music, the girls had decided to walk down the aisle to a Chinese folk song.

As it turns out, the song the young Chinese mother had been singing to her injured son on the way to Beijing was the same one Jung's mother had sung to her as a child. It was the only thing Jung remembered about her mother, so Grace and Danielle insisted it be part of the ceremony.

"You ready?" I lifted my eyebrows.

"Are you?"

"I think so."

We stepped out of our back door and started down the path through the middle of our wooded backyard. We had nearly two acres of grass and shaded flowerbeds, which had been carefully manicured over the last few weeks in preparation for this moment. The trail was spread with fresh pine needles, and the beds were bursting with autumn blooms.

The one thing we couldn't control was the weather, but God had kindly sent us clear blue skies. Even the temperature was just right—cool, but not too cold.

Everything was perfect.

At our approach, everyone stood to their feet from the chairs we had placed in neat rows on either side of the trail. On the left were the rest of my kids, all lined up in matching outfits, the littlest ones waving at their big sister, barely able to contain their enthusiasm.

On the right, Jung and Chen stood alongside their new parents, my boss and his wife, Mike and Janet.

Who'd have guessed when I promised Mike a souvenir from China, I'd end up bringing home the children he and Janet had always wanted? It had taken three full months to get the adoption transferred, but it had been finalized just in time for the wedding.

During the process, Hank and Grace had actually gotten to know one another and had decided maybe their arranged marriage wasn't such a bad thing after all. Naturally, after Seth and Danielle had announced their intention to get married right away, before finishing college, the two couples immediately began plotting a double wedding.

At the end of the path stood the massive, split-level tree fort my boys and I had built several summers ago. Seth and Danielle smiled at us as they waited arm-in-arm beneath it. Danielle's father had already walked her down the path and had taken his place on the right, next to his wife.

I would sit on the left next to Lauren, just a few steps from where Hank now waited so patiently, his face beaming.

He was letting his hair grow back also, so we matched. More than one person had asked if we were related during those weeks we'd spent at the gym doing rehab together and getting better acquainted. Hank's leg was nearly back to normal, his limp gone. Even his bullet wound was nothing more than another scar to use as a conversation starter.

Grace stepped up beside Hank as I sat down. The minister rose and stood between the couples, facing the audience.

"When things don't go according to plan," he said, "it usually means God is trying to teach us something. The past several months have held enough surprises for these four young people that they've decided it might be easier to learn their lessons if they had a good study partner." Everybody laughed.

"Seth and Danielle have seen their relationship develop slowly over many years—literally growing up together. Hank and Grace have seen their relationship blossom in a few short months. Although the two couples have arrived at the same point by different pathways, each understands that it is God who has been directing their steps all along. He has a plan, and that plan is that they go forward, hand-in-hand and heart-to-heart, learning and growing together. Seth and Danielle will no longer be two people, but one. Likewise, Hank and Grace will no longer be two, but one."

The couples smiled, and I squeezed Lauren's hand. The minister turned to the next page of his notes and continued.

"Being one with another person is not an easy task. It often requires the type of self-sacrifice that was demonstrated by Christ on the cross—who died, so that others might live. In other words, it means putting someone else's needs ahead of your own—even when it hurts. This isn't a natural thing for fragile humans like us

323

to do. Truly I say to you, self-sacrificing love is a supernatural act that requires a strength only God can provide. Both these couples have demonstrated that kind of strength in a variety of ways already..."

He recounted several anecdotes from our trip to China to support this claim. Although he lost his place in his notes momentarily, he got most of the details right. I confess that hearing those stories afresh sent my mind wondering all over Asia again. I didn't snap back to the present until the ceremony was almost over.

"Therefore," the minister was saying, "it is with confidence that I marry them now, knowing that both these couples will see their new road together to the very end. May we have the rings?"

Chen brought the rings to Hank and Grace on a little pillow. Aaron did the same for Seth and Danielle. The two couples exchanged the vows that each had written before being officially pronounced "man and wife." They then attempted to outdo one another for the longest kiss, which embarrassed their mothers to no end.

For the grand finale, both brides climbed cautiously up a ladder into our tree fort—quite an undertaking in those billowing wedding gowns. They retrieved two velvet-lined seats the grooms had hidden there earlier and quickly attached them to our zip line.

Grace hooked hers on first, perched herself delicately upon it, and with a carefree kick, came sailing down the aisle into the waiting arms of Hank. Danielle followed right behind her, squealing with glee when Seth caught her at the bottom.

The conspiring couples laughed merrily as they bounded back up the pine needle path to our house for the reception.

The zip line exit was a surprise to everyone in attendance, including myself, and the general consensus was that no one would soon forget it. The younger children all claimed they were going to do the same thing when they got married.

I spoke briefly with a number of old friends and extended family members, all of whom congratulated me on the genius of getting two kids out of the house for the price of one. I humbly explained I had nothing to do with it, but was strictly the beneficiary.

Maybe I was finally realizing that there are many things in life for which we can accept neither credit nor blame. We must simply do the best we can with the hand that is dealt us, and leave the rest to God.

Noticing Grant Simpson speaking to Eric Smith in a corner of the yard, I made my way over to them.

"Well, what did you think of the wedding?" I asked.

"Absolutely wonderful. Not only was the ceremony beautiful, but it had the usual Gunderson flare," Grant said amiably. "Eric and I were just agreeing that the weather was perfect, the brides were lovely, and the zip line provided the perfect ending. Who could ask for anything more?"

"Thank you, Grant. I appreciate your coming halfway around the world to see it."

"Wouldn't have missed it. Besides, now that I'm retired, I can do what I like."

"Retired?" I asked in surprise.

"Oh, yes. I was just telling Eric here that they are reorganizing the embassy in Guangzhou. The new arrangement doesn't seem to require the services of a librarian, so I'm calling it quits and seeing the world, starting right here in America."

"I'm sorry to hear that," I said, glancing at Smith, who only shrugged.

"Not at all. It was long overdue, and I was ready for a change of pace anyway, as was my assistant. You remember Miss Mercer—she is finally getting to study tribal languages in Papua New Guinea, which she has dreamed of doing for some time now. I believe she has arranged to give weekly updates on her progress to Chen and Jung via the Internet."

Simpson took a sip of punch before changing the subject. "So, tell me, Jon. Are Seth and Danielle still planning to holiday in China for their honeymoon?"

"Only if you still think it's safe," I said.

"Far safer now than it has been in a long, long time. Of course, Zhou's death was a terrible loss to all of us, but the girl you rescued, Ling, has almost completed her training and seems to be a natural as an agent. I anticipate she will pick up where Zhou left off and will eventually be a great asset, especially in the fight against human trafficking."

"Oh?" I asked, popping a grape into my mouth from my nearly empty plate.

"Oh, yes," Simpson continued. "We have already put a substantial dent in the slave trade, simply by exposing Lao's involvement. The Director had already become quite unpopular with the other Chinese generals, so his black market dealings gave them all the excuse they needed to oust him."

"You're kidding!"

"Not at all. I imagine they resented the fact that he was always siphoning off money to fund his research projects—money they thought should be used for more traditional things like tanks and guns. However, I think the thing they found most unforgiveable was Lao's flashiness and extravagance. It is highly looked down upon amongst the old school Chinese to have things your comrades do not—especially expensive western things. It's ironic, too, given how much Lao hated America."

"You know, someone recently told me something very similar about the rural Chinese," I said, smiling at the thought of Angelo in his old army truck full of peasants. "I guess the old Communist ideal of share-and-share-alike is pretty deeply ingrained."

Simpson nodded knowingly.

"What about Hank and Grace?" Smith asked, "Did I hear they're headed to French Polynesia—to the very island where Ranch picked Hank up just a few months ago?"

"That's right. Hank seems determined to finish his vacation before he and Grace go back to college."

"Back to college? Is that the plan?"

"Sure is. All four kids have decided to finish their education and settle down. They've even rented apartments across the hall from one another, just down the street from our local university."

"Well, I hate to hear that," said Smith.

"Why so? Lauren and I think it's a wonderful plan."

"Sure—for ordinary people, it is. But your family has a special gift. I hate to see all that talent go to waste, especially with the amazing assignment that just came up."

He winked at Simpson, a twinkle in his eyes. "You guys would make the perfect team—now that you're all on the same page. Why don't I give you a quick synopsis?"

"Oh no, you don't," I warned, pointing sternly at Smith and backing away from him. I turned and started for the house at a quick trot.

"Come back, Gunderson. I'm only kidding," Smith shouted after me, but I was already passing through the doorway and heading for the wedding cake.

I'd take no chances by going back to continue *that* conversation. Not this time. Not on my kids' wedding day.

ACKNOWLEDGEMENTS

First and foremost, I want to thank all those who helped in the editing process, especially my wife, Jennifer. I handed her the rough copy and said, "Be merciless." She was, and the book is better for it.

My kids offered both constructive criticism and enthusiastic encouragement. I appreciate their listening to me read the entire manuscript aloud and convincing me *not* to throw it in the fire when I grew discouraged with the project. A special thanks to my daughter Bethany for doing a final edit and for being so thorough.

Several friends made wonderful suggestions that helped further refine the story and the text. These include Mitch and Jenny Bernhard, Christi Caldwell, Hector Cecolli, Chelsea Cook, Steve and Shelli Cox, Chris Jones, Karen Lewis, and Tim and Meridith Twaddell. I appreciate your taking time out of your busy lives to help with this project.

I want to thank Steve Babitsky, Tess Gerritsen, and Michael Palmer for sponsoring the "Fiction Writing for Physicians" conference each year. I found it to be a wonderful and enlightening experience, and I am so grateful that these phenomenally successful people are willing to pass on their knowledge to others.

Likewise, I am indebted to Stephen King's memoir, *On Writing*, which convinced me to simply write what I enjoy, and to Steven Pressfield's *The War of Art*, which taught me that the hardest part of writing is just sitting down and getting started.

I drew inspiration from several non-fiction works, as well: The possibility of using endogenous retroviruses as a biological weapon came to me while reading *Survival of the Sickest* by Sharon Moalem and *The Language of God* by Francis Collins. I got the idea for "artificial intuition" while reading *Gut Feelings* by Gerd Gigerenzer, shortly after I finished *On Intelligence* by Jeff Hawkins. The concept of a "prodigy project" occurred to me while reading about China's Cultural Revolution in Jung Chang's epic work, *Mao: The Unknown Story.* Joshua Ramos' *The Age of the Unthinkable* provided many insights into geopolitics. Ian Ayres' *Supercrunchers* gave me a glimpse at the intersection between creativity and technology. Finally, the stories behind "sink the boats, smash the pots" and Augenblick came from Malcolm Gladwell, whose brilliant works always make me want to be a better writer.

Thanks to L. Max Buja and Joseph Miller for letting me work in their research lab a couple summers during medical school. My apologies to the mice.

Thanks to the Army Reserves for exposing me to the basics of biological warfare and to all my fellow soldiers who help protect our great nation from an endless array of threats, biological or otherwise.

Thanks to the makers of the film, *Call + Response*, who raised my awareness about the atrocity of human trafficking, to Todd Hinkie, who insisted I watch the film in the first place, and to author Francis Chan, who gives the proceeds from his many excellent books to fight this lingering scourge of mankind.

Lastly, thanks to my kids' pediatrician, Hal Everett, to my college roommate, Scott Smith, to my co-worker, Darren Tapley, and to thousands like them who have adopted children out of China, especially those with special needs. The world's a better place because of you.

11363484R00213

Made in the USA
Charleston, SC
18 February 2012